Out
of Focus

CHOSEN PATHS BOOK 3

L.B. SIMMONS

SPENCER
HILL
PRESS

Out of Focus
Copyright © 2016

This book is a work of fiction. Names, characters, places, and incidents are used fictitiously. Any resemblance to actual persons, living or dead, business establishments, events, or locales is entirely coincidental. Use of any copyrighted, trademarked, or brand names in this work of fiction does not imply endorsement of that brand.

Please visit www.lbsimmons.com

First Edition: February 2016
L.B. Simmons

Out of Focus: a novel / by L.B. Simmons—1st ed.
ISBN: 978-1-63392-099-6
Library of Congress Cataloging-in-Publication Data available upon request

Summary: For years, Cassie Cooper has convincingly played a confident young woman who couldn't care less about what others think of her actions. But in reality, beneath the bold facade lies a frightened, broken little girl who is suffocating under the weight of her secrets. Out of control, Cassie continues whirling down a treacherous path, searching for anything that will numb her pain—that is, until she meets Grady Bennett.

The martial arts instructor doesn't just look at Cassie; he *sees* her.

With painstaking patience as their relationship grows, Grady helps Cassie see herself. As Cassie faces her tortured past, her walls come down. With her vulnerabilities exposed, she loses sight of her new perspective and plummets once again into her void.

Sometimes it takes hitting rock bottom to find the necessary strength to land safely. And sometimes life has to be completely *Out of Focus* in order to finally *see*.

Published in the United States by Spencer Hill Press.
This is a Spencer Hill Press Contemporary Romance.
Spencer Hill Contemporary is an imprint of Spencer Hill Press.
For more information on our titles, visit www.spencerhillpress.com

Distributed by Midpoint Trade Books
www.midpointtrade.com

Cover design by: Hang Le
Interior layout by: Scribe Inc.

Printed in the United States of America

For Luna . . .

Thank you for loving Cassie as much as I do. You knew she had a story to tell and you were right. Because of your love for her character, your belief in her journey, this book is just as much yours as it is mine. Love you dearly, my friend. Times two.

Chosen Paths Series

Book One: *Into the Light*
Book Two: *Under the Influence*
Book Three: *Out of Focus*

Prologue

Only twenty-three years old, and I'm so goddamn tired.

I used to be so much stronger. I somehow kept the voices at bay, the memories locked away safely, contained within the confines of my mind. But with each passing day, I feel the glow of my once-luminous strength fading. Darkness encases me now, bowing the walls of protection I put into place years ago. My past is an ever-present nightmare, repeatedly tapping, slowly fracturing the window of my sanity.

I have no doubt that it's only a matter of time before the glass finally breaks. Blackness will eventually seep through its cracks and deliver me from the safety of my façade into a reality that will destroy me.

My reality.

I've done my part. I've kept the secrets thrust upon me with dedicated believability. My portrayal of who I am has become a blurred, hazy version of the once very distinct Cassie Cooper.

I read an ungodly amount of trashy romance novels.

I'm the overtly sexual and foul-mouthed friend who will say anything to get a laugh.

And I have exactly zero fucks to give to what anyone else thinks about my actions.

But the reality, the actuality, is this:

I read obsessively to escape my own world. To live the dreams of others when, for so long, the reoccurrence of my nightmares has been *my* reality. I read to fall in love and find a happily-ever-after, even if it is purely imagined. With each story I read, I'm able to *live* and *love* vicariously through the characters in my books. It's the only plausible way for me to survive.

I threw away my virginity at the age of thirteen just to prove something. And when I found that proof, that vindication I was looking for,

I sought it every chance I could. Sex is about control for me. Nothing more. The act will never be about making love, like it is for the heroines in my books. I will never be granted the beauty of that gift.

I use humor as a form of avoidance. I draw upon laughter to block the pain. And I smile to mask the agony of the eight-year-old soul who weeps within me.

And the fucks . . . well, that's not entirely accurate either.

I have given two to be exact: One to my best friend of seventeen years. She knows nothing of my past, and although she so willingly disclosed the horrors of hers, mine remains hidden for no other reason than to avoid the pity she would undoubtedly cast my way if I were to ever tell her. I don't want her pity. I would sooner die than have her look at me in any other way than with pride.

The other died with the person to whom it was given. Anthony "Rat" Marchione. He was my one allowance of naïveté. The one person I actually *wanted* to touch me, to hold me, to love me. He was going to rescue me from my brokenness as though I were a character in one of my books. Young and senseless, I thought he was to be my eventual happily-ever-after, but tragically, he was murdered five years ago.

Black coldness waits in vain to leech into the void where his once beautiful existence filled the pieces of my irrevocably shattered heart. Where he temporarily healed the hurt of the innocent child and quieted the voices that tormented her.

He's gone now. I've accepted that. And in turn, I have relinquished all dreams associated with finding the light at the end of this miserable tunnel.

I will keep trudging through this life . . . this *sentence* handed to me for someone else's crime, my payment shackled by secrets and weighted with lies. I will continue to do so with the same fraudulent smile on my lips and play the part of the strong heroine so convincingly, that even I believe it.

It's only a matter of time before my fictional strength wears out— when I'm no longer hidden safely inside my protective blur—and I have to face the very real and lurid image of my past.

But until that time comes, I'll do all I can do.

All I have ever done.

I will pretend.

Chapter 1 ✳

Bonded

Past—Six Years Old

The sun hits the tops of my new black dress shoes, making them shine with each step I take as I cross the street. I'm skipping with excitement, and my smile is as big as the poufy skirt of my dress. It's my most favoritest Sunday dress. It's yellow and happy and I love the sound it makes each time one of my feet leaves the ground.

Swish.

Swish.

Swish.

Five *swishes* later, I finally step onto the sidewalk.

I grin so wide, my cheeks ache. I knew I would finally wear Mommy down. As soon as I saw the yellow-haired, skinny little girl pull a huge My Little Pony stuffed animal out of the moving truck, I knew we were gonna be best friends. So I bugged Mommy all day long, asking her when I could go across the street to meet my new friend—at breakfast while munching on peanut butter toast, at lunch while eating a big bowl of ravioli, at dinner while chomping down on a burger my daddy made on the grill outside, and a couple hundred times in between.

Finally, she threw up her hands—*really*, she did—and told me I could run over after and introduce myself, but only if I finished my dinner first.

I've never eaten so fast in my life.

As soon as the burger was gone, I jumped out of my chair, put my plate in the sink, then ran upstairs to my room and threw on my prettiest dress. On my way out, Daddy yelled that I only had half an hour until bath time before the door slammed shut behind me.

My long dark hair, in a ponytail that I did *all* by myself, swings as I walk down her driveway and skip around the back of the moving truck. As soon as I pass the bumper, I see her. She's sitting on the top step of her porch, wearing the same pink glittery T-shirt and blue jean shorts I saw her in earlier today.

I start to say something, but my mouth slams shut when I notice shiny tears as they roll down her cheeks. My smile falls straight to the ground, and my eyebrows pinch tightly together. I slow my steps, not sure if *now* would be the best time to introduce myself to my new best friend. My feet stop moving and I still, watching her for a second or two before deciding against it. I lift my shiny shoe and slowly begin to take a step backward, but a dumb twig cracks as soon as my foot hits the ground. I freeze, just like I do when Mommy catches me stealing cookies out of the pantry right before dinner.

I'm pretty sure I'm even making the same *Crap!* face.

Her teary blue eyes meet my dark-brown ones, and I just stand there, still like a statue with my arms stuck midswing. I don't know what else to do, so I begin to move like a robot, making the same *er-er-er* sounds my daddy does to make me laugh.

She watches my moves, and after a couple of seconds, she finally giggles.

My body relaxes, a relieved grin tugging at my lips to match hers. I can't help it.

I straighten my body, then take a step in her direction, and another, and another. When I finally come to the porch, I reach forward to shake her hand, finally making the introduction I've been waiting to make *all day long*. "Hi, I'm Cassie Cooper. I live across the street." My thumb points over my shoulder as I speak.

She wipes the tears onto her jean shorts, then stands and links our hands, giving them a good shake before answering, "Hello, Cassie. I'm Spencer Locke."

Spencer looks down as the breeze blows, and another *swish* fills the air. "I like your dress." Her voice is soft, and she tucks her hair behind her ear.

I smile my thanks and curtsey, while her pretty blue eyes—thankfully now dry—grin back at me. "And you can do the robot *almost* as good as I can."

My smile becomes a laugh, and she turns to take her spot on the porch, then pats the area beside her. I sit, happy to have a funny friend.

After a few seconds, she looks at me and says, "I'm sorry I was crying. I, uh, well . . ."

The screen door behind us creaks open and I turn my head. Behind me stands a beautiful lady around Mommy's age with glasses on the edge of her nose and light-brown hair in a pile on the top of her head. Her eyes are the color of her hair, and they crinkle at the sides when she smiles at us.

They don't look anything alike, so I'm not sure if this is Spencer's mommy or not. I don't know what to say to her, but she takes care of that for me.

"Hello, I'm Deborah, Spencer's . . ."

She pauses to glance at Spencer, who says in a strong voice, "*Mommy.*"

Her mommy's mouth dips down at the sides and her chin trembles. Now tears are in *her* eyes.

Why is everyone crying?

"Yes," Mrs. Locke continues, "I'm Spencer's mommy." She says it almost to herself, then looks to me.

"I'm Cassie." I point across the street. "I live over there."

Her mommy smiles back at me. She has a really pretty smile.

She glances back to Spencer. "Well, it's good that you'll have a friend so close, isn't that right?"

Spencer nods her head and Mrs. Locke adds, "Spencer, can I talk to you for a second?"

"Yes, ma'am." Her voice is soft when she answers. Mrs. Locke steps onto the porch when Spencer stands, and the screen door bounces a couple times before it finally shuts behind her. She's wearing a fluffy, pink robe and ties it around her waist as Spencer walks toward her. That makes me smile. As soon as Spencer stands in front of her, she places her arm gently around Spencer's shoulder and leans to whisper in her ear. Spencer nods and whispers back. This continues until they finally stop and smile at each other, as though they've decided on something.

Mrs. Locke hugs Spencer then lets her go, looks at me, and winks. "Nice to meet you, Cassie. I think you and Spencer will be very good friends."

A man's voice calls her name from within the house, and she smiles again at both of us before she leaves. I glance shyly at Spencer, who's taken her seat next to me. She lets out a long breath, then she looks back at me. She tucks her hair behind her ears again, brings her knees to her chest, and lays her cheek on them before finally speaking.

"She just wanted to tell me it was okay for me to talk about why I was crying. I wasn't really sure if I was allowed to tell people, but she told me if I wanted to tell you, that it was okay with her. And I want to tell you, because if we're going to be friends, we shouldn't keep secrets from each other. If you still even want to be my friend when I'm through."

I place my cheek on my knees just like she's doing and give her a happy smile to let her know I will still be her friend. "Well, I live across the street, so *I'm* not going anywhere."

At that, her face splits into a wide grin, before she clears her throat. I watch her smile as it falls and slowly disappears. "It's not easy to talk about, so it might be hard for me to say."

My happy face turns into a sad one, but I stay still and wait for her to start.

And then she does.

I always thought when grown-ups whispered about someone's heart being broken, it was just something they said. Like, when Mr. Keyes *kicked the bucket* or when Grandpa tells me he's *fit as a fiddle*. I had no idea that a heart could actually break. I didn't know that by just listening to Spencer share her secret, I would feel real pain in my chest.

But I do.

My heart hurts for her as she tells me how her mommy isn't really her mommy, that Mr. and Mrs. Locke adopted her because her real parents didn't want her. It crumbles into tiny pieces when she shares how her new mother found her. Her own parents had locked her in a pantry for weeks with very little food and water. And when I realize that's *why* she's so skinny, my heart breaks a little more. She tells me how scared she was in the darkness, and how she cried for days, but they never let her out. She doesn't understand what she did to deserve her *punishment*, but she says that Mr. and Mrs. Locke always hug her and tell her she didn't do *anything* wrong.

By the time I know everything there is to know about Spencer's secret, Daddy is calling me to come home and *both* of us are crying. I reach over and pull her into the tightest hug I've ever given, promising in my mind that I will be strong and protect her. I will never let anyone hurt her again.

We both let go and smile as we wipe away our tears. The wood beneath me creaks as I stand, signaling to Daddy with my finger that I'll be home in *just a minute*, then look at my new friend and smile. "Wanna come over and play tomorrow?"

I think she's surprised by my offer to still be her friend because she answers me by widening her eyes. The pain I felt earlier is gone, replaced by a warm feeling as I watch happiness fill those wide eyes.

And I'm *proud* I did that. *I* did something to make her happy.

"I would like that very much. Thank you, Cassie."

I nod excitedly and turn away from her, looking both ways before I cross the street and walk toward Daddy, who's *still* on the porch. I fight to not roll my eyes—that'll get you into heaps of trouble at my house—and as my steps carry me farther away, a new feeling begins to spread throughout my chest. One I've never felt before.

Pulling is the best way to describe it, I guess.

Like two invisible ropes, hers and mine, tying a knot to keep us together.

I let out a heavy breath and keep walking.

I'm relieved when the feeling is still there once I make it to my house. Daddy holds the door open for me and I turn to give her one last wave good-bye before entering in front of him.

The last thoughts I have before climbing into bed are wondering how far this rope-thing actually stretches, and being thankful I live across the street.

Because as I still feel the strong pull in my heart when I shut my eyes, I know it's in no danger of breaking anytime soon.

And that makes me very happy.

Chapter 2

Inevitable

Friendship.

It's a truly fascinating wonder to experience. I'm not speaking of those meaningless relationships built out of convenience, due to proximity or the need to just have someone to talk to in order to pass the time.

I'm referring to true friendship. A true *friend*. Someone who, within seconds of meeting for the first time, provides you the gift of security, granting an indescribable awareness that they will stand by you for the rest of your life. An unbreakable bond is built in that moment, and you just know, through the good times and bad, they will remain by your side, fiercely loyal with absolutely no hesitation or judgment.

And as your relationship blossoms, as you laugh until tears fill your eyes and cry within each other's arms until there are no tears left, that bond is strengthened until it becomes so intricately woven between the two of you, you quite literally become inseparable.

That's exactly what started seventeen years ago, the day I met Spencer Locke. Our initial bond has only strengthened over the years. So much so, that regardless of our recent time apart, while she went to college and I stayed in Fuller drinking myself into oblivion, the minute she moved back and into my apartment, it was as though no time had passed between us at all. We just picked up right where we left off as best friends.

Yet, right now, as she bounds into my room screaming at the top of her lungs, I kind of want to take that rope-thingy—as I used to call it—and strangle her with it.

"Wakey, wakey! Eggs and bakey!"

I shake my head and groan out loud. My entire body practically seizes in protest at the mention of food, and I force the current contents of my stomach back where they belong with a deep swallow.

The lyrical laughter of my roommate fills my ears, and I moan again because, though I normally enjoy the sound, this morning it's just too much. The freight train currently blaring its horn in warning, clearly having forgone its tracks for a joyride around my skull, is about all I can handle at the moment.

"Go away, hooker," I croak, then roll onto my stomach. Which isn't the best idea because as it sloshes with the movement, I remember the reason I swore off tequila last night. And the night before that.

Spencer remains rooted in place, and I'm sure her bright-blue eyes are burning two gaping holes into the back of my head. I can picture her right now. Long, blonde hair in a messy bun on top of her head, hands on her hips, fingers drumming madly, and her eyes tapered at the sides, glaring. Predictable and expected.

What's completely unexpected is the sound of quick shuffling followed by the wet finger assault in my earhole.

"Spencer! Ewwww!"

The throbbing in my head increases as I repeatedly try to bat her hand away from the side of my head. Still face down, a grin somehow manages to cross my face at the sound of her shrieks with each of my misses. I try to fight it, but I'm helpless against the traitorous smile. Something about her joyfulness is just . . . contagious.

By the time I finally manage to grab her wrist and roll over onto my back, we're both laughing so hard there are tears, and hiccups fill the room. Her body lands beside mine, and as her head falls onto my pillow, the laughter slowly fades and our eyes scrutinize the ceiling.

Simultaneously, we breathe in deeply.

Spencer inhales again. "Cass . . ." She leans to sniff my hair, then brilliantly concludes, "You reek of alcohol."

A breath of laughter passes through my lips, and I twist to face her. "What? You don't approve of Eau de Cassandra?" I waft the air in front of my face. "I like it. I find it rather . . . intoxicating."

I laugh shamelessly at my joke. Spencer grins, then adds, "Your jokes are as bad as your breath. You need to brush your teeth, Cass."

A snort works its way through my nose. I decide to spare her the agony of melting off her face and turn my gaze upward. She says nothing else but laces her fingers between mine. It's in moments like these where we're linked physically that our past reconnects with our present somehow. As if, from our stillness, our comfortable silence, sadness is allowed to blanket the air around us, and I'm again reminded that I'm not the only one who lost someone five years ago.

The same night Rat was taken from me—shot and killed alongside his sister—the love of Spencer's life, Dalton Greer, disappeared. Mysteriously. I've watched her morph from frantically worried to absolutely furious over the years, until finally she worked her way through her deep-rooted fear of abandonment, said good-bye, and let him go. At least that's what she *says*.

Regardless, she's back now, headstrong and working on her master's in sociology. She's fearless, primed to take on the world.

I, however, am pitifully weak in comparison. My still-drunken state this morning is proof of that fact. I barely managed to graduate high school, then flunked out of college. And although I do have a cosmetology license, and can work magic with even the most appalling of hair mishaps, my job is far from the aspirations of my youth.

But those dreams were stolen long before the loss of Rat. Rat was just another one of fate's cruel reminders that I will never be whole.

Spencer hasn't had the easiest life. I've known *that* since the day I met her. Yet, no matter the hardships she's had to endure, she's always chosen to fight her fears, and time and time again has emerged the victor.

I, however, chose to cower. I still choose to cower, drowning the voices in alcohol. I choose to have meaningless sex to prove I still have control over my body. And I choose to live with the constant, degrading chatter in my head in complete and utter silence.

Maybe one day I'll find the strength to choose a different path. Maybe, if I can manage to hold on to Spencer long enough, her strength will somehow trickle its way into my bloodstream and give me the courage to strip myself clean and face the world without this constant haze surrounding me.

That's not what you want. Not what you need.

Besides, you're not strong enough.

You're ours. You will always be ours.

We will never let you go from the darkness.

The voices quickly invade my mind, stifling any foolish hope conjured.

I quickly succumb to their wisdom as it numbs me, reveling in the much-needed comfort of feeling absolutely nothing. Feeling means pain, and I've experienced enough agony to last me through eternity.

As though reading my last thought, Spencer squeezes my hand and whispers, "It's a new day, Cass."

Emotion clogs my throat and I nod, willing the tears that have suddenly sprung not to spill. The burn in my eyes is not bred from sadness, however. It's a side effect from the scorch of the deep flames that constantly ravage me.

Anger at the loss of my childhood.

Anger at the circumstances that have become my penance in my adult life.

Anger that I wander through my existence, not able to fully live.

And anger that with each new day that passes, I could very well lose Spencer.

Our joined paths will eventually fork, and while I will be forced to continue down the one obscured in darkness, she will gracefully make her exit and follow the one brightened by the promise of a happy future.

I'm still not sure how far our bond will stretch. Will it be strong enough to maintain our friendship when this happens? Because it *will* happen.

I barely survived one severed bond.

The shredding of the second will undoubtedly kill me.

But I don't tell Spencer that.

I simply squeeze her hand right back, flash her my always brilliant, carefree smile, and respond, "Well, then. Let's get this bitch started."

Groaning yet again, I scrape myself out of bed while Spencer happily hops onto the floor like a fucking bunny. I fight for balance while running my fingers through my matted hair. She practically skips past me, only to stop and turn back in my direction.

"Hey? Where'd you go last night?" Her blue eyes scrutinize my appearance, and I lower my arms slowly to display my skintight, black leather skirt and matching bra.

Black, not leather. Because a leather bra would be absurd.

"Out with Jimmy, again. Like the skirt?" A sugary smile accompanies my question, covering the battle against my stomach's urge to upchuck with the admission. I *do* a lot of things lately that I'm not proud of, and Jimmy Thatcher is one of them.

Spencer shrugs her shoulders. "I guess? It's just so short. I mean, even shorter than those Daisy Dukes you used to wear in high school."

As soon as the words leave her mouth, all air is sucked out of the room, and our inaudible gasps replace it.

Dalton used to call me *Daisy Mae* all the time in high school, for obvious reasons. I hated the name, because I knew what he thought of me, his immediate assumption that I was a bad influence on Spencer. But in all honesty, I guarded her virtue as though it was mine. Well, mine before I so recklessly gave it away.

Once I recognized Spencer was in love with Dalton, and that he was equally in love with her, I encouraged her to lose said virtue . . . to him. That being said, if I had known he would leave later the same night, I might have steered her in another direction. Maybe . . . but, I doubt it. Their *union* was pretty much inevitable, and their denial had been exasperating.

Silence ensues and I watch her face fall along with her stare. In this moment, her sorrow equals mine. They are one and the same because it was my loss that led to hers.

Rat and Dalton were best friends. And they're both gone.

That one look is all I need to know. She hasn't ever really let go of Dalton, regardless of how hard she tries to convince herself. Both of us, for that matter. She still clings to the hope that he will magically reappear just as quickly as he left.

Blue eyes rise to find my dark ones, both sets lined with tears. I bite the edge of my lip and offer her my hand. "Like you said, it's a new day, Spence."

She nods weakly and curls her fingers into my palm, giving me a light squeeze.

"Then let's get this bitch started." Her tone may be tinged with sadness, but always the fighter, her eyes still display elements of both hope and determination. It's that optimism that makes Spencer, well, *Spencer*. And I wouldn't change her for the world.

In fact, it was her phone call asking if I needed a roommate that encouraged me to get my shit somewhat together. Even though I know better than to dare hope for myself, I think a part of me stubbornly clings to what her fight and resolve could do for me. Deep down, while I admit I'm a lost cause, just being around Spencer makes me feel stronger, as though maybe one day I will finally be able to silence the whispers in my mind.

Right on cue, I'm reminded of my weakness.

You're pathetic.

You will never be anything like Spencer.

She's pure and untainted.

You're dirty and disgusting.

Your entire existence is vile.

The phrases circle my mind. Each of their passes slice the already gaping hole in my chest, the pain they bring almost as crippling as the knowledge that they're absolutely true.

I swallow my tears, knowing I may have lost my chance at happily-ever-after, but I'm sure as hell determined to find my friend hers. As long as she holds on to her hope, then so will I. I will lose myself in it. I'll do so selfishly so when the inevitable happens, when my strength is depleted and I'm finally overcome by the monster etching the outskirts of my mind, it will be *her* hope that remains, strong enough to hold me so I'm not lost forever.

I don't want to be lost forever.

She releases my hand and smiles. "Love you, Cass."

I can't help the smile that crosses my face as I respond with the familiar words shared so often between us.

"Love *you*, times two."

Chapter 3

Krav Maga

I have good days, and I have bad ones. I imagine that's normal for anyone working his or her way through a traumatic experience. Some days I'm barely able to pull myself out of bed, and others, I wake to the sun shining through my bedroom window and bask in it. I allow its warmth to wash over me, and in those few precious moments, my memories don't define me. I'm just me.

Those are the best days.

And today just happened to be one of them. I was relaxed the entire day as I worked my way through mounds of hair. Coloring, cutting, waxing. I smiled the entire time, my memories dormant. I felt . . . normal.

I'm grateful for the much-needed reprieve as I head home to my apartment.

As soon as I hit the door and I'm inside, I toss my purse on the kitchen counter and call for Spencer.

No answer.

I pull a piece of bubblegum from my purse, unwrap it, and pop it in my mouth. I listen for her, and when I still hear nothing, I head toward her room to investigate. I'm two feet away when heavy breathing mixed with strange, somewhat obscene, grunting noises sound from behind Spencer's slightly ajar door. I stop dead in my tracks and tilt my head to the side, ceasing the smack of my bubblegum so I can better hear.

Another low grunt hits my ears, and I cover my mouth to mute a very mature giggle as I press my fingertips on the door. As it inches slowly open, I note how much I *really* like the dark-gray color of my nails, then lean forward to find Spencer's long blonde hair whipping from side to side as she hops on the balls of her bare feet.

Standing in front of her full-length mirror, she's dressed in black yoga pants, the white of her sports bra peeking out at me from underneath the straps of her turquoise tank top. My eyes widen at the scene playing out right in front of me.

Exercise?

My head jerks backward in refusal before I shake it to clear the evil word from my mind. I haven't done a lick of exercise in years.

Although I do definitely exert myself quite often. Last night with Ben Jackson, for example.

I think it was Ben.

A satisfied grin forms on my lips and I mentally applaud my heart-healthy efforts before barely poking my head into Spencer's room. I watch her throw what is probably the worst right hook I've ever witnessed at her own reflection, and the grin stretches into a broad smile.

"I pity the fool," I shout in a low, gravelly voice as I enter the room.

A tiny scream escapes my roommate before she stops, removes her headphones, then glares at me in the mirror as I walk up behind her. Spencer's hands land on her waist and her brows rise, but she offers no commentary or praise regarding my excellent portrayal of Mr. T.

My lips press to the side before I inquire, "Not a big Rocky fan, I gather?" Her blank stare is my only answer.

Blowing a bubble while examining myself in the mirror, I finger through my dark, tousled curls and adjust the straps of my cami before pulling it taut over the top my frayed jean shorts. Once satisfied with my appearance, I direct my gaze back at Spencer, who's still staring.

"Mr. T? You know? *Rocky III*, 'I pity the fool'?" My voice drops three octaves in effort to better my impersonation, but still nothing. I think I may have even snarled.

Releasing a defeated sigh at her lack of response, I decide it's better to just start over. I launch myself on her bed, bounce twice, then ask, "Whatcha doin'?"

She turns, pausing to eye me smiling back at her like a loon, then responds, "Krav Maga."

I nod as though I completely understand, then ask, "Krav Ma-whatthehellareyoutalkingabout?"

She giggles and enunciates slowly. "Krav. Ma. Ga."

"Oh, well since you said it that way, I *totally* understand what the hell you're talking about."

Spencer rolls her eyes, then continues. "I found a flyer on my car for this type of self-defense called Krav Maga. I looked into it and it's pretty freaking cool. So, I enrolled myself in some classes."

The clear image of her sad excuse for a right hook races my mind. "Yeah, good idea. You punch like a girl."

Her mouth opens, but no sound comes out. I snort-laugh because it's true. She does.

"You do."

Spencer's mouth stretches into a thin line, and that ever-present determination displays itself in her tightened features.

"Well, I *am* a girl," she retorts.

"Yeah," I answer. "But you should never punch like one. Or throw like one, for that matter. It gives us all a bad name. You need to take that shit by the balls and own it like a man."

Her mouth remains open, and I fight back laughter at the insulted expression on her face. Biting the inside of my cheek, I watch her find her words.

"Like you know how to punch." She cocks her hip for emphasis.

Contrary to what she believes, I *do* know how to punch. I gave Brian Thompson a right cross to the jaw, and it was perfection, if I do say so myself. I've never told her about that though.

We were in first grade, and I overheard Brian Thompson calling Spencer a "skinny scarecrow" at the place where everyone who was anyone hung out, the *jungle gym*. I heard laughter from his entourage and made my way over because I knew exactly *why* Spencer was so skinny, and honestly, that shit pissed me right the hell off. I strode up to him, and when he leaned on the painted bars in his designer jeans, I smiled my really sweet smile. As soon as I saw his lips curve upward and the whites of his teeth, I grinned wider, then clocked that fucker right in the nose.

I think he fell in love with me that day, because anything with a penis just seems to be bred to be *that* stupid.

And because of that fact, I fucked him years later in the school parking lot, just because I could.

"Helloooo, Cass." Spencer snaps her fingers in front of my face. "Where'd you go?"

"Thinking about Booger Thompson," I answer honestly.

Her mouth dips and her brows draw together. "The guy in the first grade that used to pick his nose until it bled?"

I smile to myself, knowing those nosebleeds were most likely the result of my fist connecting with his face. "The one and only."

"Why?"

I laugh out loud, then segue back into the present. "So, Krav Ma-couldntthinkofabettername. That's what you're doing in here?" She nods and I nod back. "Good. I took some self-defense classes when I moved away from home. You can never be too safe, so I say go for it."

Her nose crinkles in response. "You think?"

"I do. It's always better to be safe than sorry," I answer immediately. The need to protect oneself is of an importance often not realized until *after* the damage is done.

Sad, but true.

Spencer's eyes light up, and I know what's coming before it even leaves her mouth. In fact, I'm already shaking my head no when she claps her hands excitedly and yells, "Come with me! It'll be fun."

"Nah, I have plans. Next week?" I redirect.

Spencer narrows her eyes, then relents and gives me a sad shrug. "Okay, next week then."

I smile, then rise from her bed. "See ya in the morning?"

The sudden urge to clear the tightening of my throat tells me my good day is taking an emotional turn for the worse. I'm on a constant roller coaster of highs and lows, and I know, as a thin sheen of sweat begins to line my upper lip, I'm about to take a nosedive.

I need a night out, an alcoholic beverage in my hand, and a warm body to help me forget.

She watches me closely, then takes the two steps she needs to embrace me, whispering once her arms are around my neck, "I'm here if you need me, Cass."

Damn it all to hell if I don't want to break down and cry, but I don't. I close my eyes and will the threatening sadness away.

"I'm fine," I answer, then release her. "Just tired. Long day."

Her jaw tightens, and I know it kills her to let me be, but that's how Spencer has always been. She gives the room needed to breathe. And I love her for it.

After giving her my much-practiced, all-is-well smile, I walk out of her room, leaving her to get ready. I'm lying on my bed when I hear the front door open then close. As soon as the locks turn, I grab my cell from my nightstand and begin dialing. Thirty minutes later, Spencer's gone, and I'm still looking for a way to pass the time, but no one answers.

My throat constricts at the idea of having to spend the night alone, but I know what I need to do. I drag myself off my bed and head to the kitchen where my beloved Grey Goose awaits.

Pouring a glass, I down it completely alone in the middle of the kitchen, then pour another one, impatiently longing for numbness to set in. Once my cheeks are warm and I'm laughing at my own internal monologue, I know I'm right where I want to be.

Drunk.

Taking the third glass with me, I change into some awesome *Jem and the Holograms* pajamas that I found online and somehow land myself in bed. My head is fuzzy and my body is heavy, but it's not enough.

Taking a deep swig from my glass, I lean over and begin to jerk the pull chain on the lamp by my bed. Over and over I pull, darkness giving way to light, then back again, until my eyes begin to glaze over and I have to fight to keep my lids open.

As they lower, I think about how incredibly happy I am to have this lamp, because its light is so pretty. So safe. So familiar.

My safe haven.

With each yank of the chain, I find myself muttering under my breath.

Dark.

Light. Safe.

Dark.

Light. Safe.

Dark.

Light. Safe.

I continue doing this until my arm becomes too heavy and I can no longer pull the chain. The lamp remains on while my hand drops to the surface of the end table.

I inhale deeply and force my focus on that light until sleep finally finds me.

Chapter 4

The Beacon

Past—Twelve Years Old

"God . . ." I choke back a sob. "Not again."

The weight of absolute horror squeezes my chest, and all I see is the white of the ceiling above me as I look upward, spitting the words through gritted teeth. "Not. Again."

I close my eyes and try to breathe in deeply, shaking my head as warm tears seep from my eyes and trail down my cheeks. My hand trembles as I reach to the side. As soon as my palm grazes the sheets underneath me, a cry is wrenched from my lungs.

They're soaked. Again.

Tremors rake through my entire body, and I'm unsure if they're from the terror of the nightmare that startled me awake, or the embarrassment of admitting I'm twelve years old and I just wet the bed.

My mouth pinches in disgust as I climb out of the warm dampness. Before my bare feet even hit the ground, goose bumps spring along my skin from the shock of the cool air. I strip my nightgown over my head, throwing it on top of my bed, then quickly grab the one stashed away in my dresser drawer for when this happens. Once dressed, I gather my bedding—mattress pad, sheets, and throw blanket—and hold it close to my body as I tiptoe toward the basement.

As always, I close my eyes and reach for the railing. My palm glides over the slick wood and I hurriedly make my way through the darkness, counting the steps as I go.

One.

Two.

Three.

I chant the numbers one by one, and when my feet finally land on the cool cement floor, I make a mad dash across the room, then throw the wet contents inside the washer. Selecting the quickest cycle, I pour some detergent inside before quietly shutting the lid, knowing that I have exactly fifteen minutes until they're ready to be dried.

Repeating the same reciting ritual, I make my way up the stairs and quickly cross the house toward my bathroom, thankful my parents' room is on the other side. Not once in the past four years have they ever been awakened by my stirrings in the night.

I don't know how that's possible, but I'm thankful.

They will never know. They must never know.

My jaw tightens as disgusting screams and shrieks fill my head. Their words turn my stomach, and I'm forced to swallow the bile rising in the back of my throat.

You're dirty.

Weak.

Disgusting.

The chanting continues as I sit on the side of the bathtub and turn on the water, wishing I could run it full force to try to drown out the nasty voices.

But it doesn't work.

Nothing ever works, really.

I run enough water to cover the bottom of the tub, then strip off my gown and climb inside. I scrub furiously. By the time I'm done, my nails ache and my skin is raw. Yet, regardless of my many attempts, I never really feel clean. After several minutes spent focusing on the washing of my body, the shouts finally dull into whispers, fading into their usual low hum, and I step out of the tub.

Ten minutes down, five to go.

I wrap a towel around my sensitive skin and pad to my room. Folding the nightgown, I place it back into its usual spot in my drawer, then grab yet another change of clothing. I quickly yank on my panties and shorts, then pull a tank top over my head, before finally heading back down to the basement. The familiar smell of detergent fills the air, and I shake my head to rid it from my nostrils.

The soft fragrance once provided me a sense of security. Now, it just serves as a reminder.

Angry tears fill my eyes, but I won't cry. I refuse to cry anymore because each tear is just a reminder of my weakness. I can't afford the outward display. It will only lead to questions I don't want to answer.

Once the bedding is drying and I'm back upstairs in my room, I line my mattress with clean sheets and throw an old comforter over my body pillow—just in case—then tread to the window and open it, searching for the light I know will be there.

Once I find it, my body is on autopilot.

I know exactly how many steps it takes to cross the street.

I know exactly how long I have until I need to be back.

And I know exactly where I'm going to crash for the next couple hours.

Because with her lamp always on, Spencer is the only person I know who truly understands living a nightmare . . .

Even though I will *never* tell her mine.

Three more steps . . .

Tap.

Tap.

Tap.

The dimly lit window unlatches and slides open with no greeting. Questions such as, "What are you doing here?" and "Do your parents know where you are?" are no longer necessary. I've been escaping into this very bedroom across the street for a while now. The one always lit by a desk lamp, no matter how late, or early, it may be.

Once I've landed safely in her room, I shut the window behind me and watch Spencer climb back into the safety of her warm sheets in drowsy silence. For a brief moment, I allow myself to remember that feeling of safety, and a small pang of jealousy worms its way through my stomach.

Immediately, I push it aside and curse myself for being a shitty friend, because I know exactly why she sleeps with her light on. It's not the sheets that provide her security; it's that damn lamp sitting on her desk. So many years have passed . . . yet Spencer still cannot handle being left alone in the dark.

She offers me a sleepy smile as she nestles her head into her pillow.

"Bad dream again?" she asks, tucking the purple comforter under her chin.

"Yeah. It was horrible. I dreamt I was forced to attend the homecoming dance wearing a fuchsia dress that fit me like a potato sack. A real fucking nightmare."

"Cassie Cooper!"

I grin as she snort-giggles at my inappropriate use of language and head to her closet, where my floor-pallet makings await. Pulling out the pillows, I add softly, "Sorry to wake you. Again."

Spencer yawns, then simply shrugs. "No biggie."

My mouth dips as I think about how much I wish I could tell her how big this is for me. How comforting it is to know that when I knock at her window, freshly bathed from waking in sheets soaked with urine, I have this small, safe haven of time before I have to go back home, where horrific memories lurk around every corner.

Everything.

It means *everything*.

And she may never know.

Not once have my parents noticed me missing. They remain asleep, content in their dreams, while I try my best to escape my nightmares. It's become a dreadfully *familiar* routine. I wake, wash, bathe, dry, then escape here for a couple hours. Then I wake again and climb back through my window, only to pretend to be asleep when my mother finally enters my bedroom, completely oblivious to any changes in bedding. Already exhausted, I lower myself into Spencer's Wonder Woman sleeping bag and clear the emotion lodged in my throat.

It's so easy to avoid your own problems by busying yourself in someone else's life. I happen to find immense joy in the times I get to lose myself in Spencer's, so that's exactly what I do.

"So . . ." I draw, settling my head into the pillow.

Spencer shifts and her tangled blonde hair tumbles over the side of the bed when she leans to meet my eyes. We've had countless late-night conversations in these exact positions—me lying flat on the floor and Spencer hovering above me with her chin digging into the side of her mattress.

Seconds later, the distraction that *is* Spencer begins to work its magic and I clench my teeth to keep from smiling before I continue. "So, that boy that your mom emergency-fostered a while back, Dalton was it? Didn't I see him at school today?"

With the mention of his name, Spencer's cheeks redden, and her eyebrows hit her hairline.

She is so busted. *Crush busted.*

She nervously tucks a strand of hair behind her ear before answering, "Yeah, Mom worked to get him in on a full scholarship. He had to be tested, and she said he did well. His scores were better than most of ours." She sighs, then adds, "He was recently placed with the Housemans. They're a good foster family. He'll do well there, I think."

Her tone is hopeful, but her eyes give away her uncertainty. Her fear that he won't be okay, regardless of what both she and her mother have done to try to give him a better life. One safer and more stable than that from which he'd been running, most likely since the day he was born. I could see it in his guarded expression the day she introduced us, and I think he saw my need to escape too, but he never said a word.

He has never said much, as far as I can tell. Sadly, I completely identify with his need for silence, to keep his secrets hidden. I get it.

Secrets aren't meant to be shared. They're to remain hidden, safe from the judgment of others as they remain a burden for you, *and only you*, to carry alone.

As I watch unsure emotions depress Spencer's features, I'm reminded why I have never told her what happened to me, even though she so willingly offered the explanation of her past.

Oddly enough, that lamp was the beacon that saved me, but I never told her why. Why I suddenly started knocking at her well-lit window in the middle of the night. Why her presence, just having someone near that I trusted, soothed me to the point of finally being able to shut my eyes again to sleep, if only for a couple hours.

And although I know she wanted to ask, she never did. She gave me, and has continued to give me, the space to work through it on my own.

Does she have any idea of what I've experienced? No. I don't think so. I feel she senses something isn't right, but not what exactly.

Honestly, I would never tell her because of that troubled expression displayed on her face as we discuss her need to fix Dalton Greer. And I say that with the utmost respect and love.

Spencer is a bleeding heart, but I don't want to be her *project*, as Dalton may or may not turn out to be. The focus of *her* need to right the wrongs in this world.

I want no part of that side of Spencer.

"He'll be fine, Spence. Just give him time," I offer with a sigh and then turn on my side to face her. She gives me a halfhearted grin in return. Pulling the sleeping bag over my shoulder, I continue with my original line of questioning. "Any-whooooo, I saw him after school in the parking lot talking to another boy. Olive complexion, hazel eyes, gorgeous smile. Sound familiar?"

Her giggle fills the room, and I mischievously smile while waggling my eyebrows.

She laughs outright, then answers, "That's Rat."

My face pinches tightly in refusal of this horrid name that has been bestowed on the beautiful creature I spotted earlier today. "Rat? What the hell kind of name is that?"

Still smiling, she responds, "My thoughts exactly. Dalton said his name is Anthony, but he picked up the nickname Rat when he was younger and it just kind of stuck."

"How unfortunate for him," I state.

Another giggle from above. "I don't think he cares what other people think. That's the vibe I get from him."

Hmm. I like him already.

"Well . . ." I try to fight it, but a yawn manages its escape before I can finish my statement. "He's hot. Like, he should be on a book cover hot."

"Gah, Cass. You and your books. I don't know how you get away with reading all those grown-up romance novels."

It's my turn to laugh. "I don't. I keep them under my bed, hidden from Mom. But I'll tell you what, the minute they come out with electronic books, it's on. I'm all for that shit. Digital would be way easier to hide."

Spencer shakes her head, stifling her own yawn. "You're addicted to romance."

I nod. "I am, but fictional only. Real-life romance doesn't exist."

As soon as I say the words, the air in the room changes. I don't know if it's because of Spencer or me, but there's heaviness surrounding us.

As usual, I say anything I can to avoid this feeling. "I mean, think about it, Spence. All the time in my books, men are *ripping* the women's panties off. Impossible. And ridiculous. That would never happen in real life."

As usual, my words are meant only for pure shock value. It's a sad form of entertainment for me.

Spencer shakes her head with a horrified expression on her face.

I grin to myself.

She loves me.

The smothering air around us disappears as she laughs, and we fall into comfortable silence. After a few minutes, her sleepy, raspy tone hits my ears. "Love you, Cass." She rolls over, and I know she's finally finding her way back to the sleep I interrupted.

My throat tightens with her words, and I think about the meaning of love as I respond in my usual, high-pitched, joy-filled response. "Love you, times two."

But my mind refuses to sleep.

Love.

People toss the word around so freely, almost as though it's merely an afterthought, but the power within that one word can change a life. It can be used to manipulate and control, or it can provide healing and soothe the wounds of the broken.

Sometimes I wonder if I will ever know the love of the latter with someone other than Spencer. Someone who will love *all* of me, including my past and the torture it brings.

I know without a doubt that Spencer loves me unconditionally, even though I've never found the courage to tell her my secrets. I know she would love me even if I found the strength to share. And although I choose not to for my own reasons, the knowledge that this kind of love actually exists gives me the hope that maybe I will find my way through the darkness and overcome my nightmares.

Spencer is living proof that it can be done.

I stay on my side and listen to sounds of her deepening breaths. Clutching tightly to the fabric surrounding me, I give my normally guarded thoughts freedom as I imagine myself as the heroine of some romance novel. I envision myself as the unsuspecting, incredibly broken girl, who finds the one person who can help her, heal her, save her . . .

Reality will soon cloud my mind. I will be forced to peel myself out of this rare calm and go back home.

But for now, I allow myself the relief of pretending.

I imagine what it would be like to love romantically.

I replay the images of the boy I saw today—the hero, as he would be in my book if I were ever to live in one—and the warmth of his imagined presence slowly lulls me into a deep, peaceful sleep.

Chapter 5   ✦

Protection

"Come on, Cass. We're going to be late."

Parked outside Spencer's door, I listen to the sounds of her mad shuffling as she hurries to get ready. I, however, am already dressed because unfortunately, I don't have shit to do. Somehow, within the last ten minutes, I fell victim to Spencer's ploy in getting me to attend Krav Ma-whatthefuckdoesthisevenmeeeean??? class with her. I've been avoiding going with her for weeks, but tonight, she dug her claws in deep and wouldn't let go until I agreed. Plus, she mockingly humped my leg while pleading with me to go. It was so ridiculous, I couldn't *not* say yes.

Just as I blow what is quite possibly the largest bubble I've ever managed, her door flies open and my eyes land on her exasperated expression.

I suck the gum back through my teeth and inquire, "What's your deal with this Kung Fu shit?"

She glares back at me, clearly frustrated with my lack of interest. "It's *Krav Maga*. I told you that already. And it's awesome."

Pressing myself off the wall, I shake my head in mock disappointment. "If only we could get you this excited about dating. Instead, for the last three weeks you've chosen to hang out in a smelly gym with sweaty guys who are most likely overcompensating for the small girth of their dicks. I don't get it."

I fight back laughter at her expression. Getting under Spencer's skin just makes me so damn happy. God, I really need to get a life.

She huffs back at me. "I didn't ask you to. The only thing I've asked you to do is accompany me to this *one* class. It's 'bring a friend' night, and since you're like my only friend, you're officially obligated to attend. And you never know, you might actually learn something useful."

Another bored bubble is masterfully inflated through my lips before Spencer pops it, then wipes the palm of her hand onto my favorite retro Star Wars T-shirt. I open my mouth to scold her careless actions, but she continues, "Plus the instructor's hot. Like, *really* hot. Not my type, but maybe for you."

All thoughts about the preservation of my precious T-shirt disappear and I smile. I *do* love me some man-candy. "Well then, what the hell are we waiting for?"

Spencer rolls her eyes and turns on her heel while I laugh and follow her down the hall. I grab two water bottles then join her as we exit through the front door. Spencer dangles her keys in front of my face. "We're taking my baby."

My humor-filled expression plummets in defeat. She just giggles.

My steps are lazy and definitely unhurried as we walk down two flights of stairs and make our way to where Spencer's blue '68 Mustang awaits in all her glory. I hate that car. Why someone would ever want to possess a car that threatens permanent hearing loss every time you start the goddamn engine is beyond me. My poor auditory nerves will never be the same.

I glare at the Mustang before sliding inside and silently cursing myself for not calling dibs on the ride. After a lovely session of Spencer revving the engine every time I try to speak, which she knows I loathe, we finally make the ten-minute drive to the building my roommate has been practically living in over the past few weeks.

Crow's Gym.

As soon as we walk inside, I breathe in the pungent scent of plastic mats and sweat, the smell oddly comforting. It's been years since I attended self-defense classes, but I remember the feeling of empowerment they brought and suddenly I'm saddened I didn't continue. It sure beats the regular crushing shame I feel on the mornings I wake in random people's beds after getting wasted the night before.

While I found hard-earned relief and growth in the instruction, the voices somehow managed to divert my attention and reset my priorities. *They* offered what I craved.

Numbness.

On one very weak day, I more than willingly accepted their promise as I chose to party instead of attending class in search of a much more convenient form of escape. One night led to another, then another, until I just quit going.

But as I enter the pungent room, I find a renewed sense of resilience.

I make a mental note to find out more about this class, then find a place by Spencer on the mats. We busy ourselves by stretching until a collective silence fills the gym. I watch the back of the instructor as he confidently makes his way through his students toward the front of the class.

His hair is the first thing I notice. It's a very light shade of brown, almost blond, and shaved on the sides, but a long, thick strip lines the top of his head and is fastened tightly in the back with an elastic band. My eyes graze slowly over the rest of his muscular features as he walks—the thickness of his neck, the movement of his back underneath his white shirt, the flex of his triceps with each sway of his arms, the curves of the powerful legs that carry him through the crowd.

My entire body begins to tingle with awareness. A pull I haven't experienced in years tightens, and I suddenly find myself unable to break away, fixated on his every movement.

I'm sure Spencer is gloating next to me, but as much I want to turn to her and discuss why the hell she didn't force me to come to this class sooner, I cannot for the life of me disengage my stare. I'm hypnotized.

I'm also in trouble, because I swear to God, the minute he turns and I'm given my first glimpse of his face, I can no longer breathe. His eyes. They're the most beautiful I've ever seen. Dark blue—inviting—yet intense as he scrutinizes the crowd in front of him. I'm completely lost in them.

Somehow, through the mass of people, we lock gazes. His sapphire stare unwaveringly holds mine, and warmth floods my cheeks. Everything around me begins to slow and my normally spiraling world crawls to a standstill with my focus finding its center on him. There's an overwhelming sense of peace in this moment of stillness, and I find myself smiling at the relief it provides. In response, his rounded, perfectly shaped lips rise at the corners, and he holds my stare for a bit longer before finally breaking the connection and redirecting his attention to the class.

Air rushes my lungs the second he looks away, and I inhale deeply.

What the hell was *that*?

Completely baffled, I shake my head from side to side, then watch as he clasps his hands in front of his chest before addressing the class.

"Welcome to Krav Maga. My name is Grady Bennett and I will be instructing you this evening. For those of you joining us for the first time this evening, thank you for coming."

Hands now joined behind his back, Grady weaves his way through the rows of people as he speaks.

"Krav Maga, which translated from Hebrew as 'contact combat,' is a line of defense developed and initially only used by Israeli armed forces until the 1970s, when its instruction began worldwide. The most important thing to remember in the philosophy of Krav Maga—avoid confrontation when at all possible. Only when offered no other option do you utilize the techniques that will be taught tonight. The art of Krav Maga is not about violence but protection. We will go through various strikes and kicks, then pair off to visit particular situations that may be of use, which is the reason for this open class—take what is taught and utilize it as necessary."

Now back in position in front of us, there's a tender quality in his tone as he adds, "Although I hope you will never be in a situation that requires the use of these defensive techniques."

Grady's eyes are soft and caring as he shifts his gaze to each of the females in class before dismissing us to warm up. It's a gesture that tells me that, for whatever reason, he is extremely invested in those he teaches.

I turn to Spencer, who by the way is *totally* gloating, and ignore the shit-eating grin on her face while we throw some punches and launch kicks. Just as I begin to break a sweat, Grady's soothing voice filters through the air from across the room.

"Ladies, please pair up with someone of the opposite sex. It's crucial for you to learn how using the energy naturally carried within your center can overpower someone larger than you and for you to understand where the vulnerabilities lie in someone who could be *perceived* as a stronger opponent."

Immediately, I freeze and my mouth dries to the point that I'm forced to swallow what feels like pure sand. Avoiding any potential stares, my eyes are drawn to the mat below me, and I say a silent prayer that no man will be putting his hands on me during this exercise.

I hear nothing but my racing heartbeat as it whooshes through my ears; each of its rhythmic pounds borders the point of deafening. I close my eyes and draw in a deep breath, trying to calm my frantic nerves. On my second influx of much-needed air, the sound of footsteps approaching ceases and warmth spreads along the entire right side of my body as someone makes their move to stand beside me. I drive the dread from my mind and force my lids open. My eyes refuse to break from the ground, remaining locked on the mat as I swallow my fear. After releasing a long, calming breath, I finally manage to tear them away, only to find myself once again lost in a captivating shade of blue.

"Hi."

Grady Bennett stands in front of me, and as he offers that simple hello in introduction, the tenderness of his tone unleashes a floodgate of calm. It rushes through me, washing away my apprehension, and I have no choice but to breathe in a sigh of relief and grin at its effect. It's funny how the intonation of one tiny word has the power to invoke a feeling so paramount.

Is it me?

Or is that how every single female he comes into contact with responds to his voice?

"Hi," I respond, suddenly unable to speak above a whisper. My cheeks warm as the side of his mouth lifts, forming a crooked grin. His bright eyes are relentless as they hold my stare, their intensity a bit overwhelming. I clear my throat and extend my arm. "Cassie."

Grady's hand wraps around mine, and as his fingers curl and graze my skin, a shiver races through my entire body. The feeling morphs into one of comfort and my earlier grin stretches into a wide smile, thankful for the absence of nausea that typically accompanies having someone touch me.

"Grady," he answers, then squeezes my hand. Still holding it within his firm grasp, his eyes finally break from mine, dipping downward. His lips twitch as he adds, "Nice shirt."

I glance down, then back at him, goofy smile still present on my face. "Thanks. It's Star Wars."

"I can see that."

Then, he smiles. Like, full-on, breathtakingly beautiful smile.

It's shameful really. Very rarely will you find me being a girly-girl, but standing here, in front of this handsome stranger with the warmest of touches, whose strength *doesn't* overwhelm, and who also seems to have impeccable taste in clothing and quite possibly the most beautiful smile ever, I'm about two seconds from melting into a puddle right here on this mat. It's when my knees actually begin to buckle that I take action and force myself back to reality. Although, I will admit, this visit to *Never-Gonna-Happen* has been a nice, brief reprieve.

Stepping backward, I extract my hand and gesture toward the mats. "I guess it's time to teach me about the energy naturally carried within my center."

And that's when it happens.

An unfamiliar, nervous energy replaces the calm, and all of a sudden I'm the equivalent of a twelve-year-old boy.

I'd like to teach him about the energy in my *center.*

I bet if my center *and* his center *got together, we'd definitely have plenty of* natural *energy. For days.*

I've got your energy right here, blue eyes . . .

I can't help it.

Evidently ill-equipped to handle Grady Bennett and his smile, my brain completely shuts down and I go full-on stupid.

And giddy.

I am now, much to my mortification, *stupid-giddy*.

I give him my back to hide my laughter, but I'm fairly certain he heard the snort right before I turned. I try to choke back the amusement with *myself*, which only makes me want to laugh harder.

My body protests and tears begin to fill my eyes just as he steps closer behind me. The mat dips with his weight and his breaths tickle the back of my neck, and I'm so consumed by my own hilarity, my defenses have shut down right along with my brain. Strong hands wrap themselves around my hips, and caught completely off-guard, my entire body goes ramrod straight. My laughter ceases and my breathing stalls while all focus homes in on the fingers gripping my waist.

He's too close.

Too. Close.

Can't. Breathe.

His head peeks over my shoulder, edging into my peripheral vision. Breathing shallow breaths, I turn toward his face and my eyes latch on to his like a lifeline. Grady narrows his stare with the further stiffening of my body, and I force the biggest, broadest smile that has ever graced my face.

Unable to speak, I continue to hold that smile while he cocks his head so minutely, most wouldn't notice the movement. But I see it.

And he sees *me*.

His eyes are shrewd as they assess my reaction, then he finally relents, loosening his grip. I inhale deeply, but still holding his gaze, I offer him a slight dip of my head, signaling the permission for his touch to remain. All of which happens in the matter of seconds while the same fake-ass smile remains on my face.

The smile is for show, yet the language between the two of us is anything but.

Invisible to others, it's a silent conversation of lines drawn and boundaries learned.

Without me knowing the how or why, it's me connecting with someone who understands.

He sees me.

Grady clears his throat, then proceeds with teaching. "Your core is here. Your strength. You can use it to draw upon if and when a threatening situation presents itself."

My eyes are locked with his as I give him another indiscernible nod. One hand leaves my waist, latching onto my wrist, while the remaining hand tightens and draws my hip backward into the security of his frame. I face forward and rely on his strength to hold me as he masterfully twists both our bodies, guiding my arm into throwing a perfect right hook.

I feel like a puppet, and fuck me, I actually *like* it.

He. Sees. Me.

I bypass the need to revoke my own kick-ass woman card and sink into him. My entire body relaxes and melts into his frame. Something about him speaks to me. I can't put my finger on it, but I know I haven't felt this level of trust with another man since, well, since Rat.

Yet, as much as the memory of his loss pains me, I cannot stop this feeling of much-needed relief from overriding my naturally guarded intuition for self-protection. I'm no longer in control, and the knowledge of that fact scares the absolute shit out of me.

So in response, I do what I do best.

I reinforce my protective walls and pretend, because *that*, at least, I can command.

My reaction to Grady Bennett . . . not so much.

But I manage to mask it, and I do so masterfully.

For the remainder of class, I plaster the same bogus grin on my face. I fulfill my duty as the quirky friend for this class in which I'm thankfully unknown, because that's what I need to do to get through it without experiencing a full-fledged anxiety attack.

I squelch the feeling Grady's touch rouses as he guides me through more defensive exercises.

I hide my anxiety when he later pulls me in front of the entire class to demonstrate how to disarm a threat with a gun, which I manage with ease, much to his surprise.

I evade the situation at hand, catching Spencer's eyes and making inappropriate innuendos as Grady stands behind me. And when she giggles, I find myself laughing too.

My anxiety lessens as class continues, because once I'm able to shove my fears into the abyss where all avoidance is stored, I find my new focus.

Grady continues his instruction, but I totally zone out, watching Spencer with her partner. I'm lost in their interaction, intrigued by the peculiar awareness shared between them. He's huge, more of a bulky musculature to Grady's lean. His hair is long, the color of coffee, and gathered into a man bun, snug against the back of his head. His keen eyes are a shade darker than that of the hair on his head, as well as the beard that *almost* conceals his full smile in reaction to something Spencer says. I very much like the way he watches her closely as they spar. There seems to be an air of protectiveness in the way he touches her, very reminiscent of . . .

Dalton Greer.

That, however, is the only resemblance between the two. With Dalton's light-blond hair and clear blue eyes, they couldn't be more opposite in appearance.

Spencer laughs, and the sound of it as it travels the length of the gym . . . well, it warms me from the inside. I haven't heard her laugh, *really* laugh, in years. And as soon as it hits my ears, a true smile crosses my face.

Satisfaction envelops me, and I return my attention to our instructor, who has stopped instructing. He stands a mere two feet away, silent in his observation of my impromptu grin. My brows rise in surprise, and I break my stare from his to glance around the gym. People walk slowly, tired and sweaty as they scoop up their water bottles and head toward the exit of the gym.

Hmmm.

Class must have ended while I was spying on my best friend.

Time for me to get the hell out of here.

Just as I turn on my heel, I hear, "You're beautiful when you do that, you know."

My forward movement comes to a jerky halt, and I slowly pivot back in the direction of Grady. I jut my chin in his direction and angle my ear to better my hearing. "I'm sorry?"

His eyes are locked onto mine as he steps forward, repeating what I was sure I just misheard. "When you let yourself smile. You're beautiful when you do that."

"Um, thanks?" is my brilliant response, because what the hell do you say to something stated so blatantly sincere, it literally steals your breath? I, for one, would like to know because that shit never happens to me.

Ever.

So I do the only thing I know to do in response. I conjure a grin in thanks, then begin to walk away, but what he says next stops me dead in my tracks.

"Nope. Try again. That one doesn't count."

I know what he's trying to do, and damn if an ornery grin doesn't try to cross my face at his brashness. But if I'm nothing else, I'm consistent, and I have always, and will for the rest of my days, refuse to abide by other people's expectations. So, I clamp down on my back teeth and wheel around, completely straight-faced.

By the time I'm facing him again, he's a step closer. "I'd like to see more of that smile. Maybe, outside of class?"

Automatically, I shake my head.

I'd like to see more of that smile.

He can't know how much I want to touch those words and bring them close to my heart.

You're beautiful when you smile like that.

How nice it would be to be able to hear that daily, immerse myself in such luxury.

You will never deserve true love, Cassandra.

It will never be in the cards for a slut like you.

But as flattered as I may be, I know I'll refuse.

There's just too much to lose. I know this with all certainty based on my initial reaction to him today. Whether it's allowing his voice to soothe, or his touch to rile, or his stare to penetrate . . . there's just too much potential for *feeling* when it comes to Grady Bennett.

And I cannot allow that to happen.

I was broken a long time ago, and when I was put together again, I was forever changed. My broken self didn't really piece back together in a way that allowed me to be the same as I was before. *Feeling* is something I stay far away from, because if I were to shatter again, I know with absolute certainty there would be no coming back from that.

Therefore, I don't *date*.

I fuck.

I get what *I* need.

Then I leave.

Spencer's familiar giggle draws my attention, and I turn away from Grady to see her joking with her partner. Pleased as hell to hear the sound, my mouth curves upward on its own accord as I watch them walking side by side. *She* deserves to be happy.

Grady clears his throat, reeling my stare back in his direction. His eyes leave mine briefly, following the same path from where my gaze just came, then he looks back at me.

Remembering that I'm midconversation, I open my mouth to politely decline his offer, but he cuts me off. "And seeing as those two have been the only ones to coax that beautiful smile onto your face for the last half of my class, I say we bring them along."

My head jerks backward and my brows pinch in confusion. "What?"

Grady closes the distance between us, then leans into my personal space and gestures to the couple. "That's my friend, Liam Kelley. I happen to know he's very interested in learning more about your friend, and I'm very interested in learning about your smile. It's a win-win."

Is this guy for real?

I shake my head and offer a snort in reply. "You're interested in learning about my *smile*?"

He tilts his head to the side and narrows his eyes. Then those eyes fill with such intensity, I'm held captive as he states, "I am. I want to understand why you feel unworthy of your own smile. I've watched you this entire class and you want to know what I see?"

I want to tell him no. To tell him I'm scared to death to know what he sees. But I don't get a chance before he answers his own question.

"What I see is exactly this: You refuse to smile for yourself, but you smile for her. With everyone else, including me, it's forced, but with *her*, it's real. And it's beautiful. I'm interested in understanding why." He shrugs. "Call me selfish, but I also want to learn what it takes to get you to flash that gorgeous smile at me. *For* me."

Grady finishes with another matter-of-fact lift of his shoulders, as though he didn't just say the most profound thing anyone has ever said to me. And also, the most romantic.

My damn knees weaken *again* and I know it's time for me to skedaddle before I'm forced to acknowledge the effect his words have on me. I break my stare just in time to see Spencer give Liam a farewell wave. She turns to head in my direction, a wide grin on her face and a light in her eyes that's undeniable. Liam's protective stare follows her retreat, and as I watch, I know I have to do this for *her*.

And with her fast approach, I know I have to do it now.

I accept his invitation with one word.

"Tonight," I whisper, then explain. "It has to be tonight, before she has time to think about it."

He gives no noticeable reaction to my answer. He doesn't look disappointed. His face demonstrates nothing as he nods while taking my number.

Grady, a very perceptive individual as demonstrated about five seconds ago, does not miss the fact that this date will take place for Spencer's benefit only. As much as it saddens me, that's just the way it has to be. It's the way I *am*.

But it's his poised expression that betrays him. He's determined. And even worse, he's confident.

I steel my walls and give him a curt nod, resolute in my decision, before turning to intercept Spencer and guiding her to the exit.

I am doing this for her.

I *am* doing this for her.

Maybe if my head keeps repeating it, my heart will finally catch on.

But as it rouses, as it begins to pound relentlessly against my ribcage, I have a feeling my heart may be even more stubborn than Grady Bennett.

Chapter 6

Big Reveal

"He's gone, Spence. He's not coming back."

The words I'd spoken to Spencer a little over an hour ago still wreak havoc in my heart. It hurt me to say them out loud, knowing the sting she would feel from my brutal honesty.

But they needed to be said.

I know she still hasn't let go of the dream that *was* Dalton Greer, and I totally get it. I get that she fell in love with him the day she found him sitting on her porch, bruised and beaten. I understand they had a connection that formed that day, a bond that only strengthened through the years they spent together as friends. And I'm not going to lie, I was fucking *over the moon* when they finally got together.

But more than that, I can relate to losing someone important. One minute they're there and everything is hunky-dory, the next they're gone, with no explanation of *why*.

I've had my closure. We buried Rat. I know exactly where his body was laid to rest.

But Dalton, well . . . I can't imagine the agony Spencer experienced. *Experiences.* Hoping and wishing he'd show up one day, then the next, then the next. And I think she still believes he will miraculously appear, because that's just Spencer. Forever the optimist.

I, however, am not. And it's my duty as her best friend to bring her back down to earth sometimes.

So I had to remind her of the obvious in the midst of her tantrum about going out this evening. I know what I saw between her and Liam, and I'd be a shit friend to turn down this date just because being around Grady makes me all weird and awkward. I may suck at my own love life, but Spencer's I have mastered beautifully since we were in high school. I was the push needed to get Dalton to admit how he felt about Spencer, and so help me, I *will* help her find love again.

Starting with the ruggedly handsome Liam Kelley.

I have a good feeling about him.

And so will she before tonight is over, I just know it.

So as we pull into Bambino's parking lot, with Spencer's ridiculously loud engine drawing much unwanted attention, I affirm my plan. I will focus all efforts on Spencer, while pretending to be on a date with Grady. Totally doable.

We coast into an empty spot and once she cuts the engine and only silence exists, we look at each other and nod resolutely, grins on our faces.

At the same time, we step out of her car, and arms linked, we make our way to the front of the restaurant. As we approach, I take in Spencer's appearance, and almost laugh. We could *not* be more opposite. Yet, that's how we've always been. My yin to her yang.

I've donned a sleek, seductive black minidress that clings to my every curve, with matching six-inch, black heels that could be lethal weapons if need be. My dark hair is in a tight bun secured to the base of my neck, and my eyes are framed with a smoky outline a shade lighter than my dress.

Spencer is *hippie*-Spencer, the only modern thing on her body being skinny jeans. She's clad in a peasant top the color of rust, beige heels that I would deem practically flats (probably only three or four inches), and her hair is loose, tousled blonde waves, with two tiny braids crowning her head. Her blue eyes are bright with excitement, and I smile to myself at the sight before releasing her as the two men come into view.

Looking down, I carefully step ahead of Spencer, and the woodsy smell of Liam's cologne wafts in the air as he passes to greet my friend. I grin slightly, then my eyes lift from the pavement. As soon as I see Grady, all breath escapes me. It's an involuntary reaction, an effect I try to push to the back of my mind, but I'm helpless against it.

His light-brown hair is still secured at the back of his head, highlighting his perfectly pronounced jaw as he smiles back at me. He looks absolutely gorgeous. His muscular upper body is covered by a navy-blue button-down, sleeves folded at quarter-length, showcasing his corded forearms, flexed as he reaches for me. My eyes drift downward, noting the perfect fit of the charcoal dress pants that hug his hips and how they break at just the right length above his black dress shoes. Slowly, my gaze lifts, and I'm met with the same striking blue eyes that captured my attention today in class, seemingly brighter as they taper at the corners with his widening smile.

"Hi," he breathes, equally bereft of air as he takes my hand into his.

"Hi," I answer. The soft, low tone of his voice is surprisingly powerful as it strikes against my chest. Again, my protective walls tremble with its force, but I reinforce them, refusing to acknowledge the warmth of his free hand pressed gently against my lower back. His touch remains as he guides me into the restaurant, and I also force myself to disregard the sad truth that *no one* has ever done that for me.

It feels *nice*.

I focus my attention on the low rumble of Liam's voice from behind as he and Spencer fall into easy conversation. As we wait to be seated, I chance a glance at Grady, who seems to be eyeing the two with a bit of apprehension.

Odd.

He's the one that asked for this date because of Liam's interest in Spencer, yet uncertainty tugs at his features. After a few seconds, he disengages his stare from them, bringing his brilliant eyes to meet mine. All signs of hesitation disappear, and he smiles.

Those damn eyes.

I'm so screwed.

I give him a grin back. Grady tightens his stare and cocks his head to the side, a devastating smile still present on his face as he considers me. I narrow my eyes back at him, knowing those damn eyes have tagged the falsity of my smile. Which makes him grin . . . *wider.*

My expression doesn't change in the slightest, with the exception of the tightening of my jaw preventing the reaction he's looking for.

I repeat. I am *so* screwed with this guy.

And not the normal screwing involved with a guy.

Fuck.

I'm totally out of my element.

As soon as we're seated, both Grady and I order glasses of Cabernet; Spencer, Pinot Grigio; and Liam, water.

It's then that I really look at Liam for the first time tonight, and I have to say, he's even more handsome up close. His dark hair is down, shaggy waves brushing the shoulders of his dark-gray shirt. He watches Spencer intensely from the side as she says something to me, something that causes his bearded mouth to quirk into the tiniest of smiles. But I'm unable to comprehend what she's saying because as I watch him, I'm struck again by a sense of unnerving familiarity.

"Cassie." Spencer's voice draws my attention away from Liam. I shake my head then slide my stare to meet hers.

"Sorry," I state, clearing my throat. "I just zoned right on out there, didn't I?"

Spencer giggles, then adds, "*Ya think?*"

I smile with her laughter just as the waitress sets down our drinks on the table. We proceed to order our food, then I decide to take matters into my own hands by giving her the shove she needs. Metaphorically speaking, of course.

Angling away from Spencer, I give her my shoulder, twisting in my seat to fully face Grady. When his right brow lifts in question, I lean into him and explain nonchalantly under my breath, "Those two need to get better acquainted."

"Ah, I see." Grady whisks my glass of Cabernet off the table and hands it to me before grabbing his own. He brings it to his lips, and as he swallows, the movement of his throat momentarily mesmerizes me. Visions of my teeth nipping the skin underneath his perfectly sculpted jaw fill my head, so pronounced, I bite down on my bottom lip. His stare falls to my mouth, and his eyes remain there as he casually leans to set his glass onto the table before finally raising them to meet mine. He grins a mischievous, lopsided grin, then states, "I think perhaps *we* should get better acquainted. Don't you?"

The seductive tenor of his voice enters my mind and travels my body, striking me in a place least expected. Warmth pools between my legs and I cross them to relieve the sudden ache his voice alone elicited. Heat courses through my body, searing upward, until finally ending its deliciously torturous burn as it settles onto the tops of my cheeks.

As though sensing my body's traitorous reaction, Grady's eyes turn molten as he watches me take my own much-needed sip of wine. The sip turns into a long draw, then with shaking hands, I set the glass on the table beside Grady's.

I fight the urge to fan myself.

When did it get so fucking hot in here?

Before I can answer my own rhetorical question, all warmth is lost as a shower of chilled Pinot Grigio rains down mercilessly upon me. Or my dress, rather.

A loud gasp escapes me as I frantically begin swiping the droplets off the soaked, now freezing, material. Wide-eyed, I look across the table just in time to see Spencer steal my Cabernet and down the entire glass before announcing to the entire restaurant, "Cassie, we need to go to the bathroom. *Now.*"

The men stand as we rise from our seats.

"*Ya think?*" I repeat her earlier question, then watch completely dumbfounded as she apologizes to our dates. She latches so mercilessly on to my arm, it's quite possible she's drawing blood as she pulls me from the table. Her legs move at lightning speed, and I trip approximately five hundred seventy-four times in my six-inch heels before we finally make it to her mark: the bathroom.

The door closes and as Spencer turns, I inquire through my teeth, "What is *wrong* with you?"

Her face is flushed and her breaths are shallow. She raises her hand to her chest, and I begin to look around for a paper sack for her to breathe into before she passes out. The closest I come is the brown paper towel hanging from the dispenser.

My eyes find hers again and she shakes her head. "I'm losing it, Cass. Losing. It."

"I'm about to lose it if you don't tell me what the hell is going on," I respond, half-worried and half-pissed that wine is dripping onto my very expensive shoes. I lean toward the counter and hastily pull the paper towel from the dispenser, then lift my foot from the floor to dry off the leather.

My poor babies.

Once they're dry, I place them on the floor, then glare at Spencer, who says nothing, but continues shaking her head while the blood drains from her face. I narrow my eyes in frustration and step forward, fully intent on flicking her forehead, but my movement seems to prompt her ability to speak.

"I just saw Dalton. Well, what looked like Dalton, only not really, but kinda."

My neck jerks, and I subtly shake my own head. "What? I'm not following. What are you talking about?"

"Cass. Please don't freak out, but Liam . . . he looks like Dalton, kinda. In the right light, I mean, I know that's completely crazy but . . ." She bounces excitedly, and adds, "Oh. And he said something outside that made it sound like he knew you. I thought it was odd, but now . . ."

At that, I suck in a breath. The familiarity I felt earlier suddenly doesn't seem so far-fetched.

Spencer inhales deeply, then pauses in reflection before reaffirming, "Okay, I am *definitely* losing it, Cass."

After allowing myself a few seconds to think and forcing a few calming breaths, I come back to reality. And when I land, I'm understandably disturbed because now I feel like *I'm* losing it. This entire conversation is ludicrous. There's no way Liam Kelley is Dalton Greer. Absolutely no way.

And I refuse to allow Spencer to talk herself into believing it either.

So I plant my hands on my hips, cock my head, and give her my best I-know-you-don't-want-to-but-you're-coming-back-to-reality-with-me glare.

Her eyes grow wide, then she states in a low, strangely calm voice, "I swear on your Kindle, Cass."

I can't help it. I gasp out loud. Spencer knows the importance I place on my Kindle and everything downloaded onto it. She also knows the meaning of daring to swear upon it. It's not to be taken lightly. My Kindle is *my everything*.

I open my mouth, and only one word manages to escape as the gravity of the situation begins to sink in. "Noooooooooo . . ." She nods, and still in disbelief, I can do nothing other than repeat, "Noooooooooo . . ."

She keeps nodding, but when I open my mouth again, her hand clamps over it as she breathes, "Yesssssssss . . ."

Our stares remain locked, but in this moment, I *need* to know. Not so much for me, but for Spencer. I place my feet back into my drying heels, throw open the door, and exit the bathroom, Spencer's own heels clicking madly as she races behind me. Somehow we find ourselves hidden by a six-foot plastic monstrosity covered in leaves, and once we're settled, I push an annoying branch out of the way and lean forward to better assess Liam Kelley as he sits at the table. I watch him and Grady as they seem to be in a somewhat heated discussion. Well, one-sided discussion, as Grady seems to really be laying into Liam, judging by the hardened expressions on both their faces. Liam's darkened eyes are glaring back at Grady, who has just gained points in the badass department, because no joke, Liam Kelley looks downright terrifying right now. Not that I'm tallying.

But as I watch their interaction, I find myself squinting in effort to see Dalton Greer somewhere in Liam's fierce appearance. "I don't know, Spence. I mean," I tilt my head to the side, "maybe?"

"*Maybe* I'm just losing it. I saw it, but from far away, now I'm not so sure," she whispers. I watch as Liam's face tightens further into a scowl, a look I find extremely memorable. Dalton wasn't a very happy boy, and neither is Liam Kelly at the moment.

My voice is practically quaking when I finally speak. "No, I can see it. Kind of . . . Now that you've pointed it out, I mean, I see the resemblance."

Spencer's fingers curl over the tops of my shoulders. "What the hell are we going to do?"

I begin to answer, but instead my words are cut off and my body jerks in surprise when I hear a voice call, "Are you ladies okay?"

Perhaps we're not as covert as we thought.

Together, we twist our bodies in the direction of a somewhat alarmed waitress. "*We're fine,*" I state at the same time as Spencer.

Together, we silently watch her face screw up with our simultaneous answer. Her uncertainty is clear about whether or not to announce the two crazy ladies hiding behind this fake-ass tree, but then she makes her decision and leaves well enough alone by hauling ass to the kitchen.

I tear my eyes away from the swinging doors and direct them at Spencer. "What do you want to do?"

She shrugs and inhales deeply before answering. "I guess just have dinner without looking at him? Maybe my mind is just superimposing Dalton's face on Liam as payback for the last five years of useless pining?"

It's then that my own face screws up with my response. "Highly unlikely."

We look back to the table, and I can feel Spencer's nerves rolling off her in repeated, anxiety-ridden waves. I'm about to make the decision for her when she finally releases her grip from my shoulders and stands on her own, resolute. "Well, I guess we just go over there and act normal. Like nothing happened."

"Right," I scoff, because I know Spencer. Unlike me, Spencer is very *bad* at pretending. No way in hell is she going to be able to act as though nothing happened. She may intend to, but the minute we get to the table, she'll say something. It's just her nature.

We lock gazes, and once she has composed herself, we nod, then make our way back to the table. I can feel the blood draining from my face as we approach, because if Spencer's right, if this is in fact Dalton Greer, then fuck me.

Where the hell has he been for five fucking years and what the hell is he doing here now pretending to be Liam Kelley?

I watch from the side as Spencer eyes him with caution while he stands. Then he confirms our theory with what could possibly be the best plot twist ever, when he extends his hand in her direction and asks, "Wanna take a ride?"

His voice is so unlike that of the Dalton I remember. Liam's is raspy and gritty and low. Dalton's was more similar to Grady's, soothing in tone. But then I see it, the torture in his eyes when she refuses to take his hand. The look alone negates any previous doubt as to whether or not, after five long years, Dalton Greer is alive and standing in front of me. It's the same pained expression he always wore when around Spencer.

Why now after all these years? After everything?

I know now, and have since news broke about Rat's death, all about Dalton's past. Detective Kirk Lawson explained it to Spencer in a sit-down at her house shortly after he disappeared, which she later shared with me.

Dalton had been forced to take refuge in the house of Silas Kincaid, an infamous drug lord in our area. He did so in order to find protection from those who'd abused him, driving him to live a double life, so to speak. There was the Dalton of the streets, and the Dalton who aspired to be what Spencer deserved. And as I observe the look on his face as he warily gauges Spencer's reaction, it's so very reminiscent of the tortured nineteen-year-old who disappeared years ago without a trace.

That day, I also found out that Dalton hadn't been the only one sucked into Silas's world. Rat had also been pulled under, working side by side with Dalton since they were kids, both forced to prove their allegiance to Silas Kincaid. Presumably, when Rat faltered, he was shot and killed on the spot. Dalton disappeared the same night.

I take my time to examine the man standing in front of me.

While his appearance is completely opposite of that of the Dalton Greer I remember, his presence, the familiar air of intimidation that often cleared a five-foot radius around him, is still very much present.

I tighten my gaze and my mind wanders.

He had always been protective of Spencer, swearing he would never let anything hurt her, then he just left. It makes no sense.

What could possibly have driven Dalton to leave so abruptly, doing exactly what he swore he would never do, completely shattering her? And what makes him think it's okay to show up now? What does he want with Spencer?

My mind circles back to what I learned after he left.

After Rat's death, did Dalton make his declaration of allegiance? And if that was the case, his loyalty did not fall with Silas Kincaid. Maybe Dalton understood the ramifications of his decision, knowing Silas would come after him, and left in order to do the only thing he's ever wanted. To protect Spencer.

So the question still remains, why did he come back?

Spencer's stare connects with mine, and I lift my brows in question. She shrugs her shoulders in silent response, then focuses her attention once again on Liam . . . Dalton. Just as when we were kids, she remains impervious to the power of his presence. She simply narrows her eyes, but then turns back to him and asks/implies, "We can take my car?"

As I watch their interaction, I find myself fighting the most inopportune smile. The whole scene playing out in front of me between them might as well be happening back in high school. And from what I remember, all fingers point to the fact that Dalton Greer is about to get his ass chewed.

Dalton says nothing, but dips his chin. Accepting of his answer, Spencer then turns her sights to Grady and points. "I'm going to get your license plate number, just in case. Cassie better make it home safely, because I *know* people." And by people, I know she means Detective Lawson, who has become a very important fixture in both her and her mother's lives, especially her mother's.

Grady squashes his laughter, then responds, "She'll be home by eleven. Scout's honor." Then he dares to present her three extended fingers, sealing his promise.

I release a heavy breath in refusal, because who the hell, at the age of twenty-three, is home at fucking eleven o'clock? I sure as hell don't plan on that happening, based on premise alone. Grady looks to me and winks, and for the first time since meeting Grady Bennett, I smile back at him. A full-fledged, real smile.

I could blame it on being mentally weakened and worn from my nonstop musing about Dalton's reappearance. But I don't. Honestly, I grin because I happen to find Grady Bennett extremely funny.

My eyes remain on him, and his on mine, while there's further interaction between the still-feuding couple across from us. I hear nothing but the beat of my own heart as he mouths, *beautiful*. Masterfully, he disconnects our stare, then redirects his gaze to the couple now seemingly at a standoff, never missing a beat as he offers to Dalton, "Looks like you're going to have a fun evening."

At that, I laugh. I try to cover it, but unfortunately, it does not go unnoticed. Spencer glares at me before returning her eyes to Dalton.

In turn, he reaches for his wallet, throws a couple hundred-dollar bills on the table, and proclaims, "Dinner's on me."

Grady's brows skyrocket as he takes in the money, then he grins and garners the attention of our waitress as he announces proudly, "Well then, I'm changing my order."

I can't help it. I laugh again, and Spencer's glare is removed from Dalton and redirected at Grady. "Then cancel ours."

Grady is still smiling, but he respectfully dips his head in concession. "You got it."

Dalton gives Grady a look of warning, but eventually relents and hooks his fingers around Spencer's arm, leading her away from us and out of the restaurant. Once they're out of sight, Grady gestures toward my now dry, empty chair and I oblige. I slide into the offered seat just as the waitress approaches. Grady turns in his chair, says something that makes her giggle, and I'm mid eye roll by the time he twists back to face me. His smile widens as my eyes settle back into my head.

He says nothing, but allows me the time I need to digest this evening's whirlwind of events.

Grady Bennett knows not just Liam, but *Dalton*, which means he knows about his past.

If Grady knows about Dalton's past, it would suggest that Dalton is back to address that past. Possibly to avenge the death of his best friend by wiping away the existence of Silas Kincaid and his organization.

And to do that, he would need the help of local police.

I nibble on my lip as the pieces slowly begin to click together.

In all of his conversations, Detective Lawson never seemed particularly worried about Dalton's disappearance. Which now, if my theory is true, would make complete sense if they've been working together this entire time.

But Lawson is also fiercely protective of Spencer, which means he wouldn't allow Dalton to show his face again in this town unless she was safe.

Another click.

It's not Dalton's face, it's *Liam's*.

Oh my God.

Dalton is working undercover for Lawson.

I glance back at Grady and narrow my stare, studying him.

And as I do, I become more convinced of my theory.

Lawson would need a team behind him to take Silas down. That *has* to be Grady's connection to Dalton. They're both cops. It's the only thing that makes sense. So as the conclusion is drawn and cemented in my mind, I candidly ask, "Is your name really Grady Bennett?"

His face falls serious and he answers without a lick of hesitation. "Yes."

The lack of his uncertainty regarding my question is all I need. Each piece of my theory clicks together. And once it's formed, Dalton's reemergence and Grady's role in his revenge are presented in an undeniably clear picture. The puzzle is finally complete.

I lean closer to him, and for a beautiful life lost and for the past five years of happiness stolen from my friend, I state on a stern whisper, "I hope one of you shoots that motherfucker right between the eyes."

Grady's mouth jerks upward in clear understanding before he confirms, "You got it."

"Good." Satisfied, I nod, then relax back into my seat before continuing. "I will ask you nothing else, other than this. Is Spencer in any danger?"

He shakes his head and responds, his tone a bit angered. "Dalton planted the flyer for my class on Spencer's windshield so she would be capable of protecting herself in the *extremely* remote chance she would need to do so. Your apartment has been secured and is being watched by my men twenty-four hours a day. We've taken the necessary precautions to keep *both* of you safe."

I fight a smile at the mention of the flyer, because that is such a *Dalton* move. But when he mentions the nightly stakeouts happening at my apartment, my head jerks in surprise. "You've been watching my apartment?"

Grady's mouth quirks, and when my eyes fall directly to his perfect lips, the heat from before resurges between us. I swallow deeply as he slowly inches forward, the warmth of his body searing my skin as he hovers near me. Then those lips pass my own to land on the shell of my ear before he whispers, "*My men* watch your apartment."

He chuckles and his heated breaths fan my ear, sending a wave of goose bumps rising along my skin. "For the first time in my career, I was forced to take *myself* off surveillance. Because while my main objective was to keep an eye on your surroundings, all I could focus on was beautiful, irresistible you. I *couldn't* tear my eyes away from you, and because of that, my involvement was compromised."

By this point, I'm no longer breathing, so as soon as he retracts his presence and is once again relaxing in his chair, a whoosh of air enters my lungs. After drawing a long breath in and releasing it, I do the only thing I can do.

I blink.

Grady chuckles.

I blink again.

Then I clear my throat and break my one-question rule, again. "Exactly how *long* have you been watching me?"

Grady leans forward, pressing his forearms on his thighs and lacing his hands so they dangle between his knees. Then he opens his mouth and completely blows my mind.

"I've been watching you long enough to know something broke you. Something you keep hidden, something that weighs on your soul. You pretend, but your eyes betray you. There's pain hidden within them, but when you smile, *really* smile, the pain is gone and you're *you*. Not the person you pretend to be. And like I said earlier, I find that very interesting. I want to know what makes you smile, how to make you smile, and how to keep that smile a permanent fixture on that gorgeous face of yours. And more importantly, I want to know why you feel unworthy of that smile, and how to fix that too." He gives me a crooked grin and shakes his head. "I guess what I'm saying is, I would very much like the chance to get to know *you*, if you'll let me."

I blink, then swallow. Because once again, there is nothing I can say that could ever match that.

He laughs silently, gorgeous smile on full display, then extends his hand. "Do you trust me?"

Trust. It's another one of those small words that carries such profound meaning.

I trusted once.

And it was that trust that broke me.

I dared to trust a second time.

And the evil hands of Silas Kincaid slaughtered that.

I don't know if I have it in me to trust a third time. I really don't. Not with someone who makes me laugh, or someone who makes me feel things completely unprecedented. Someone who without a doubt carries the power to completely shatter me.

Right on cue, voices slither through my mind, screaming their protest. *Their warnings.*

Only Spencer deserves light and sunshine.

Not you, Cassandra. Never for you.

You will always be alone.

All alone.

As you deserve.

I look away to the empty chairs across the table.

The voices rejoice in their victory while the obvious fact in front of me slices another gash in my chest.

I'm all alone.

Grady's voice is barely heard above their yelling. But soon, the soothing tenor enters my mind and stifles their screams. "Don't get lost in that head of yours. I'm right here. Focus on me."

I tear my gaze away from the chairs to find myself immersed in a beautiful sapphire stare, so earnest and sincere as his outreached hand remains, waiting for me to find the courage to take hold. My chin trembles and moisture coats my eyes. I swallow and allow his stare to fortify me as I attempt to will the voices away.

I'm so tired of pretending.

And maybe it's the prolonged exhaustion, but as I root myself into those damn eyes, I find myself succumbing to their comfort.

I know I cannot fully grant his request.

Or can I?

As I search deep within myself, I find there's just not enough courage left in my reserve.

But still, I want.

But you don't deserve that. You never have.

I want.

But you can't have.

God, do *I want*.

Inhaling deeply, I hold his gaze and after several heavy seconds, I finally release my breath. My arm reaches forward, and as his hand wraps around mine, I revel in its warmth. It travels through my body and its heat settles in my cheeks. I narrow my eyes, but decide in this moment, I will give him all I can give. "I *want* to trust you."

Much to my surprise, what I think I see in Grady's expression is . . . triumph.

I've been watching you long enough to know something broke you. I want to know why you feel unworthy of that smile, and how to fix that too.

The corners of his mouth kick up as he states victoriously, "That's enough for me."

That's enough for him. Who is this man?

Not to be deterred, Grady then glances down at his watch, snatches Dalton's hundreds from the table, and signals to the waitress as she passes by, swiftly concluding our time at Bambino's.

"Then let's get the fuck out of here. You have an eleven o'clock curfew."

Chapter 7 ✦
Comfort Zone

"Um, no." I shake my head manically. "Not gonna happen, blue eyes."

Grady's shoulders wrack against the seat next to me as he laughs, unabashedly. I wait patiently for him to cotton to the fact that (a) there's nothing remotely funny about the building in front of me, (b) his laughter is not setting a good precedent for this whole trust thing he's so keen on, and (again) (c) there's nothing remotely funny about the building in front of me.

Once he finally manages to get control of himself and kindly stops laughing in my face, he removes all evidence by wiping his eyes before twisting to face me.

"Oh, it's gonna happen." His voice is suddenly scary fierce and his stare is equally determined.

"Um, no," I repeat, then add in a much more vicious tone, "One does not roller-skate in a minidress, Grady."

"Come on," he beckons. "It'll be fun."

"It'll be me, falling flat on my ass in two seconds, while wearing a *minidress*."

Grady grins while shrugging innocently. "Not really seeing the problem with that, Cass."

I hate him.

I also hate how the way he just called me *Cass* makes my insides all wonky.

"Of course you don't see the problem, *Gray* . . ." I mimic the endearment. "Seeing as you only have a penis residing between your legs." I gesture at my lap, which only makes him smile wider.

"Therefore, you know nothing about the rules of the minidress. Number one being, you don't roller-skate in one. Ever."

"Your argument's for shit, *Cass*. I happen to have a very good friend who does, in fact, have a penis between his legs, and has demonstrated many times how much fun you can have while roller-skating in a minidress."

I take note to ask about said friend when not so irritated, because he sounds all kinds of awesome, then counter, "I'm not going."

"Yes, you are. And it's going to be fun."

I roll my eyes, then cross my arms over my chest, turning to gaze out the window. I breathe in deeply and shake my head, my voice a mere whisper as I admit to the glass, "I'm going to fall."

Grady's humor sobers, and he immediately reaches to take hold of my hand. I reluctantly give it to him, then force myself to meet his stare.

"You said you *want* to trust me. Well, consider this the first step." He firms his grip, and his eyes pierce mine. "I will *never* let you fall."

He pauses, drawing in a breath, then cocks his brow. "You need to do something fun. Conquer something outside your comfort zone. Lose control. That's what I'm offering you, right here, right now. A chance to have some fun, and maybe . . . I don't know, call me crazy, but maybe even laugh a little."

The image of the gorgeous badass beside me in a pair of roller skates forms in my mind, and fuck me if I don't have to keep the hint of laughter from being displayed on my face.

Grady eyes my reaction and lifts a challenging brow, grinning while he does it.

I remind myself that I hate him.

Then I think, *How much can you hate someone if you have to remind yourself to do so?* So I amend, thinking that I *dislike* his cocky self very much, and release his hand while offering, "Fine. But if this is some sick roller derby fetish, you're going to be sorely disappointed."

He shakes his head and chuckles to himself before opening his door while I do the same. I tuck my clutch under the seat for safe-keeping and begin to step out of the car. As soon as my heels hit the pavement, he's there, warm hand extended as I make my exit. I take hold, allowing him to guide me safely, and keep my grip tight as we make our way to the front doors of Skate Place.

As we enter, blaring music from the DJ booth in the corner blasts us. The door shuts behind us and I happen a glance at my kick-ass heels. My metaphorical lightbulb ignites, and I grin to myself before shaking my head in mock disappointment. "Darn, I don't have any socks. Looks like I won't be skating this evening." I shrug. "But I'll be happy to watch you relive your elementary years from the sidelines."

Clearly disregarding my excuse, Grady's hold remains as he tugs me gently behind him toward the front counter. Skate Place T-shirts, key chains, bumper stickers, and the other memorabilia that line its glass shelves come into view with our approach. My eyes flit to each in appreciation before finally landing, then hardening, on a lone pair of highlighter-yellow Skate Place tube socks dangling from a tiny rack by the cash register.

They're hideous.

They're blinding.

They're also taunting me, so I glare harder.

"Two adults, two skates, and the *last* pair of socks." Grady faces me, his face bright with sardonic joy. "Well, well, well . . . aren't you the lucky one?"

Aborting my illogical personification of a pair of tube socks, I redirect my glare to him. He, in turn, waggles his eyebrows, then pays the man with Dalton's money.

Once we have our roller skates in hand, Grady leads me to a bench lining the white walls of the skating rink, and I reluctantly take a seat. An old eighties ballad begins, and I watch as kids of all ages begin circling the rink, noting the absence of any adults in the moving crowd. Well, ones not attached to a youngster of their own, that is.

"Grady . . ." I swallow and begin nervously nibbling my bottom lip.

Already kneeling in front of me, Grady's slicked-back hair shines as light from above is reflected in it. My eyes lose sight of the ponytail at the base of his neck and connect with his as he looks up at me. His stare continues holding mine as he slides the kick-ass heel off my foot, and I fight the shiver as his fingers graze, then tighten, around my calf muscle, giving me a reassuring squeeze. "I won't let you fall, Cassie. Okay?"

Embarrassment heats my cheeks and my heart kicks up its rhythm. Twenty-three years old, and I've never skated. The knowledge of why begins to saturate the air around me, and suddenly I find it difficult to breathe.

After a certain point in my youth, I just kind of checked out. I remember being a very sociable child at one time, but after . . . well, after . . . the only person I really ever spoke to was Spencer. I shunned all my other friends. I hid any birthday invitations received, often chucking them immediately in the nearest trash can, knowing the parties would only make me a nervous wreck. Because being around people I didn't know, adults I didn't know, well . . . those situations I couldn't really handle. In fact, I rarely spoke to any adults at all, my parents included.

Needless to say, I missed out on many skating parties during my youth, hence my inability to skate.

I grew out of it eventually. I found some strength in my pretending, I think. I reinvented myself in a way that my past was no longer my weakness, because it simply didn't exist. I erased it from my mind, and in turn, the ever-present anxiety disappeared.

Except, it didn't. Not really.

I sure as hell pretended that it did though. It was the only way I could cope and feel *somewhat* normal.

Grady's confident gaze remains fixed on mine, and I give him a hesitant dip of my head. He gifts me a wink, then proceeds to slide the sock over my foot and tugs it gently upward until it covers my calf. He performs the same ritual on the other leg, all while I remain silent as I watch, amazed at his unwavering patience.

Again, who is this man?
And where the hell did he come from?
And why is he here with me?

After both feet are weighted heavily with skates, his warm hand cups my knee, giving me another encouraging squeeze before he rises off the ground to take a seat next to me. I test the wheels, alternating each skate as I glide them slowly along the carpet while Grady finishes lacing his own. When he's finished, he rises to his feet, then masterfully executes a half-turn, positioning himself directly in front of me.

Grinning down at me, he announces, "Go time."

I swallow deeply as Grady reaches for me with both hands, and I willingly slide mine into his, allowing him to lift me from my seated position. Once standing, I'm surprised to find that my feet don't immediately fly out from underneath me. I glance down, shock and a tinge of triumph working their way through my body by way of a relieved chuckle. I grin, then cast my eyes upward. The white of Grady's teeth shines brightly with his smile, and his own eyes delight as he begins to wheel backward, taking me with him.

I skate-walk, the loud *clunk* with each step making me smile wider at the ridiculous sound. With our grips locked together, we continue making our way to the main floor. I scan for a beginner's lane, but don't see one. All I can see are people zipping past at ungodly speeds. My head begins to shake back and forth and my entire body locks in clear objection to this madness, my recent bout of self-assuredness beginning to wane.

Grady pinches my chin between his thumb and forefinger, tearing my horrified gaze away from the floor and forcing it onto his narrowing stare. "I've got you. Eyes on me. Only me."

My throat clamps shut, but I force a breath and with my eyes bolted to his, I move my right leg forward. Then my left, and my right again. My confidence grows with each successful step taken. And it continues to do so, until the inevitable finally happens. It's then that I realize the ill-colored red carpet is this rink's evil ploy to lure novices such as myself into a false sense of security.

As soon as I set foot onto the slick surface of the skate floor, my left leg flies forward while the rest of my body shoots in the opposite direction. My life flashes before my eyes upon my rapid descent, until a strong arm clamps itself around my waist and I'm heaved into the muscled wall of Grady's chest. My feet slip every which way, continuously searching for some sort of traction beneath them, but unfortunately the floor doesn't seem to be equipped with *any*. At all.

"Jesus *Christ*!" The sound of my cry is muffled into Grady's chest as he tightens his hold, allowing me the time I need to find my footing. Adrenaline spikes my blood as it surges, and my body trembles in response, overcome with its release as I continue trying to get my wheeled feet under control. Once my legs are solid and located firmly underneath me, I slowly unclench my fingers from the security of Grady's navy-blue shirt. My heart pounds against his chest, its beat threatening to break through my ribcage as it drums mercilessly beneath it. I inhale deeply in attempt to calm my body's reaction, then lift my eyes. They continue to climb upward until they find Grady's wide-eyed stare, a stare that tells me without a doubt, he thought I'd embellished my inability to skate.

I try to fight it, but the recent wave of adrenaline now flooding my system overpowers me. The suppressed giggle inflates until it's finally released, freeing itself from the depths of my deadened soul. As it rises, its effervescence carries with it a portion of the heaviness constantly draped over me. The weight dissipates, and with its disappearance, I do something I haven't done with someone other than Spencer in years.

I laugh. *Really* laugh.

"I'm so sorry," I somehow manage through multiple hiccups. "I tried to tell you."

I fist the back of his collar, making sure I have a damn good hold before releasing my other hand to wipe the tears from my eyes. Both of Grady's arms are now around my waist, holding me securely, and his body is also shaking from laughter.

Once it tapers off, he shakes his head and his eyes are full of mirth as he states, "You have completely *annihilated* my roller derby fetish."

My smile remains intact as he speaks, and his stare dips to my mouth then lifts back to my eyes before he amends, "Or not."

Our laughter subsides, leaving heated stares in its wake. Still high on adrenaline and *clearly* not thinking, I link my hands behind his neck and press my body against his. Grady inhales deeply upon contact, and with one arm still secured tightly around my waist, the other is freed as his hand lowers to caress my ass. Our bodies are flush, so close, I'm sure he can feel my heart pounding against his chest.

Holding his stare, I urge his face closer to mine, and my eyes drift shut as he consents. The arm around my waist aligns with my spine, and his strong fingers curl around the base of my neck. With his grip still firm, he tilts me backward, and my body willingly takes his direction as it leans into his hold. Breathlessly, I wait to feel his mouth touch mine, but it never does. He continues to lower his head until his heated breaths mercilessly strike my neck. His mouth hovers over my skin, deliciously tortuous, before inching farther to press his parted lips against the area where my pulse beats erratically beneath my skin. Desire snakes through every inch of my body and I swallow in response, which seems to encourage him. His mouth opens wider and the tip of his velvet-soft tongue glides gently along my skin. Any fight I thought I had flees me, and I allow the shiver he elicits to run its course. He smiles into my neck, then ends the kiss, sealing his lips against my skin, before breaking away and righting our bodies.

I'm practically panting when he sets me upright, and my breaths increase as Grady leans to press his forehead against mine, his breathing just as affected. His piercing blue eyes bore into my returning stare, searching for something I know for certain he will never find.

As much as I would love to drown in this feeling, as much as I would love to surrender and give myself to him completely, I can't.

I'm damaged.

Shattered.

I can only offer pieces of what he seeks because pieces are all that remain.

I open my mouth to explain this, but he cuts me off, pressing away as he asks, "Dance with me?" His eyes are earnest and pleading, and if I weren't already broken, the look in them alone would destroy me.

"I can't." My voice trembles with my refusal, from fear or sadness, I'm unsure. I begin to remove my linked arms from his shoulders, but he lifts his hand to secure them in place.

"One dance. Then we can go."

Right on cue, a new song begins and it is quite possibly the best—and worst—song to hit my ears at this very moment. Foreigner's "I Want to Know What Love Is" blares through the speakers, and if I were writing a book, this would be the perfect song for this scene.

I choke back all sentiment brought forth by my own memories. So many nights I would listen to this song, alone in my room, with tears streaming down my face, wishing I could find love. I would dream that somewhere within my hidden depths I possessed the ability to feel the emotion and somewhere in the world, waiting, was a hero strong enough to dig deep enough to find it and teach me how to experience it without fear.

The words of the song fill the air, and as I remember each one, I revert to that sixteen-year-old girl who dared to dream.

I lower my walls just enough to whisper, "Okay."

Grady's mouth curves upward, and he removes his hold from my wrists to encircle my waist with both arms. My skates remain facing forward as he begins wheeling us backward. I break my stare from his to glance at others who have taken to the song. Some skate side by side, holding hands, nervous smiles flitting on their faces. Their youthful innocence compels my own goofy, girly grin as I observe them passing by.

"Eyes on me, Cass. Stay with me." Grady's voice is husky as he garners my attention. Still grinning, I twist my neck back in his direction. He leans forward and his soft lips barely touch my ear as he whispers, "Beautiful."

We continue to skate, and by the time we make our second revolution around the floor, I'm at ease and allow him to lead me, which is a strikingly novel first. Never before have I allowed anyone to take the lead.

Our stares remain joined and I even dare to push forward on my own, which earns me a prideful grin from Grady. Just as we turn another corner, someone zips by us and brushes up against me, throwing me off balance. A person whips past, my eyes are ripped from Grady's, and I feel the security of our connection splinter as our joined stares break apart. With my defenses already lowered, and now the loss of Grady's eyes, I'm helpless against what happens next.

My stare locks onto the whites of the wall nearest us, drawn by the colors fluttering along them from the strobe light overhead.

Their pull is unbreakable.

I can't tear my eyes away.

I'm frozen, forced to watch the movement of the colors dancing along the walls, leaving me defenseless and unprepared for when I'm pulled under as the wave of my past crashes all around me.

No one else exists. There is only blackness surrounding me as I'm left alone, submerged in my darkness. My eyes are permitted to see nothing, no one, except those lights on the wall. Memories rush my mind, and the revulsion and disgust accompanying them extinguish any spark of hope Grady somehow managed to ignite.

My entire body begins to quake. Tears escape the corners of my eyes as they remain glued, bound to the revolutions of flitting color. My knees buckle, and with the sudden loss of strength, I begin to collapse. A weak whimper escapes me and I barely register the fact that I never hit the ground, but instead, I'm lifted off it. I shiver from the cold, even though warmth now surrounds me.

You're a disgrace.

You don't deserve someone like him.

Tell him to leave you, before it's too late.

You will only pollute his perfection with your foulness.

"Look at me, Cass." Grady's voice slices through the vile murmurs, but I can't break my stare. Our bodies are jolted as he steps off the floor and onto the carpet, but there's no safe haven from my fears. Blues, reds, yellows, and greens follow me everywhere we turn.

A gentle hand is placed against my cheek and it presses firmly, forcing my eyes into the crook of Grady's neck. His touch remains, never leaving while I stay cradled against his chest. I focus on the sound of his heart as it repeatedly strikes the inside of his chest, its soothing whoosh calming my own. I breathe in deeply, but the tears are relentless as they continue coursing down my cheeks. I grip the material of Grady's shirt, pulling myself as close as I can, and force my face deeper into the safety of his neck, the security he offers my only saving grace in this moment.

We jostle as he takes a seat on a bench, and terror constricts my chest with the idea that he will release me or force me to break my hold. But he doesn't. Somehow I'm able to remain within the safety of his arms as my skates are removed, and my upper body is drawn closer into the heat of his chest as he leans to take off his own. After some maneuvering, I'm jostled once again as he rises, and a cool breeze stirs around us with each of his swift steps. Grady turns and presses his back against the front door, and a gust of much-needed air washes over me as we exit.

Goose bumps line my arms and legs as I heave an exhausted breath, all fight within me gone. Grady continues with his strides, carrying me across the parking lot, and my grip on his shirt remains tight. Gravel crunches beneath his shoes and I listen to the sound until those steps finally cease. It's only then that he breaks the silence.

"Cassie, I need to put you down now. Is that okay?"

I nod into his neck and breathe him in deeply, for the first time noting the scent of his skin. Fresh and clean, like the soothing waters of the bluest ocean. An influx of emotion swells inside my chest. Blue. His eyes. I *need* his eyes.

What am I thinking?

I don't need anything, or anyone.

As I continue trying to convince myself, the longing for the peace he offers becomes frantic and my walls splinter with its force.

I peel my face out of the safety of his neck to find those eyes gazing curiously back at me. There is absolutely no apprehension in them. No fear. And thankfully, no pity. Just pure strength and resolve emanating from his returning stare. Releasing his shirt from my clutched fingers, I press the tips firmly just under my eyes, clearing the remnants of my tears. I give him an apologetic smile and nod, sniffling once in the process.

My heart braces itself for the impact. For him to drop me like a hot potato and take off running. I wouldn't blame him one bit. In fact, I kind of expect it. Instead, and much to my surprise, he cradles me into his body and presses his lips against my forehead, breathing in deeply before finally releasing me and setting me on my feet.

With my kick-ass heels dangling from his fingers, Grady lifts his free hand to cup the side of my face, tenderly stroking it with the pad of his thumb. The sensation of his repeated touch along my damp cheek continues to soothe. His mouth forms a half grin, then he releases me, leaning forward and opening the passenger-side door of his gray Maxima. Just as before, his hand finds the small of my back as he guides me into the passenger seat, then his body crosses mine to buckle my seat belt before he gently sets my shoes in my lap, stands, and shuts me safely inside.

No longer trembling, I curl my fingers over the tops of my heels and watch as he rounds the front of the car, trying to push aside the absolute mortification threatening me. As soon as he slides into the driver's seat, I twist to face him. My voice is shaky as I speak. "I'm so sorry, Grady. I don't know . . . I can't explain why . . ."

Grady reaches across the console and his hand envelops mine. "No need to explain, Cass. None at all. The only thing I need you to do is tell me what you want to do. Do you want me to take you home, or do you want to come home with me?"

My brows shoot up, instigating a chuckle from beside me. I would typically pounce on the chance to go home with someone, fuck *anyone*, just to avoid being alone, but my conscience won't allow it this time. Grady is different. I'm in unfounded territory with him.

I don't want to see him as my conquest.

I want him to be so much more than that.

So I evade his offer by asking, "What about my curfew?"

This spurs another beautiful grin. "I'm sure Mother Bear will understand. I'll even talk to Spencer myself, if you like, but only if you're comfortable. We still haven't eaten, and honestly, I'm not quite ready to let you go. So I'd like to continue our time together, but only if that's what you want to do." His eyes implore mine as he ends his proposal. "I'll be a complete gentleman. Scout's honor." Grady lifts three fingers, sealing his promise, and I shake my head, laughing freely at the gesture.

"That's what you told Spencer about the curfew."

His expression is still filled with humor, but his voice is laced with sincerity as he states, "Yeah, but this time I mean it."

I narrow my eyes and assess him, weighing my options. I can go home, where I'll be left alone to fend for myself against the impending darkness still skirting my mind. I can still see the colors but they're more of a vague mist.

How did he manage to ground me so easily?

Normally by now, I'd be . . . I'd be . . .

Don't go there, Cass. Don't . . .

I *could* accompany Grady to his apartment, enjoy some company, and temporarily distract myself from the inevitable. Because the memories will eventually overtake me—they always do. But as I root myself in Grady's patient stare, I feel . . . *safe*.

I allow the sensation to wash over me, then inhale deeply, disbelieving of the words coming out of my mouth. "All right, but no funny business, blue eyes." I point a warning finger in his direction and my conscience sings its approval.

Grady dips his head, acknowledging my one condition with a wide grin as he turns the key and starts the engine.

I lean forward and finger for my clutch under the seat, and once it's in my possession, I flip it open, removing my phone as I relax back. "I'll take care of Spencer," I remark, just as Grady exits the parking lot. "I need to check up on her anyway."

I slide my finger across the screen, noting the time of 9:48 p.m. before tapping on Spencer's name. Four rings sound with no answer. Just as I begin to lower the phone and disconnect the call, Spencer's voice hits my ear. "Cassie?"

"Hey, hooker." Grady chuckles beside me and I smile into the receiver. "Everything go okay with Liam-slash-Dalton?"

Her voice is shaky with her response. "Yeah. It will be, I think. It's just a lot to take in, his being back after all these years, you know?"

I nod. "Yeah."

As much as I want to ask her more, I don't. I don't know what she can share and what she can't, but I *do* know I don't want to put her in a difficult position. So I ask the next best thing. "Are *you* okay? I mean, I was going to stay at Grady's to give you more time to talk and reconnect, but I can come home if you need me."

Spencer's answer is immediate. "This is your apartment, Cass. Come home if you want. Don't stay away on our account." Then her familiar giggle hits my ear. "But if you want to stay with Grady, go for it. He seems like a good guy from what Dalton said. Plus, I have a good feeling about him. About the two of you." Another giggle. "So, consider your curfew lifted. Indefinitely."

There it is. The light. The hope. It's in her voice. I haven't heard that since her eighteenth birthday.

I take a quick thankful breath, and despite my nagging demons, I feel somehow at peace for her. She'll be okay. I smile and give Grady a sideways glance. "So, you're saying you approve of Grady Bennett?"

The side of his mouth kicks up as he signals left, checks all available mirrors, then merges into the left lane.

"I do," Spencer resounds.

"Got it. I'll keep that in mind." Still grinning, I face forward and inquire, "See ya tomorrow?"

"It's a date." Spencer laughs, then states, "Love you, Cass."

"Love you, times two."

Before hanging up, I add, "I'm really happy for you, Spence. You deserve this. After all these years, you're gonna get your happily-ever-after with the love of your life. It's an amazing gift you've been given. Treasure it always."

Before she can respond, I hit the end call button. Tonight has been emotional enough without going down that road.

Road.

Path.

I draw in a long breath, trying to fortify myself against the degrading whispers, but they zip right through my defenses and infiltrate my mind.

Spencer and I were on the same path, at one time. *You were never meant to be on that path. It was too good for you.*

When I was eight years old, I was plucked right off and placed onto another. *As you should've been. You found your rightful place.*

And although they remained conjoined for years, this is the moment I was certain would happen. *It's for the best that you're separated. Your existence will only darken hers.*

The fork in our road has come.

I swallow back the tears as *all* the happenings of the evening invade my mind.

The sad fact is, regardless of my present company, the *truth* of the matter is undeniable.

After five difficult years, Spencer has finally found her happily-ever-after. She will continue along her happy path, joined hand in hand with the man she loves.

And I will remain on mine, nothing more than the absolute disaster who has a panic attack because of some fucking strobe lights.

The voices mock me as they begin to celebrate in my acknowledgement. I shake my head and exhale deeply in defeat as I gaze out the window, their wicked, gleeful laughs all I'm able to hear as Grady drives.

Chapter 8

Unconditional

Past—Eight Years Old

"I'm sorry about your daddy, Spencer."

We're sitting side by side on her porch, knees tucked into our chests, cheeks pressed on top of them as we look at each other. I watch a tear disappear from the corner of Spencer's eye into the material of her black dress.

My own chin trembles at the sight, and as a strand of her long blonde hair catches with the breeze and blows onto her face, I pluck it away with the tips of my fingers, sliding it carefully behind her ear.

Spencer's puffy eyes, red and swollen, focus on me. She gives me a sad smile. "I can't stop crying."

"I know. Me either." And it's the truth. I feel so sad seeing my friend's heart breaking right before my eyes. There's nothing I can do to take away her pain.

Seconds of silence pass, our eyes locked onto each other's. She begins to cry harder now, and her entire face crumbles as she wails openly, "I only had him for two years. I loved him so much, and now he's gone."

Mommy explained to me that even though he was very young, Mr. Locke died of a heart attack. I can't imagine what I would do if I lost my daddy. Just the thought makes me cry harder.

I close my eyes and take a deep breath, reminding myself that Spencer needs me to be strong for her now. I can cry later, when I'm talking to Mommy, but now, I need to make her feel better. And I can't do that when I'm just as sad as she is.

"I know you miss him, Spencer. That's how I felt when I lost Ernie, my favorite fish. One day I found him floating in his bowl, even though I fed him every day like I was supposed to. I was so sad. I cried because I thought it was my fault that he died, but Mommy said it was just *his time*. She hugged me and told me to be thankful for the time I had with him, and to always remember the good times we shared, like when I would read to him before I went to sleep and talk to him when I was bored. And after that, whenever I was sad about him dying, I would remember how much it made me laugh when I pretended he was talking to me by making up words every time he would open his mouth under the water."

Even now, I can't help but grin. I smile softly and shrug my shoulders. "Maybe just try to remember the good times you had with him, and that will make you feel better too."

Spencer nods, then lifts her hand, wiping a tear as it crosses the bridge of her freckled nose. I give her a half smile and raise my arm to stroke her hair. We stay like that for a long time, never once moving through all the many people carrying huge pans and dishes of food up the steps beside us. Spencer is very lucky to have so many people that love her and her mother so much. I know Mrs. Locke does a lot to help out people in need around our community; it's nice to see people doing something nice for her.

The sound of heels clicking on the pavement suddenly stops, and I glance up to see Mommy standing in front of us. Her voice is soft as she states, "Dinner's ready, baby. I know you want to stay here, but it's time to come home. Maybe we should let Spencer get some sleep now?"

She's still dressed in the same dark dress she wore to Mr. Locke's funeral earlier today.

"Okay, Mommy," I answer, then look back to Spencer and whisper, "I gotta go, but I'll stay awake all night, in case you need me."

This makes Spencer smile and I grin back, happy I made her happy. Mommy leaves us and walks toward the street in the direction of our house. Just as I stand to follow her, the screen door opens, and Mrs. Locke steps onto the porch, her eyes more swollen than Spencer's. The sight sends more tears to my own, because Mrs. Locke is such an amazing person, and no one as wonderful as her should ever have to be so sad.

"I'm sorry, Mrs. Locke. I wish there was something I could do to make y'all feel better," I state, my voice a bit shaky.

What I say makes her smile and she continues walking until she's standing right in front of me. She crouches down, putting us at eye level, and swipes a tear from my face with her thumb.

Her hand remains on my cheek as she says, "My sweet, sweet Cassie . . ." She smiles bigger. "We are so lucky to have you in our lives."

This makes me grin and I see Spencer agree with a nod as she remains seated on the bottom step of the porch. I look back at Mrs. Locke, who continues. "And yes, we are very sad, Cassie, but that's a part of this glorious thing called *life*. Things may happen that we don't understand, but we have to be brave and strong so we can get through the hard times to truly appreciate the precious moments life will also offer us. Such as this one, right now, that I'm experiencing with you."

I lean into the warmth of her palm, and cover her hand with my own. Tears line the bottoms of her eyes, but she sniffs them back and stands, placing a gentle kiss on the top of my head before turning to leave. As she passes Spencer, Mrs. Locke bends at the waist and presses her lips lovingly on Spencer's forehead, before whispering, "I love you, my beautiful, *brave* girl."

"Love you too, Mommy."

Mrs. Locke kisses her again, then extends her hand for Spencer to take hold. As she does, Spencer stands, then looks to me. "See you tomorrow?"

I nod and answer, "It's a date."

"Come over anytime, Cassie. You're always welcome," Mrs. Locke adds with a wide smile and a wink. She wraps her arm around Spencer's shoulder and together they enter their house.

Joy fills my chest that Spencer was given a second chance, a second family, to experience all the happiness she deserves. After experiencing so much pain, to see her loved and wanted as she should be, well . . . I know she and Mrs. Locke will be just fine on their own, because they have each other.

I turn just in time to see my daddy driving into our driveway. After looking both ways, I skip my way across the street. A mischievous smile crosses my face as I approach the car, and just as Daddy opens the door, I shout, "BOO!"

His chuckles sound as he steps onto our driveway, and he holds his arms open wide, something he does every day when he gets home from work.

Except, today is Saturday.

"Where'd ya go?" I ask from within his tight embrace, sniffing the familiar spicy smell of his cologne.

He sweeps his hand down my hair, then releases me. I squint as I look up, screening my face from the sun with my hand as his caring brown eyes smile back down at me.

"Well, I have a surprise. We have a visitor."

Daddy looks to the side, and I watch as a younger version of my daddy rises out of the car. Surprised, I gasp, then look back to Daddy, who's grinning widely while the man walks to where we stand.

"Cassie," Daddy says, then adds my full name, "Cassandra. This is Uncle Alan. He's going to be staying with us for a while until he gets back on his feet."

I grin at Uncle Alan, my hand still glued to my forehead.

"You look just like my daddy," I announce excitedly. I love when we have company, and knowing I have a new relative has me hopping up and down on the soles of my favorite shoes (brand new, with a heel).

Uncle Alan laughs, and his smile is warm, just like his eyes. He leans toward me and shields the side of his mouth, whispering, "If anyone asks, I'm the better-looking brother. Deal?"

I giggle and nod. Uncle Alan rises and my daddy claps him on the shoulder. "I'll help you bring in your luggage. We've got you set up in the basement, for the time being." Daddy looks down at his watch and announces, "Dinner should be ready soon."

"I'll get the luggage, wouldn't want you to throw out your back or break your hip, would we, Daniel?" Uncle Alan winks at me and I laugh. "Cassandra here can help, can't ya? Show me where the basement is?"

"At your service," I shout, then salute before rounding the front of the car. Leaning into the still-open door, I grab the bigger bag of the two with all my strength, and lug it out onto the cement of the driveway.

Both men chuckle to themselves. I look up to see Uncle Alan's grin widen as I try to lift it. "Why don't I take that one? You grab this one." He hands me the much smaller one and leans into the car to grab a pillow, tossing it to Daddy. "And I think *he* should be able to handle this one."

Daddy shakes his head after catching the pillow, then heads into the house. Uncle Alan follows, as do I, the bag brushing the side of my leg with each step I take.

"Carol," Daddy calls. "Alan's here."

"Oh good," I hear her yell back before Daddy turns the corner.

"Basement's this way," I remark, stepping in front of Uncle Alan and proudly leading the way to the basement door. Once we arrive, I fling it open and flip on the light. The steps creak behind me, telling me Uncle Alan is still following. I continue down them, and once my feet hit the floor, I head to the couch and proudly toss his bag onto the middle cushion.

"This folds out into a bed so you should have plenty of room to sleep. And the washer and dryer are down here too, so you should always have clean clothes."

Uncle Alan sets his bag next to the other, then places his hands on his waist and turns, observing the room. As soon as he faces me, he grins. "This will do just fine. Thank you, Cassandra. You're an excellent hostess."

My cheeks warm with the compliment, and I smile back at him. He takes a step in my direction and adds, "That's a very pretty dress."

I glance down at it and run my fingers over the black satin sash. "Thank you. I wore it to a funeral today. My friend's daddy died."

"I'm very sorry to hear that." My stare lifts to find Uncle Alan standing in front of me. He offers me an apologetic smile. "She must be very sad."

"Yeah, but she's strong," I state. "She has a good mommy. She'll be happy again soon."

Uncle Alan nods. "Yes, family is very important. Family can make you very happy. And we're family, right, Cassandra?"

"Mmm-hmm," I agree, then add, "You can call me Cassie. No one really calls me Cassandra."

Uncle Alan shakes his head, then lifts his hand to touch my cheek. "Cassandra is a beautiful name, just like you. So, I think I'll just call you that, if you don't mind. It can be something shared just between us, our special secret."

I grin. I like very much that he thinks I'm beautiful. It makes me feel special.

"Cassie. Dinner is on the table. Go wash up and bring Uncle Alan with you." Mommy's voice sounds from the top of the stairs.

My eyes lift toward the sound. "Yes, Mommy."

I redirect my attention to Uncle Alan and extend my hand. "Come on, Uncle Alan. We'll be in trouble if we don't hurry up and get to the table."

Uncle Alan grins down at me and nods, taking hold of my hand.

And I smile back as we walk side by side out of the basement.

Uncle Alan would quickly become one of my favorite people in the world. I loved and trusted him with all my heart. Unconditionally.

Six months later, he disappeared without a trace.

Except, he was never really gone. Every inch of my house would serve as a permanent reminder of the time Uncle Alan spent with us. Yet, for as strong as his remaining presence was, no one in my family ever mentioned his name again after he left. We never spoke of him.

It was as though he never existed.

But still, he was everywhere I looked.

A ghost . . .

One that would haunt me for the rest of my life.

Chapter 9

Comfortable

"Well, here it is, my humble abode."

Grady unlocks his apartment and opens the door, gesturing with a wide sweep of his arm for me to enter. Since I never put them back on, my heels are hanging from the tip of my index finger as I stride by him, highlighter-yellow socks still proudly covering my calves. I'm sure I look *fabulous*, but honestly, I'm too emotionally wiped to give a fuck.

Plus, the socks are kind of growing on me.

The door shuts behind me and I consider Grady's living room. Clean, but definitely lived in. Large TV mounted to the wall. Lamp in the corner. Brown leather couches and matching recliner. All in all, a very standard bachelor-pad design and layout.

My eyes carefully scour the apartment as I walk, until they land and freeze on something I can't help but grin at it. Because sitting right on his coffee table is a half-empty coffee mug with *Fuller Police Dept.* printed right on the front.

I knew it!

I smile and look over my shoulder at Grady, who's also eyeing it with a smile.

He winks.

I blush.

Then turn away to hide it.

Grady tosses his keys onto a table in his entryway, then fully enters the living room behind me, the sound of his shoes hitting the floor muffled by the beige carpet. I begin to survey his apartment further, when I feel the weight of my shoes lifted off my finger and the clutch pinned under my arm removed.

"Thanks," I remark, watching as he carefully sets both in the recliner before heading to the kitchen. Silently, he grabs two wine-glasses from the cabinet.

I continue to ramble, looking at the floor. "For *everything*. I'm so embarrassed."

Grady uncorks a bottle of wine and begins to pour. When he turns, I glance up just in time to see him relax back against the counter with a glass of red wine in each hand.

"Come here." His tone is gentle and his eyes are kind with his demand.

I stay where I stand, the stubborn part of me remaining rooted to the carpet. Grady's mouth quirks up at the side in a sly, crooked grin before he adds, "*Please.*"

Clearly my feet bypass my brain, automatically taking me in his direction. I walk the steps necessary to close the distance between us, landing me at the island, where I now stand in front of him. He extends a glass, and I willingly accept, mirroring his stance as I lean back against the edge of the granite. Taking a sip, my eyes remain on his as he does the same, before setting his glass next to him. He crosses his feet at his ankles and his arms over his chest.

"Want to talk about it?"

"Not really, no." I lift the glass and take a large gulp, lowering it when I'm through, and offer nothing else.

Grady narrows his stare and cocks his head to the side, gaug-ing me. After a couple seconds, he inhales deeply, then relents. "Hungry?"

Right on cue, my stomach rumbles, answering for me. Grady's brows lift slightly. "I'll take that as a yes." He uncrosses his arms, then lays his palms on the counter, curling his fingers under its edge. "I'll cook, you get comfortable. Sound like a plan?"

I lift my foot and wiggle my highlighter-yellow-covered toes. "Already comfortable."

Grady grins, chuckling and shaking his head. "Not exactly what I had in mind."

He presses off the counter, then reaches forward. His fingers are warm and strong, yet they curl gently over the top of my hand. "Trust me?"

Those damn eyes pierce right through me with his question. My heart jumps in my chest and my throat constricts. Tears surface in my eyes as they remain held by his, and I swallow them back. He remains quiet, watching me. *Seeing* me.

The intensity of the moment builds as we remain silently locked in our stares. Conflicting feelings war between my heart and my mind, seemingly at battle with one another for dominance.

Fear.

Excitement.

Need.

Longing.

Fear.

Fear.

Fear.

Grady's grip on my hand doesn't lessen, and his eyes don't disconnect from mine. He waits patiently for me to say something. *Anything*.

But I can't.

A tear breaks free and trails its warmth down my cheek. Still silent, Grady squeezes my hand, then tugs softly.

I want.

I want.

I want.

My body complies, and I step forward. With his hand still enveloping mine, Grady brings his free arm to circle my shoulders and pulls me into an embrace. I press my cheek against his chest, inhaling his fresh scent deeply while another tear is lost, bleeding into his shirt. Soft lips touch the top of my head and warm breaths sift through my hair, soothing me with each of his exhalations.

With every caress he offers, I wonder how in the world Grady Bennett is able to understand exactly what I need in this moment.

Grady releases my hand to wrap me safely within his frame, securing me tightly against his body. I lift both hands and drive them between our bodies to fist the material of his shirt. I hold on to him, permitting the first real feelings I've allowed myself to experience in years to wash over me.

No words are spoken. Tears, breaths, and the beats of our hearts speak for us.

I tell him I want nothing more than to trust him.

He tells me he understands and will wait patiently until I can do so.

I clench his shirt, pulling him closer in thanks.

He presses his lips firmly against my head, then moves his hand to cup the base of my neck, reassuring me with each stroke of his thumb along my skin.

I allow him to hold me while I cry silently, and with each fallen tear, weight is lifted.

We stay like that for some time, until my eyes are finally dry and his shirt is drenched. I breathe in deeply while still in his arms, then press away from him, bringing my eyes to his.

Thank you.

Grady winks.

You're welcome.

I blush. Again.

He grins and I do the same.

Beautiful.

Wonderment floods me with the simplicity of the shared moment between the two of us.

Never.

Never before have I felt so understood.

So cherished.

Clearing my throat, I finally find the courage to break the silence. "Thank God for waterproof mascara, huh?"

His chuckles fill the air. I sniff, then inquire, "We were discussing my getting comfortable?"

"Ah, that we were." He nudges his head toward the living room. "Follow me."

His arms fall from my shoulders and he hooks my pinky with his index finger, then leads me out of the kitchen. I trail behind him, taking my time to once again admire his living space. Once through the large room, we enter a darkened hallway and approach one of the two doors in this section of his apartment.

Fingers still linked, he turns the knob, casts the door open, and flips on the light. My eyes take a few seconds to adjust as we enter what looks to be a spare bedroom. A simple cream duvet and huge brown throw pillows line the fluffiest comforter I've ever seen. I fight every instinct I have not to fling myself on top of it. I bet it feels like heaven.

I sigh to myself, then smile at it. Not really sure why.

Still following Grady's lead, we approach a white dresser. Grady releases my hand and leans forward to open one of the drawers while I eye the contents on top.

Books! Lots of books.

I'm sure there are other items on it, but all I can focus on is the plethora of books in front of me. Multiple piles line the wooden surface, and as I eye the spines, I see some of my favorites within the stacks. I grin widely as I pick one up, bring it to my nose, and sniff its pages.

Grady sifts through the contents of the drawer, selecting various items and placing them in his arms, then turns to face me just as I fan the pages with my thumb. He laughs under his breath and shrugs. "Well shit, all I had to do is take you to the library to get that smile. Who knew?"

I grin. "I'm sorry. I read a lot, but I read on my Kindle. This is one of my favorite books, and I've never seen it in paperback." Or smelled it. "It's beautiful."

"*You're* beautiful," he counters. Not giving me a chance to disagree, he lifts the clothes strewn over his arm and continues, "Change of clothes."

Girl clothes.

Oh my God. He has a girlfriend.

Had a girlfriend?

One that he obsesses over to the point of stashing her clothes in a dresser, removing them only to gaze longingly at them, maybe even sniffing them every now and then because they still smell wonderful, like her. She was gorgeous, of course . . .

I drift into my imagination, thoughts about Grady and his girl-friend looping around my mind.

"Eyes on me, Cass."

Startled out of my thoughts, I focus on those eyes, which are laughing at me as he speaks. He gestures at the books, then dips his head toward the clothes. "My sister's."

Oh.

My face heats to the point that I actually break a sweat. I clear my throat and shake my head, throwing my hands out in front of me while I sputter, "No . . . I wasn't . . . I mean, I didn't . . ."

Grady offers me no help or pardon as I try to explain my misjudgment. He just stands there and watches me flail.

I stop speaking and glare.

He tries not to smile, but it's a fruitless effort. He succumbs, giving it free rein, and his perfect white teeth flash as he wordlessly removes the book from my grasp, setting it back on the dresser before taking my hand. After giving it a little squeeze, he links our fingers and leads me out of the room toward the other door in the hallway. He opens it and once the light is on, my eyes land on a pristine vintage claw-foot tub, white with dark iron claws at its bottom. A fluffy white towel hangs over the side, just above a black-and-white-checkered bath mat that looks as though it might be softer than the heavenly down comforter I spied a few minutes ago.

My stare remains locked on the tub, and the question escapes me as I whisper in a trance-like state, "Can I?"

"Of course," Grady answers with a satisfied smile, before releasing me to set the change of clothes on the counter. He turns to leave, but as he passes me, he stops and leans to place the softest of kisses just above my temple. I practically melt into him as he tenderly whispers in my ear, "Take your time."

The door closes behind him as he leaves me alone in the bathroom, my eyes never leaving the tub.

There is only one word that could adequately capture how I feel as the door clicks shut.

Surreal.

Without even knowing this man, I feel as though he understands exactly what I need, when I need it.

And he gives it to me.

Grady may never truly come to know the actual meaning of this moment, but I knew as soon as the question left my mouth, a part of me—I'm not sure how small or large that part may be—does in fact trust Grady Bennett. I have no idea why. Maybe it was his eyes as they connected with mine, or the way he promised never to let me fall, or the fact that he carried me out of a skating rink while I had an unexplained panic attack, or the way he let me cry without asking why . . . I don't know.

What I *do* know is I haven't submerged myself in a tubful of water in years. Not since I was forced to take hurried baths in the middle of the night before escaping to Spencer's.

But here, right now, standing in this bathroom, I actually *want* to take a bath.

My memories are surprisingly absent as I look over the tub and smile.

It's just me, standing in a bathroom, listening to the clanging of pans as Grady begins to cook our dinner.

I was definitely wrong about the comforter.

Because I'm one hundred percent sure this moment, as I experience the serenity it offers, *this* is what heaven feels like.

And I have Grady Bennett to thank for it.

Chapter 10 ✳

Better Acquainted

With a fluffy white towel wrapped around my head, I make my exit from the bathroom wearing a pair of yoga pants and a heather-gray T-shirt with the words *Wherefore art thou* . . . stamped beside a picture of . . . Waldo. I think I could end up enjoying the company of someone like Grady's sister. I can't wait to meet her. Between the books and her awesome choices in casual wear, I think we will get along perfectly.

My cheeks are still warm and flushed from the heat of the water as my bare feet tread quietly down the hallway. As I near the kitchen, I inhale deeply, the savory smell of garlic and cooked pasta filling my nose.

After another deep breath, I note that the smell of Grady's cooking is the only reason I didn't take up residence in that damn bathtub for the rest of the evening. My stomach growls its agreement and I lift my hand to pat it, mentally applauding it for its patience and promising its reward soon. I grin down at it, then at the comfortable clothing selected as my attire this evening.

Cradled next to my chest is my black minidress and rolled into a ball lying on top are the hideous Skate Place socks. My smile broadens. They may be dreadful, but they're equally as beautiful because they will forever remind me of this very *odd* night with Mr. Grady Bennett.

And speak of the devil, just as I round the corner to enter the living room, my eyes catch the sight of him standing in front of the stove, and as I take in *his* attire, I damn near drop my belongings.

His faded navy-blue athletic shirt has been sliced open on each side, leaving the ridges of his six-pack visible as he bends to open the oven. I watch, mesmerized by the constriction of his muscles as he rises, lifting a white casserole dish. I swallow as my eyes practically glaze over, fixated on his movement, until they find focus on his gloved hands. I choke back laughter at the sight. His hair is still secured in a low ponytail, and together with his corded muscles flexing as he sets the dish onto the counter, his ripped T-shirt, and the gray sweatpants hanging low on his hips, he emits complete *badass vibe*. Yet, the oven mitts covering his hands . . . are pink.

A giggle is wrenched free, and I clamp my hand over my mouth to mute it, but the sound has already alerted him to my presence. Grady turns his head, looking at me over his shoulder. His eyes are bright, highlighted by the coloring of his shirt, and filled with warmth as they rake over me.

They flit from the towel on my head, down to my bare feet, then back to my face. My cheeks begin to burn with his gaze, so I turn away and walk into the living room, placing my dress and now-beloved socks on the recliner with my other belongings. I pivot around to see he's still watching me, and my face heats another hundred degrees.

What the hell is wrong with me?

I am *not* a giddy schoolgirl.

I'm Cassie Fucking Cooper, damn it.

I do not blush.

I do not giggle.

And I sure as hell don't get flustered by a guy.

As though reading my thoughts, Grady chuckles, then grins triumphantly.

Jerk.

I roll my eyes but decide to end the standoff by heading to the kitchen, announcing upon entry, "I just had a very interesting talk with my stomach in which I convinced it to hold off eating itself until we try your cooking."

Grady laughs. "Is that so?"

"It is. Also, my taste buds would like to know what we're eating. They like to be prepared."

More laughter, then Grady jerks his chin at the stove. "Chicken Parmesan. I've been craving it since Bambino's."

I glance at the pan of cooked pasta already mixed with sauce and the casserole dish with four Parmesan-breaded chicken breasts.

My stomach growls for joy.

"Pipe down, you." I point at it in warning.

Grady's shoulders shake as he turns, hefting the dish and placing it onto the island, pink mitts and all.

I grin and gesture toward his hands. "Also your sister's?"

He shakes his head. "Hell no. These are all mine. Pink is the new black, or haven't you heard?"

"I must have missed the memo," I retort.

Smile still on his face, he lifts his arm and brushes the tip of a mitt down my nose. "I have so much to teach you, young grasshopper."

A breath of laughter passes through my nostrils and I shake my head at his boldness.

"Can I help?" I inquire.

"Dishes are in the cabinet. Silverware is in that drawer." He points, then continues, "Grab those. I'll get everything else."

"On it, boss," I state with a salute.

After setting out the dishes and silverware, Grady plates our food—which looks amazing, by the way—and we take our seats. Before we eat, Grady lifts his wineglass in my direction. "To getting better acquainted."

I smile and raise my glass, accepting his offered toast. "To no more skating. Ever."

A flash of sadness dims his eyes. "I'm sorry about that. It wasn't my intention, obviously."

I shrug my shoulders and look down at my plate. "It happens sometimes. I don't really have any control over it. It wasn't anything you did, or didn't do. It's just *me*," I end, my tone bordering defeat. "It should be me apologizing. I'm sorry if I embarrassed you."

Grady's eyebrows shift downward, creasing his forehead. "You could never embarrass me, Cass. Not in that way. Not under those circumstances."

Cass.

My insides tumble and warmth spreads through me with his use of the nickname, and once again I find myself stunned by how much I love the sound of it coming from his mouth.

The air grows palpable, and I sense the conversation veering down a very treacherous path, so I reroute. "Well, I definitely have a knack for it. Just ask Spencer. I embarrass her all the time. It provides me much joy."

I conjure a grin.

Grady narrows his eyes.

I cast my stare down to my plate and slice a piece of chicken, bringing it to my mouth. My eyes widen as the chicken melts onto my taste buds and garlic butter floods my mouth. I look back to Grady, covering my very full mouth as I speak. "Thith is amathing, Grady." I savor each chew, then swallow. "How did you learn to cook like this?"

He lifts his shoulders, bringing his eyes to his own plate. "My sister taught me. Our parents worked nights, so we kind of had to fend for ourselves growing up."

I nod, then ask, "You're close? You and your sister?"

Grady swallows his own bite, then looks to me and smiles sadly. "We were, yes. Very."

I finish my sip of wine, setting the glass down onto the countertop. "Were?"

Grady perches both elbows on either side of his plate, allowing his fork to dangle as he inhales deeply. "Yes. She was murdered her freshman year in college."

The fork within my grip falls, clanking loudly against the ceramic plate beneath it. "Oh, Grady . . ."

He shakes his head, cutting off my words. "One day she existed, the next she didn't. She was just . . . gone. I completely lost it after that. Went down a path I'm not proud of, but eventually I made peace with her death and moved forward."

He sips his wine calmly before continuing. "In fact, she's a big part of why I became a cop, and she's the foremost reason I started instructing Krav Maga. I wanted to teach people, women in particular, how to defend themselves if they're attacked. Every class I have is my homage to her, and every person I teach carries forward a piece of her existence." He shrugs. "To me, there's nothing more vindicating than the ability to find the strength necessary to turn the worst experience imaginable into something so beautiful, it eclipses all the ugliness. It helps to find reason, to find purpose, in something so senseless."

As I ingest his words, tears fill my eyes, brimming my lashes. I look away from him, embarrassed. Not because of my reaction, but because his words, so poignantly spoken, slice right through my heart. Each word a reminder of my own weakness and fear. Of my inability to cope with the horrors of my past and the disgust that so often overwhelms me. Of the fucking obvious fact that I have no right to be sitting here with someone as truly beautiful as Grady Bennett.

I feel it, the pain his truth brings.

You're nothing but a slut, Cassandra.

Why are you even here?

You don't deserve a man like Grady Bennett.

The words may remain unspoken, but I feel every slash they make as they race through my mind.

They hurt.

I inhale deeply as a tidal wave of nausea rolls through my stomach, unleashing its agony, and all of a sudden, I'm not so hungry anymore. Reaching for the napkin by my plate, I wipe my mouth and excuse myself. "I'm sorry . . . I just . . . I need a minute."

The legs of the barstool screech as I stand, and Grady rises along with me, gripping my arm. "Cassie."

I shake my head and flash him my palms. "I need a *minute*, Grady." Anger works its way through my system, coating my tone.

His eyes tighten on mine, his hold still firm around my forearm. "A minute to do what? To get lost in that head of yours?"

I gasp, then clamp my mouth shut, only to open it again. "I don't need you evaluating me, Grady. Trying to piece me back together. I'm broken, you said it yourself. That's what you see . . . a girl who's broken."

Fury rages within me. My defenses catapult right back into position, and I know what I'm going to do before I even say it. The words scorch as they erupt from my mouth.

"There's nothing I can offer you except a good fuck. Is that what you want? Is that why you brought me here tonight? To fuck me? Well, what the hell are you waiting for? Let's do this." I laugh manically to keep from crying, my own craziness bleeding into my brain. I feel it coming, the darkness as it threatens to swallow me whole.

And all I can think as I begin to disappear is, I need to get away from Grady. It works both ways, and I know my ugliness will eventually eclipse his beauty.

Grady's eyes remain locked on mine, warning clear in the register of his low tone. "You keep spewing that venom, sweetheart, but you're striking no one but yourself."

I scoff under my breath. "You think I care? I can't do anything to myself that hasn't already been done."

Grady draws in a deep breath through his nose, jaw clenched, and I lose the fight with my tears as they begin to gush from my eyes.

His voice softens. "I know what you're doing, and this shit isn't going to work on me. You can push me as hard as you like, but I'm not going anywhere. And neither are you."

"Why?" I sob. "Why does it fucking matter what I do?"

No one has ever cared before.

Why the fuck does *he* care?

You are worth nothing, Cassandra.

Both hands move to grip my upper arms, holding me in place. Grady bends, aligning his face with mine, his eyes all I can see as he whispers, "Because *you* matter. Regardless of what you think, of what you *do* to convince yourself otherwise, you do matter. To me."

"You barely know me, Grady," I declare.

His answer is immediate. "I know what I see. What I've been trained to see, and what I see on my own. And what I see is when you let that guard down, when you expose that vulnerable part of yourself that you try so desperately to protect, it's the most precious sight I've ever laid eyes on. It's so fucking beautiful, Cass, and if that's not worth fighting for, then I don't know what is."

Our stares are bound and I remain silent, suddenly ill-equipped to formulate a snarky response. With those words, he's taken all the fight out of me.

Grady senses it and the corner of his mouth shoots up, triumphant. Then he leans, positioning his lips inches from mine, and states, "And regarding *fucking* you, as you so eloquently phrased it, that will happen only when you can give me all of you. Not the tiny bits of yourself that you offer here and there, but every single piece. Because when I take you, I need you to be *there* with me. Not in your head, thinking yourself unworthy and sabotaging us before we even get started. I need you to be there. *With. Me.*"

No air remains in my lungs as he backs away and concludes, "I can see we aren't there yet, but I can tell you, once we are, it's going to be fucking phenomenal . . . and definitely worth the fight."

I open my mouth, but nothing comes out. I close it, then open it again. Still nothing as his words repeat in my mind.

When.

When I take you . . .

He grins, the damn sexy bastard, and gestures at the table. "Now, I'd like to work on getting us there, but I'd also like to eat. I can't have you *and* your stomach pissed at me in the same night. That's one battle I just might lose."

He winks then taps the seat of my barstool. "*You* I can handle. Your stomach, not so much."

I take the few necessary steps and slide into the seat, and as I do, my goddamn stomach decides to announce to the entire room just how pissed it actually is. Grady's brows rise with the corners of his mouth, and I make a measly attempt to not smile, but eventually a weak one crosses my face as I state, "Well, now you've gone and done it."

Grady's laughter sounds from beside me, and I turn to look at him. As I do, his smile falters a bit, and he brings both hands to the sides of my face, wiping the moisture from my cheeks with his thumbs. "We'll get ya there, Cass."

I nod and sniff, then, with his hands still cradling my face, I lean forward, silently requesting a kiss on the forehead—something I have never, *ever* done in my life.

But I decide to take this chance, knowing it's not *there*, but it's something. A new piece of myself to offer.

Which he happily accepts as he obliges.

Chapter 11 ✦

Falling

"Blue!"

"Foot!"

Our shouts are simultaneous as they fill the room from our positions on the mat. All furniture has been moved, slid carefully until flush with the wall to provide the room we need. With his eyes following my movement, Grady grins as he inches his own foot forward to place it on the blue circle.

This is exactly where three glasses of wine with Grady Bennett gets me. It lands me right here, crouched in a pouncing position, playing an impromptu game of Twister. After satisfying the demands of my stomach, we ended up back in his guestroom. I sipped wine while he catalogued the various things he'd kept that belonged to his sister, Ashley.

Her books, for example. Ashley had been an avid reader, and her collection of books rivals my own. I thumbed through them, memorizing various titles I've yet to read, while Grady explained that being four years older than him, she was the one who often tucked him in when they were kids. And she did so reading him a story. As they became older, he rarely saw her without a book in her hands, so he brought some to his apartment to ensure their safety when his family cleaned out her bedroom.

He also snagged some of her favorite clothes just to have some things of her with him. The shirt handed over so easily to me was one she wore all the time, and I expressed to him the absolute honor of wearing it, which garnered me a gorgeous smile and a kiss on the forehead.

Yet, although the moment was beautiful, voices found their way to the forefront of my mind, tarnishing it with their shouted reminders.

No one will even remember you when you die, because you mean nothing.

Their slithers and whispers lingered until another glass of wine was finally able to dull them.

Later in the evening, we also stumbled upon a drawer full of games they played when they were young. Monopoly, Yahtzee, and Uno were among the many others, including, of course, Twister. Three glasses in, I took him up on the challenge, but as I eye the mat below me with my muscles straining, I'm second-guessing the child-like eagerness with which I accepted. Each move we make reminds me that I'm definitely not a kid anymore.

After the torture of Krav Maga and now this, I'm sure I'll be hella sore tomorrow, but it's totally worth it to be crowned champion and wipe that arrogant smile off Grady's face.

I grin back, strategically planning my next move. It's my turn to call the color, his to call the body part, and we've made our way to the center of the mat. And as I plan, the weight of the decision I must make hits me full force. I can choose to go with green, which will most likely move us laterally, or I can call yellow, potentially moving us closer to each other.

Slide laterally, basically going nowhere, or take a chance by moving forward.

Suddenly this game of Twister has turned into a metaphorical game of life.

Grady patiently awaits my choice. I have no doubt his challenge was premeditated, knowing I would eventually come to making this very decision. But as usual with Grady, he doesn't force my hand. He puts me in the position to choose the next move.

My grin falls, significance weighing my expression. I dip my head, signaling to Grady the decision has been made.

"Yellow," I whisper softly just as Grady reveals his choice. "Hand."

Slowly, I press my weight onto the ball of my foot, propelling me forward as Grady does the same. Our arms cross when our hands land in neighboring yellow circles, and the warmth of Grady's body encompasses me as we come together. My cheek brushes against his, the slight stubble on his skin spawning an eruption of goose bumps along my arms. My throat tightens and I take in a deep breath of air, allowing the freshness of Grady's scent to wash over me as I approach his neck. My forehead settles into the crook, so close, I feel when he turns his head toward my throat. My skin ignites where Grady's warm lips part along the hollow, heat coursing my entire body upon their touch.

They trail slowly up the column of my neck, forcing me to swallow when the tip of his tongue glides gently along my skin. I peel my head out of the safety of Grady's neck to arch my own, allowing him more access. His teeth nip lightly as he approaches the line of my jaw, and I whimper at the sensation. A low growl sounds next to my ear, before his lips continue their path along my cheek until they find their destination, landing at the corner of my mouth. They seal together, pressing against my skin a tender kiss, then his warmth disappears as he pulls away.

As soon as I open my eyes, darkened ones return my stare, heated as they fall to my mouth. I dart my tongue along my bottom lip, and Grady draws in a deep breath before lifting his gaze. My eyes dip to his soft lips, reddened and slightly swollen, and I inch my face closer to his, wanting nothing more than to feel the heat of them on my mouth. I force another swallow, then bring my stare to meet his.

Our eyes remain locked, Grady's boring into mine, silently requesting permission to close the distance. I revel in his warm breaths as they strike before his lips finally find mine. Every cell in my body ignites, pulsating as they spark to life within me. Our mouths align perfectly, fusing together, and an involuntary moan escapes me when his velvet-soft tongue parts my lips. I open for him completely in this moment, accepting the offered caresses each deep sweep of his tongue provides.

I surrender all guilt, all fear, all anger, and melt into his kiss, allowing an all-encompassing sense of peace to warm my insides. It rushes through me, soothing the fragmented pieces of my soul. The heat of his slick mouth against mine, the sound of my whimpers and moans as I succumb, the smell of his skin pressed against mine . . . everything about this moment etches itself into my brain, because for the first time in as long as I can remember, I feel *alive*.

The ever-present cold and darkness no longer loom. They're flooded, blanketed by warmth as it surges through my body, and with it launches the realization that this is the first time I've ever been kissed.

Sure, *I've* kissed a lot of boys, or men . . . but my kisses have always been hard, angry, frenzied—impatient to find my release and always within my control. Nothing like this. Grady is kissing *me*, and I'm allowing him to do so, relinquishing control with each pass of his tongue along mine.

Grady lifts his hands off the mat, sliding his knees securely underneath him for balance as he gently frames my face. The tenderness of his hold stokes the fire within me, sending another wave of heat through my heart. I choke back the emotion the sensation brings and focus on the feel of his mouth against mine. Seconds pass, then Grady languidly softens the kiss, brushing his lips lightly over mine before relaxing back. His eyes watch me intensely, and as they do, I find solace and security. A small smile tugs at my lips at the innocence of this moment, of this kiss that has roused the dormant, youthful part of me that has been numb for so long.

Did it ever really exist?

His mouth curls upward, and I slowly slide my stare down to the mat before once again meeting his eyes. My grin widens as I softly proclaim, "I win."

Grady's gaze falls to where all my extremities remain in the appropriate circles. He chuckles to himself while his teeth find the suppleness of his bottom lip. He shakes his head, bringing those watchful eyes back to mine. Wide grin beaming on his face, he leans in and whispers, "Sweetheart, this victory is all mine."

He brings my forehead to his lips, then releases me to stand. "Time for bed, sleepyhead."

It's only then that I realize I'm yawning. Three glasses of wine, emotionally drained and physically tapped out, I have to admit I'm a very sleepy girl. I nod and take his hand, allowing him to pull me to my feet. Hands joined, silence surrounds us as we head down the hallway to the guest room.

As soon as we enter and the light is on, my awakened inner child giggles and claps for joy, and in a very *non-Cassie* manner, I happily launch myself onto the bed. Laughing as I sink into the enveloping softness, true joy illuminates from within, and I smile widely at Grady as he approaches the side of the bed. He grins back knowingly, but says nothing as he pulls the bedding down for me to slide underneath.

I tug the comforter under my chin and settle into the sheets. Grady takes a seat on the edge, lifting his hand to brush the hair away from my face. Once satisfied, he places his palm against my cheek and strokes my skin lightly with his thumb, forcing my sleepy eyes to drift shut. The movement is so soothing, my body begins to float into sleep but is awakened when I feel him lean over me. Tenderly, he kisses my temple then inhales deeply with his lips lingering on my skin. I grin from under him, and his warmth disappears as he rises.

"Sleep with me?" I request, my voice rough with sleep.

I feel his eyes on me, deliberating. I also feel my heart begin to hammer with my request. I'm taking a leap, allowing myself to plummet into the sense of security that Grady's presence provides.

Where the hell is the woman formerly known as Cassie Cooper?

Because this invitation is so *not* me.

I haven't allowed anyone in my bed for as long as I choose to remember. With every single one of my sexual partners, I've never stayed the night, and they've never been invited to my apartment. The idea of someone lying next to me, of leaving myself unprotected and vulnerable while sleeping, usually suffocates me to the point that I leave approximately five seconds after we've both come.

But as I relive the evening with Grady, the tenderness with which he handled me—the strength and resolve openly displayed tonight—I find I *want* to share my bed with him. I want him near me, knowing deep down I will feel nothing but protected when I sleep. Not afraid but safe. Not alone but *together*.

His footsteps recede toward the door, stopping just short to turn off the light. Soon after, the bed dips with his weight and the sheets rustle as he settles in. I open my eyes and turn to face him, grinning because my inner child seems to have a mad case of the giggles. He angles his mouth into a crooked smile then extends his arm in my direction, opening his body to me. Slowly, I sneak over to his side, lay my head on his chest, and exhale deeply when his arm curls around my shoulders.

"Fucking phenomenal," Grady's voice rumbles against my ear, and my cheek presses into his shirt with my smile.

I say nothing. I remain silent while listening to his steady heartbeat and his deep breaths as they begin to lull me to sleep.

My mind replays Grady's vow to never let me fall and I know, as I remain held safely in his arms, *that* promise is one he might not be able to keep . . .

Because I could definitely be in danger of falling hard for Grady Bennett.

Chapter 12 ✴

Tit for Tat

Sunlight hits my eyelids as I gradually wake, feeling fully rested for the first time in . . . well, forever. Exhaustion no longer claims me as I peel my eyes open, blinking them several times to get them to focus. I scan the room, memories from the previous night running their course and highlighting the obvious fact that I fell asleep as Grady held me, and it was bliss.

I turn to find him, but he's no longer beside me. Once I realize I'm safe from scrutiny, I roll over, centering my face into the pillow, and grin widely into its confines. My heart swells, threatening to explode with each joy-filled beat.

I feel youthful, young and alive, brimming with excitement.

I have indeed become a giddy schoolgirl.

And I kind of like it.

Rolling onto my back, I stretch to full capacity, wiggling my toes beneath the sheets as my fingers touch the wooden headboard. Once functional, I lift the covers and make a safe escape to the bathroom across the hall. Upon entering, another smile breaks across my face as I spy a brand-new toothbrush and toothpaste. Lying on the counter right next to them is a handwritten note on a paper towel.

Morning, beautiful.
Made a run to the store. Hope these work for you.
Bought some food while there. Hoping to keep you just a
while longer to continue getting better acquainted. Join me
for breakfast?

My heart flutters and I shake my head, the fact that someone like him exists completely boggling my mind.

After taking care of my morning routine, I leave the bathroom and head down the hall. The smell of bacon and eggs carries me forward and I feel like one of those cartoon characters, floating after the scent of deliciousness. Again.

Exactly like before, I round the corner and just as I open my mouth to wish Grady a good morning, I stop dead in my tracks. All the air whooshes from my lungs, and I stand there, gawking.

Because in the kitchen is a shirtless Grady Bennett. In. All. His. Glory.

Holy unfair-to-the-rest-of-the-male-population hotness.

Seriously.

I'm struck silent as I observe him without his knowing, fascinated by his every movement.

I can't *not* watch the muscles of his back tighten and flex as he flips the bacon in the skillet. I can't *not* admire the "V" cut of his waistline when he turns to the side, removing a cookie sheet full of toast from the oven. I can't *not* notice how silky soft the strands of his hair appear to be, falling in messy waves as he bends, finally released and grazing his chin. Completely hypnotized, my eyes fall, and I can't *not* remain under his spell as I ogle the definition of the muscles lining the tops of his forearms, swelling to capacity when he places the toast on the counter.

And I sure as hell cannot seemingly break my stare, or close my mouth even, when he turns to face me with—I kid you not—a fucking *eight*-pack on full display.

My entire body heats and begins to thrum wildly with the need to feel his perfection, the weight of all of those glorious, well-defined muscles, hovering over me.

Our eyes lock as my mouth clamps shut.

I swallow.

He grins.

I die.

Then I come to my senses.

My hands fly up to shield his body from my eyes, and my face pinches in mock disgust. "Ack. Cover up, would ya? You're hideous. I'm not even sure I can eat now."

Grady waggles his eyebrows, and I'm pretty sure he flexes his pecs, *not* that I'm looking.

His smile widens, then he winks.

I die all over again.

He does an about-face, taking a couple of plates from the cabinet, and my eyes drift to the dented skin just above the magnificent ass sadly hidden behind his gray sweats.

I'm onto his little game. Sexy man, mussed hair, cooking, ripped and bare-chested . . . all of which are hot as fuck.

He's baiting me.

Before I begin to drool all over myself like a loon, I decide to up the ante. A little tit for tat, so to speak.

I grin at the brilliance of my little joke, and clear my suddenly parched throat.

"Sooooo," I drawl, "shirtless breakfast. Another memo I did not receive."

Grady pivots around just in time to see my fingers curl under the hem of my shirt. My brows lift in challenge. He remains collected, shrugging his shoulders in nonchalance. Then he whips the spatula in his hand around in the air, and the slightest of grins hits his lips as he offers, "Feel free to make yourself more comfortable."

The flare of Grady's eyes is the last thing I see before I whip the T-shirt over my head. The cool air around me rushes over my naked skin upon its removal. I glance down, mentally applauding my choice in undergarment. The strapless black peekaboo lace was a perfect pick, seeing as how it demonstrates just how chilly the air really is.

Calmly, I fold the shirt and lay it on the counter before lifting my stare to meet Grady's. His blue eyes no longer wide but filled with amusement as he chuckles to himself. "I cannot believe you just did that."

I lift my shoulders innocently and walk to where he stands, reaching for a plate. "I was hot." I fan myself for emphasis. "Uncomfortable."

"Sweetheart." Grady moves to stand behind me, gliding his fingers under my hair and sweeping it over my left shoulder. Heat from his bare chest seeps into the skin of my back and his voice is low as it hits my ear. "Your tits are telling me a different story."

I suck in a sharp breath when his parted lips touch the sensitive area behind my ear, and right on cue, my nipples harden as a rash of goose bumps rise along every inch of my skin. His laughter strikes my neck, and my eyes roll into the back of my head as I refute, "I said I *was* hot. Clearly that is no longer the case."

"Clearly." Another lingering touch from his lips, then his warmth is gone.

I turn to face him, smile on my face, plate in hand. Grady scoops some scrambled eggs onto it, then adds a couple slices of bacon and a piece of toast, before gesturing to the island. I take my seat, and as I sip on the orange juice provided, Grady plates his own food then sits next to me.

Both grinning mischievously, we finally begin to eat. After a couple of bites, Grady places his fork on his plate and turns to look at me. "We discussed my family at length last night. What about yours? Siblings?"

Suddenly getting *better acquainted* doesn't seem like such a good idea.

I shake my head, swallowing a mouthful of bacon. Grady continues. "Parents?"

Inhaling deeply, I press my feet on the bottom rung of the barstool and rise. I need to reroute this conversation. "Two."

I offer nothing else, just lean over slowly to grab a jar of grape jelly from the center of the island. As I do, I make sure to press my breasts together, making my cleavage pop shamelessly. I glance over, disappointed to find Grady's eyes haven't left my face. My mouth twists to the side in a defeated pout as I recline back into my seat.

"Close?"

I dip my knife into the jar, scooping a heap as I respond, "We were when I was young. Not so much anymore."

Grady scratches the stubble on his chin in thought, then asks, "What happened?"

The mound of jelly plops onto my toast and I slather it with the knife. Tearing my determined stare away from my hands, I look

Grady right in the eyes and offer in a clipped tone, "They stopped paying attention."

Grady's brows draw together and his head jerks backward. And on that note, I decide to end the conversation. Drastic times call for drastic measures.

Folding the toast in half, I squeeze it as I bring it to my mouth, forcing some jelly to fall from the bread and land smack-dab on the swell of my breast.

"Oh, look at that. I can be such a klutz sometimes." I *tsk* and shake my head, then lower the toast to my plate. Keeping my gaze downward, I bring my hand to cup the underside of my breast and press it upward. As it lifts toward my mouth, I slowly extend my tongue and lazily draw it along the surface of my skin, clearing most of the jelly with a long, leisurely lick. Once through, I bring my eyes to Grady's and smile innocently while batting my eyelashes.

His stare is not fixated on my breast, nor following my tongue as it disappears back into my mouth. His eyes are merely filled with humor as he grins, shaking his head and relaxing back into his seat. "Not ready to discuss the parents. Got it."

My face falls and I gape back at him, uncertain if I'm more surprised that he showed absolutely no reaction to my ploy, or the fact that he so easily dismissed the conversation. His shoulders shake with more laughter, warm gaze still focused on my face.

I find myself a bit depressed at his blatant lack of interest. It must be displayed in my disheartened expression, because Grady rises from his relaxed position, leans into me, presses the pad of his thumb into the supple skin, and drags it along the path just taken by my tongue. The trail that had been cooled by the air scorches as his thumb grazes along the top of my breast. The burning fades when he lifts it to his mouth, seals the pad between his lips, and sucks the remainder of grape jelly off the digit.

It's the sexiest fucking thing I've ever seen.

My mouth dries and I can do nothing but stare as he leans closer and whispers, "Missed some."

Grady's lips are soft and sweet as he presses them against the corner of my mouth before rising and taking both plates with him to the sink.

And I watch, riveted.

Never before have I ever been treated with such . . . *care*.

It's an odd, yet captivating feeling.

I inhale deeply, just as Grady pivots to face me. His palms press against the counter as he rests his body against it. "Come here."

I remain by the stool, and Grady grins crookedly. "Please."

Slowly, I leave the safety of the island, grabbing the Waldo T-shirt as I pass by on my way to Grady. Curling my fingers around the cotton material, I walk to where he stands. He extends his hand, requesting the shirt, and I willingly hand it over because, well, it doesn't belong to me.

I watch as he unfolds it, turning it upside down and opening its bottom.

"Arms up."

I do as requested, and the shirt is carefully tugged down my arms and over my head. Grady pulls it taut over my stomach, then brings his eyes to mine. They're filled with warmth, and for some reason, the gesture of him dressing me, caring for me, prompts me to speak. "I just . . . my past . . . I can't . . ."

He lifts his hand to my face, stroking my cheek lightly with his knuckles as he dismisses my lack of explanation. "I don't need you to tell me anything you're not ready to discuss, Cass. Everyone has a past. I have mine, you have yours. When and *if* you're ever ready to discuss it, I'll be here to listen. No judgment. No assumption. But most importantly, no pressure."

I nod, then whisper, "Thank you, Grady."

His mouth kicks up at the side. "Thank *you*."

Grady's hand falls from my face, and I turn to leave, only to halt my steps when he calls, "Oh, and, Cass?"

I twist to face him, brows raised in question. "Yeah?"

He dips his head and speaks in a low register, watching me intensely from beneath his lashes. "Lucky for you, I swore an oath to remain a gentleman on *this* date. Considering I've been *rock-fucking-hard* for the past thirty minutes, I feel the need to warn you ahead of time that *next* one, all bets are off."

Well . . . fuck.

He lifts his eyebrows.

I blush.

Then I die for the third time today.

But death by Grady Bennett?

I sigh to myself then speak nothing but the truth when I answer, "I look forward to it."

Chapter 13 ✳

Apologies

Opening the door to my apartment, the alarm sounds and I nearly jump out of my skin, surprised it's been activated. Spencer and I hardly ever use the thing.

"Shh," I scold, my fingers flying as fast as they can across the keypad. Once it's been quieted, I bring my hand to my chest and breathe in deeply, trying to calm my racing heart. As it slows, I turn and gently press the door shut with my fingertips then pivot back around. With a plastic bag containing my dress and heels clutched between my fingers, my yellow sock is set upon the hardwood with a hesitant first step. Then another. And another.

As I tiptoe, it feels strangely reminiscent of performing the familiar walk of shame, but at the same time, it couldn't be more opposite. I don't feel weighed down by the usual grime of disgust and remorse. I merely feel as though I'm a normal sixteen-year-old, sneaking into her house, praying she doesn't get caught.

Tunnel vision in full effect, I focus on the hallway leading to my bedroom, steadily increasing my strides toward its safety. My stare is so intense, I completely miss the burly, bearded man leaning casually against the windowsill in my living room.

"You should lock the door." His voice is low with caution as he pulls the chain on the lamp next to him.

"Jesus Christ!" My palm hits my sternum in attempt to keep my heart from launching out of my chest as I whip around. My widened gaze lands on the altered appearance of Dalton Greer, calmly crossing his arms, still dressed in the same dark-gray shirt and charcoal pants as last night. His hair is still dark, now loose and messy from sleep as it hits his shoulder, but his deep-brown eyes no longer remain. Familiar and penetrating clear-blue irises observe my reaction from across the room.

I narrow my stare.

"Are you two *trying* to give me a fucking heart attack?" I whisper-yell, clenching my teeth.

White teeth flash from behind the brown beard concealing his face just as quickly as they disappear. He presses off the windowsill, makes his way to the door, then glances at me over his shoulder, taking his sweet-ass time to demonstrate how to lock the door.

I roll my eyes and curl my fingers around my cocked hip.

Dalton steps out of the entryway, his presence so potent, it seems to take up the entire living room upon his reentry. The low grumble of his voice is gone, replaced with the tone I remember as he speaks. "I'm not sure what Grady told you."

"He didn't have to tell me anything, Dalton. I know why you're back."

Dalton nods his head, absorbing my words. "Well, then you must also know that our situation is . . . *precarious.*"

I fight a snarky grin at his use of the word. It's just so Dalton.

He continues, "I need to know that both you and Spencer are doing all you can to remain safe. Which means," he gestures toward the entryway, "locking the door and setting the alarm at all times."

"All right, *Dad,*" I scoff.

Dalton narrows his eyes. "This isn't some fucking joke. You know just as well as I do *exactly* what Silas Kincaid is capable of."

All defiance is lost and my throat seals shut as I nod, words escaping me.

Dalton steps forward, covering the distance between us in three long strides to place his hand on my shoulder. Holding me captive with his stare, his voice is surprisingly gentle when he adds, "I'm sorry, Cassie. Rat's death, well . . . it's on me. I let him down. I lost him, but you lost him too. And I'm so sorry for that."

I shake my head. "There was nothing you could've done, Dalton."

He inhales deeply, pain and sadness filling his expression. "I got him involved. That's enough."

Memories of Rat and our brief time spent together unleash a fiery fury from somewhere deep within me, a place that has remained securely hidden for years. My head dips forward, and anger is threaded through my tone with my harsh whisper. "Then make it right."

Tenacity fills his baby blues with a jerk of his chin. His grip on my shoulder tightens as he responds, "Keep the doors locked and your apartment alarmed until it's done, okay?"

The urgency in his voice takes me by surprise. "I thought we were safe."

Dalton's brows shoot upward with that admission, but he recovers quickly. "You *are* safe, Cass. Grady and I are both making sure of that. But you can never be *too* safe. So please, for my sanity, just do as I ask."

My head bobs in answer, then he surprises the shit out of me when he tugs me into his body, pulling me into a tight embrace. All anger subsides and my eyes widen against the material of his shirt. I remain completely still, shock freezing my muscles. His hold remains, so hesitantly, I lift my arms and clumsily pat his back. His broad shoulders shake us both with his laughter until he finally releases me.

I look up at him, surprised to see a wide smile. I don't think Dalton Greer has ever smiled at anyone other than Spencer. Peacefulness settles into his eyes as they stare back at me. Rooting myself in their depths, I realize that sometime during the past five years, Dalton's wounds have healed. I know with absolute certainty; his head is finally in the right place to get his vengeance. And his girl.

I grin shamelessly back at him.

He angles his head, assessing me before he speaks. "I underestimated you, Cassie. In high school, I thought you weren't a good friend for Spencer to have. I couldn't have been more incorrect in that assumption. I'm sorry for that too. You've always . . . protected her, so to speak."

I chuckle with my response. "Well, it was my job to protect her for six years before you came along. Then I passed the torch because, well . . . she was in love with you. There was no competing after that. I knew she was always safe with you, and safe she will remain, now that you're back. I have no doubt."

Dalton stares back at my blatant honesty, and the intimacy of the moment begins to overwhelm me. So before it gets too serious, I add, "But just in case, I'll be sure to set the alarm and lock the door, as requested."

Deep laughter fills the room as he steps away. His amused stare drifts to my shirt and his darkened brows rise, a huge smile lifting right along with them. "Nice shirt. Have fun last night?"

I shoo him with my hand. "Oh my God, go away now. I'm *so* not discussing my evening with you."

"Come on, Daisy Mae. You know you want to talk about it."

I grin at the endearment and shake my head. "Not with you, I don't."

"Oh!" Spencer's angelic laughter fills the air as she practically floats into the living room. "Talk about it with *me*. I want to know everything."

"And then there were three," I remark under my breath.

Spencer's long, blonde hair is piled messily on the top of her head, bouncing with her steps. Her eyes fall to my socks, filling with humor before rising. Wearing a simple light-blue tank top and black yoga pants similar to the ones loaned to me by Grady, she happily bounds off the balls of her feet as she makes her way to Dalton. His arm lifts with her approach, and she nestles into his body. My eyes take in the sight, its completeness, and my heart lifts with the knowledge that all is right in their world.

The two halves of their broken hearts mended as they come together.

I sigh inwardly, then jerk my thumb over my shoulder. "I have to get ready. I have an appointment at eleven."

Spencer's eyes widen and she covers her mouth, but her smile is still evident. "You liiiiiike Grady," she sings. She looks up at Dalton, who's grinning back at her, explaining, "She never gives up deets about the ones she likes."

I snicker. "How would you know?"

"I just know," she retorts, offering nothing more.

I'm thankful for her discretion, because the only other person I've ever not shared *deets* about is Rat, who has already been painfully discussed in depth. Over the past twelve hours, I've officially hit my emotional quota for the next year, and I really don't think I can handle anymore today.

"We can talk about it later," I gesture to Dalton, "when *he's* not here."

With that statement, I'm pretty much guaranteeing that we will never talk about it, because I have a feeling Dalton will become a permanent fixture in this apartment. I grin knowingly at Spencer, who just frowns.

I lose the smile and lift my stare to Dalton, dipping my head, silently reiterating my earlier demand. He does the same in understanding, and before I can cry, or beat the shit out of some poor inanimate object, I hightail it out of there.

As soon as I hit my room, I close the door behind me, the whirlwind of emotion taking its toll. I fall onto my bed, inhaling deeply as I roll onto my back, taking my pillow with me and hugging it to my chest as I stare at the ceiling.

Out of everything that has happened, my thoughts keep circling back to the peace in Dalton's expression. He's not the angry kid I remember. The palatable fury felt with his presence no longer remains. With his acceptance of whatever really happened during his childhood, serenity seems to surround him now.

And all I can think is, if Dalton Greer can achieve that inner sense of calm, then maybe I can too.

Chapter 14 ✦

Kindred Spirits

Past—Seventeen Years Old

A knock at my window wakes me. Half-dazed, I pull myself out from under my covers and stumble toward the sound. With each groggy step taken, I empathize with Spencer all those nights she had to let me in through her window. A habit I thankfully broke a little over a year ago.

A barely there smile tips my lips upward as I unlock the window and slide it open. A cool breeze accompanies his entry, jet-black curls moving in the wind as he climbs over the ledge and into my room. His long arms hit the floor, knocking over a pile of books.

"Shit. Sorry."

I cover my mouth to mute my laughter just as my eyes catch the glisten of the gold Italian horn around his neck. It dangles in the air until he gets his feet underneath him and rises, landing itself against the white T-shirt covering his muscled chest.

Anthony "Rat" Marchione standing in my room is a sight I'll never tire of seeing.

About a month ago, Rat carried me into this room when I passed out in Dalton's car after a very unfortunate night of clubbing with Spencer. We began the evening with two guys who ended up being fucking douche-canoes and concluded the night with Rat and Dalton kicking their asses and then bringing us home. It was eventful to say the least.

Since then, Rat has been stopping by pretty much every night after my parents go to bed. He sits in my chair, booted feet propped on my bed, while I remain under the covers as we chat. It's a very unexpected friendship, but one I've quickly come to truly appreciate. I treasure it so much, I even asked him to prom. We're just going as friends, but I'm hoping maybe one day we'll be more.

I tiptoe to where he stands, and his hazel eyes smile in apology.

"It's okay," I reassure him. "You know by now my parents sleep like the dead."

Hooking my thumbs in my shorts, I pull them lower on my waist, then tug my gray tank over their top. Damn. Maybe Dalton has a point about the length. Not that I would ever tell him that.

"Like the shirt," Rat says on a laugh.

My eyes flit downward to see exactly what shirt I'm wearing. I really hope it's not the one that says in big bold letters *I SWAL-LOW* with tiny script underneath it *my bubblegum*. Mom hates it, so I make it a point to wear it all the time. Not that I can even recall the last time I cared what she thought.

Instead my eyes read, *Karma is like 69: You get what you give.*

I grin. Another one of my parents' favorites.

Rat's eyes dance with laughter before he turns, snagging the chair at my desk while I climb back under my sheets. The light from my closet remains on, illuminating his form as he takes his customary seat by the edge of my bed. His boots land right by the side of my legs and he leans, putting his weight on the back two legs of the chair, assuming his usual position.

"Where were you last night? I waited up for you," I inquire after a long yawn.

He offers me a rueful grin with a shrug of his shoulders. "Sorry. Couldn't get out of it."

I accept his apology with a nod of my head. "It's okay. With Dalton?"

He gestures with a jerk of his chin. "Yeah."

Rolling my body to face him, I tuck my hands under my cheek and inquire, "You guys have been friends for a while, yeah?"

"Since we were kids," he affirms. "He's seen me through some tough shit. And me, him. He's the brother I never had. Would lay my life down for him."

My lips curl into themselves, thinking how I feel the same way about Spencer.

Rat chuckles to himself, then continues. "But seriously, the guy needs to learn to lighten up. I get he's angry at life, but shit. He needs to let it go or that type of rage is going to fucking eat him alive."

"Well," I offer, "maybe Spencer can help with that."

"That's a definite possibility," he agrees.

We share sly grins. He removes his feet from my bed, setting the chair on all fours, and slants his body in my direction. "You know, I make up stupid-ass words just to fuck with him." He laughs outright. "Nothing pisses him off more than misuse of the English language. An art form I've perfected, by the way."

Laughter bubbles through my nose as he continues to speak. "I mean, it fits though. I guess we kinda picked our roles early on in the friendship. He's the genius and I'm the goofy sidekick." He shakes his head. "But honestly, I wouldn't have it any other way. It works. Opposites tend to balance each other. We make a good team."

"Yeah," I whisper, thinking about my friendship with Spencer. I understand what he's saying completely. I'm the promiscuous to her virginal. I'm the crude to her innocent. I'm the dark to her light. (Both literally and figuratively.)

But no matter how unlikely, it works.

His hazel eyes dip to my shirt, and his smile lessens. His expression is trance-like as he falls into deep thought, almost as though he's speaking to himself. "Sucks though. I mean, I could be *more* than the goofy sidekick. Sometimes life just has a way of knocking you on your ass though, doesn't it?"

I nod sympathetically, stunned by my own reflection in those words. He lifts his face. "Yeah," I agree.

"Where's fucking karma when you need it?" he asks. "I mean, you trust people and they force you into impossible, unforgivable positions. They take advantage, make you resent who you are because of choices *they* make . . . it's like you have no—"

"Control," I finish for him in a whisper.

"Yeah," he concludes, his voice just as soft.

His eyes hold mine, and in this moment, I feel the bond strengthen between us. It tightens, binding us together as mutual understanding is shared in our silence. I know in my heart Rat understands what it's like to be manipulated into keeping someone else's secrets. How after they're divulged, after they're forced upon you, it alters who you are, who you were *meant* to be.

And as the bond intensifies, pulling us together, it draws the admission of my past right along with it. I want to share it with him, because I know he won't judge me. He won't pity me. He will accept me. He will *understand* me, because in a way, he *is* me.

No one will ever understand you.

No one could possibly care enough to try.

Frustrated with their presence, hope fuels my strength and I shove the voices out of my head, because maybe, just maybe I've finally found someone who can and will.

Relief gathers at the tip of my tongue. If I can just say it, I won't be alone anymore.

I don't want to be alone anymore.

I don't want to be alone forever.

Resolute, I inhale deeply and gather my courage. Slowly, I open my mouth, and—

Rat's phone vibrates, breaking our shared moment. He disengages his stare from mine, lowering his eyes as he pulls his cell out of his pocket. His mouth tightens into a thin line and his eyes glare at the device in his hand. "Fuck. I gotta go."

I nod and swallow the tears of hope clawing my throat, driving the relief previously felt back down with them.

You see, little girl? We told you.

No one will ever want you.

You will always be broken.

Always alone.

He stands, leaning over me and ruffling my hair like he always does, same warm smile on his face. I swat his hand away like I do every time he does it, and he laughs before bending and placing his lips against the crown of my head.

"See you tomorrow?" he asks.

"Tomorrow," I respond, still barely able to speak.

I watch with saddened eyes as his frame moves gracefully across my room, placing the chair back under my desk before opening the window and climbing outside. He shuts it behind him, and I remain alone in my bed.

But tomorrow?
Tomorrow I will be open with him.
I need *to tell him.*
He . . . knows me. Understands me. I feel it in my heart.
I don't want to be alone anymore.
I'll tell him tomorrow.
Rat was shot and killed later that very night.

Chapter 15

Fuck or Flight

It's Sunday, and I am in an absolute funk.

Sunday, by the way, is the worst day for me to be in a funk. I have no appointments, so I've been lying in bed, staring at the ceiling, with memories of Rat churning in my mind. It's clogged with my last image of his smiling eyes, full to the brim with the painful reminder that I could have done something. That I *should* have done something. Maybe convinced him to stay longer, talked him out of going, anything.

Instead, I laid there like a fucking moron, watching him leave on his way to being mercilessly executed, both of us none the wiser.

Fuck.

Three times I've gotten up, ready to stalk over to Spencer's room and demand Dalton's gun to hunt that motherfucker down myself. And three times I've lain back down, knowing that's a surefire way of getting myself killed.

On my fourth time rising, my cell rings on my nightstand, aborting my mission. *For now.*

I cast an angry glance at the phone, then reach to grab it.

"Yeah," I sigh irritably in greeting, not even bothering to see who's on the receiving end of my funk.

A familiar chuckle sounds, and my brows furrow as I pull the phone away from my face to look at the screen.

Pressing it back to my ear, I add, "Grady."

"Wow, someone's in a funk today." The crease in my forehead deepens. I dart my eyes quickly, making sure Grady hasn't performed some masterful police reconnaissance mission and is standing somewhere in my room.

"You could say that," I confirm.

"Pissed?" he probes.

I fight a growl. "Yeah."

"At me?"

"No. At life."

"Hmm."

Just as I begin to crawl back under my covers, Grady proclaims in an annoyingly energetic voice, "Get your ass up and get dressed. Something comfortable. I'll be there in twenty."

He disconnects the call, and I sit up, clearing the hair from my face before scanning the room. Then I look at the phone, frustrated because I don't want to go anywhere.

But judging from Grady's tone, he's not going to take no for an answer, so I haul my ass up as requested. My feet drag the entire way to the dresser, seemingly as happy as I am about this recent development.

By the time there's a knock at my door, I'm dressed in yoga pants and a hot-pink tank that reads, *Bitch, please.* I found it fitting for my mood. My hair is in a haphazard ponytail, because again, I don't give a fuck. And just to emphasize my lack of caring, I'm not wearing a lick of makeup.

If Spencer saw me now, she'd probably have me committed.

I trudge my way over to the door and fling it open. Grady stands in front of me wearing another mutilated T-shirt, long gym shorts, and royal-blue Nikes. The grin on his face is pompous—breathtakingly beautiful, but still pompous—as his eyes graze over my appearance.

I frown at his amused expression, my lips pinching tightly. "I really don't want to go anywhere. I'm just going to throw that out there."

His smile beams, and he laughs under his breath. "Well, that's the best time to get going."

I don't even bother to grab my purse, just a square of bubblegum and my keys as I exit the apartment. I set the alarm and lock the door, shooting Dalton a pointed stare through the brick wall separating us, before joining Grady as we walk to the parking lot.

"My car or yours?" I ask, gesturing toward my cherry-red Jeep as we pass it.

"It wouldn't be a surprise if you drove, now would it?"

My eyes roll upward in defeat as I admit, "No, I suppose not."

Grady grins, then reaches, linking his index finger with my pinky. The simple gesture creates a tiny spark of liveliness, and my tired body starts coming to life. In thanks, I offer him a small smile, which earns me Grady's narrowed stare in return. My mouth falls, too exhausted to pretend.

He pulls me with him to his car, and as we approach the door, he unlocks it, leaning over me to jerk the handle open. I move reluctantly to take my seat, but he tugs my arm, urging me to remain standing. His sapphire eyes taper at the corners, crinkles forming at the sides as he watches me. Then he nods to himself as though a decision has been made.

"I know exactly what you need."

His tone is low and sultry, and an uncontrolled zing of desire whips right through me as it hits my ears. I maintain a neutral expression, but Grady must have noticed the sudden flush of my cheeks, because he grins before releasing me.

Fifteen minutes later, all desire is lost as my eyes land on our destination.

Crow's Gym.

"Seriously?"

Incredible.

Grady, clearly finding some sort of sick humor in the situation, just laughs as he drives to the front of the building, parks the car, and kills the ignition. He says nothing as he opens his door. He remains silent when he escorts me from my seat to the front door. Only when he puts the key in the lock does he speak. "Fuck or fight."

I practically choke on my wad of gum and jut my head in his direction. "I'm sorry. What?"

Clearly amused, he laughs to himself before explaining, "You're angry. Two sure-fire ways to rid yourself of anger is to either *fuck* or *fight*. Since fucking has *temporarily* been taken out of the equation," he shrugs, "fighting it is."

"What?" I screech, now bordering on my own laughter because Grady Bennett might just need to be committed right along with me. "I'm not going to fight you."

"No, you're right. But you're sure as hell gonna try."

He pulls the heavy door open with ease, then lifts his eyebrows, waiting for me to enter.

I just stand there.

His lips curl upward and the muscle lining his jaw clenches as he tries to suppress his laughter. Then, as if that wasn't enough, his brows rise even higher, challenging me.

Mine lift in stark defiance.

He mocks a yawn, covering his mouth with a closed fist.

In turn, I release a pronounced growl, declaring my irritation, before finally relenting and stomping into the building. The door shuts behind me, and I lose him in darkness. Seconds later, I hear shuffling, then the lights flicker on.

Once our eyes have adjusted, Grady points toward the red mats lining the floor. "Stretch."

Reluctantly, I do as I'm told but make sure to pucker my lips and pout like a petulant child. Grady takes a seat beside me, and together we work through some stretches and various warm-up exercises.

After a round of cross-body punches, I wipe a bead of sweat from my forehead just as Grady asks, "You've taken classes before?"

I nod, changing it up and slicing an uppercut through the air.

Grady performs the same movement, adding, "I could tell in class the other night. You've had decent enough instruction."

My body freezes mid right cross, and I stare at him, willing myself not to smile. "*Decent?*"

He shrugs. "Could use a little improvement."

"Huh," I state, then lower my body in a fighting stance.

He mirrors my position, grinning widely. He then proceeds to try to intimidate me by cracking his neck, and I force back laughter. This whole situation is beyond ridiculous. His eyes land on my fixed mouth, then he lifts his arms and taps his chest with the tips of his fingers.

"Hit me."

Beyond ridiculous, but for reasons unknown, I do it anyway.

My leg lunges forward, bending softly at the knee as I power a jab toward his chest. Unfortunately, it doesn't strike. My fist smacks against Grady's palm, and his fingers curl over the top before he squeezes it lightly. He narrows his eyes then heaves my hand toward the ground, unimpressed, and his easy dismissal stokes my anger.

He steps back, cocking his head and observing my tightened expression. "Gotta be faster than that, sweetheart."

Grady gestures toward his chest.

I dip my head, step closer, and whirl around, attempting a round-house kick.

My ankle is trapped immediately between his hands, and as though annoyed, he drops my leg to the mat and shakes his head. My molars clamp together, harshly grinding against each other as I watch him. Rage begins to boil, elevating my heart rate. Memories and past recollections burn as they flow, searing my mind with their travel. They whirl madly, seeking exit, and my floodgates bow, allowing angry tears to well.

What the fuck is wrong with me?

I haven't cried in longer than I can remember, and all of a sudden I'm an emotional basket case around this guy.

Frustration mixes with my fury, creating more tears.

Grady's expression is no longer amused but concentrated as he gauges my reaction. "Feel that burn, that anger? You need to let it out, Cass. Trust me on this."

He pounds his chest. "Again."

His raised voice snaps something in me. I launch myself at him, throwing every punch I can. And each one is deflected, followed by instruction.

Left hook.

"Widen your stance."

Jab.

"You're overextending."

Straight punch.

"Shoulder's too relaxed."

Frustration builds with each fruitless attempt, until finally, fury overwhelms me. Fire erupts, singeing my restraint. I willingly surrender as it's unleashed because it just feels too goddamn good not to allow its freedom.

I need this.

I throw everything I have at him and as I do, Grady's instruction ends. He is focused on blocking my efforts and continues to do so until I have absolutely nothing left in me.

Finally, I give out, panting as I bend at the waist.

My inescapable anger is extinguished, replaced by the thrumming of my heart. Grady's Nikes come into view, only to be followed by the swirling intensity in those compassionate eyes when he crouches in front of me.

"Feel better?"

I nod once, still trying to catch my breath.

He presses up off his feet and his fingers curl around my chin as he stands, bringing me upright with him. Our stares locked, he angles his head slightly, then asks, "Wanna talk about it?"

I begin to say no, but I'm stunted by my efforts. I'm overwhelmed. Exhausted. Both physically and emotionally. There's nothing left in me to guard the words before they explode from my mouth.

"You're not the only one who knows about senseless death, Grady. I lost someone too. Someone I cared about very deeply. Someone who left and never came back. Someone who, five years ago, was shot and killed right alongside his *sister*."

There is no look of surprise on Grady's face as he listens. And with his lack of reaction, I realize he already knows about Rat's death. Of course he does. It's a major underlying factor in the reason Dalton came back.

Grady remains silent while I mindlessly continue my rant, breaking eye contact with him to pace the floor as I speak. "I mean, he was there one minute, talking about how the effects of a choice *one* person makes can alter who *you* are as a person, then the next minute, he was gone. And it pisses me off."

Rage-filled tears begin to build with each aimless step I take.

"It fucking pisses me off because he deserved so much better than that. He was a *good* person. He deserved to live a long, happy life, but he was never given that chance."

I turn and face Grady, who watches me with empathy.

"And it pisses me off because he *understood*. He knew exactly how it felt to be taken advantage of in a way that can't be undone. He understood living with the fucking consequences of someone else's choice. We shared in that torture. Yet here I am. I *live* with it day in and day out, while he's buried six feet underground. It makes me sick."

My eyes break away from his to look upward. My voice is barely above a whisper as I admit, "I fucking went crazy when he died. And it only got worse after Spencer left for college. I was going out, getting wasted, doing God-knows-what with complete strangers just to forget. To numb the agony of knowing I lost the only person in the world who would understand *me*."

I laugh, dejected, tearing my eyes away from the ceiling and bringing them back to Grady's.

"And you know what my parents did?"

The shake of Grady's head is slight, but it prompts me to continue.

"They put an alarm on my fucking window, my only escape from the nightmares. They caged me in like an animal inside my own personal hell. For months, I was forced to remain locked in that bedroom, visited each night by the terror of my memories. I will never forgive them for that."

Tears have long since broken free, trailing down my face as I speak. Grady makes no move to approach, but his voice is as resounding as if he were standing two inches away. "Do you know why I brought you here?"

I sniff, frustrated, then shake my head as I wipe my nose with the bottom of my shirt, awaiting his answer.

"Because you're a fighter. You do what you need to do to survive, including throwing those walls up at a moment's notice to protect yourself. I get that. I *understand* that. But what *you* need to understand is that sometimes those walls have to come down, sweetheart, just so you can breathe."

He takes a deliberate step in my direction.

"You said it yourself, you get to live. *He* didn't have a choice, and neither did my sister. They were victims. You are not. You're a survivor. But you keep doing what you're doing, you keep building those walls, cutting off anyone and everything around you, and you might as well bury yourself right along with the both of them."

Another step.

"Do you think your friend *wanted* to die?"

My head jerks back. "No. What the hell kind of question is that?"

Grady takes the final step he needs to stand in front of me. His eyes bore through me, not uncaring, just penetrating as he elaborates. "I mean, do you think he would have rather died than go on living his life the way it was? Just given up? Or do you think he would have fought to make a better one?"

I answer with absolute conviction in my tone. "He would have fought."

He never had the chance.

Grady nods encouragingly. "Exactly, but he wasn't given that choice. It was taken from him. However, you still have yours. The question is, what are you going to do with it? Are you going to let your fears reign, allow them to keep you from really living? Or are you going to dig deep, face them head on, and fight for yourself to have a better life? A happier one. The one *you* deserve."

He shrugs. "The choice is yours."

He's lying.

You don't deserve anything other than loneliness.

You have no choice.

Your sentence has already been decided.

Grady ends his statement with a gentle kiss to my temple, then turns to leave.

I shake my head to stifle the voices and train my focus on the true meaning behind his words.

Do you know why I brought you here?

I do. I know with certainty he brought me here for other reasons than the one he chose to disclose.

He knew I would get angry. He knew I would exhaust myself to the point of talking. And he knew exactly what he was going to say before he even brought me here.

I watch him walk away, wondering if he also knew that by the end of this ridiculous sparring session, one of those walls would be completely obliterated, leaving me utterly exposed and defenseless . . .

As I willingly just handed him a piece of my past.

Chapter 16 ✳

Weightless

Two hours later, I'm sitting in Grady's apartment, stuffing my face with a melted ham and cheese. While watching Grady cook has quickly become one of my favorite experiences, devouring his meals is definitely a close second.

Both are delicious and equally appealing.

Setting the sandwich down onto the plate, I chance a glance at Grady next to me. His hair is still secured tightly in a low ponytail, leaving the shaved sides of his head exposed, the length of the hairs only a tad shorter than the growing scruff that covers the sharp line of his jaw.

It's amazing the clarity that comes with multiple failed attempts at assault. It's as though I'm really seeing him for the first time today.

His stare flicks upward from his plate to meet mine and widens when he notices my quiet observation of him. Brazenly, I don't look away. It's not like me to hold someone's eyes, well, prior to Grady anyway. But this man—this intelligent, unapologetic, sexy man—has me stupefied.

And as I look at him my mind begins to question.

How long has he been a cop?

How old is he?

Why is he so invested in me?

And how the hell can someone I barely know read me so easily?

Why does he even care?

My eyes remain locked with his, unyielding, astounded by the strength and confidence stemming from them. I wonder what he sees when he looks at me?

Do I even want to know?

Propping my elbow onto the granite of the island, I set my chin in the palm of my hand, steadying my stare. Grady sets his own sandwich onto his plate then pushes it aside, giving him room to imitate my pose. My mouth curves into a slight smile, and I watch as his does the same.

His tone is soft as he speaks. "Like what you see?"

My lips kick up higher. "It's *decent.*"

Grady's shoulders shake as he chuckles, eyes bright with amusement. He bends, swiveling me in my seat and gripping the bottom of my barstool. The chair screeches along the floor as he heaves me closer with one pull. My knees hit the front of his stool, trapped between his legs on either side. A shiver rakes through me when he places his hand on my knee, casually stroking it as he states, "Just *decent?*"

All sass vanishes and I swallow, his proximity instigating the hammer of my chest and the loss of words.

His eyes drift to my neck, then slowly, he shifts forward to place his parted lips tenderly on my skin. "A *decent* man would have more self-control, but," another warm touch of his mouth, "it seems I have no control when it comes to you."

Warmth blossoms in my stomach and pools between my legs. I press them together, the ache intensifying with each nip his teeth leave along my skin. Involuntarily, my throat works another swallow, and I feel Grady's grin before he rises.

His eyes are heated, the burn in them similar to the heat I feel warming my face. Smile still intact, he bites into the fullness of his bottom lip and I draw my tongue across my own, my eyes refusing to leave his. I feel youthful. Giddy. Daring.

An unfamiliar childlike innocence and awe for the person in front of me washes away the revulsion I typically feel when this close to someone. Never before has anyone brought out this side of me, this wondrous feeling of excitement due to a mere touch.

I want to feel more.

Leaning forward, I mimic his gesture, slowly propelling myself forward and pressing my lips onto the skin of his neck. I can feel his quickening pulse beneath my mouth, and without haste, I leisurely trail the tip of my tongue where it rapidly rises and falls. Grady draws in a long breath, and his free hand curls around the back of my neck while the other remains on my leg, stroking my knee.

I inhale deeply, taking in his scent, then end the brief kiss, sealing my lips against the soft skin before rising. Grady's hold remains, guiding me as he presses his forehead against mine.

"Dance with me?" he asks, voice gruff.

This is the second time he's asked me that question, and I say a silent prayer that this dance goes better than the first one. To him it may seem a simple request, but for me, it's one that holds magnanimous meaning. I've never really *danced* with anyone. In my younger years, I often attended school dances, but the dancing was definitely not why I went. I used them as an excuse to find my escape, disappearing to the nearest unlocked classroom with the first willing participant. And prom, well . . . needless to say, I missed that.

But now, looking into the depth of Grady's pleading eyes, I want to give him this. So many firsts I wish I had to offer no longer exist. But *this*, this is Grady's dance. Just for him. A part of me, a tiny piece of innocence lost that only he can render with his patience and understanding in allowing—in encouraging—me to be me.

I dip my chin and he removes his hold on my neck to take my hand. Linking a long finger with my pinky, he steps off his stool, then waits patiently for me to follow. Together, we make our way to the living room. Grady leads me to the TV then crouches on his knees, opening the doors of the cabinet below it.

With the touch of his hand, an iPod and dock power on. With the other still holding mine, he searches for the song he's looking for then hits play. As he rises to his feet, the sound of a strumming guitar and soft keys playing on a piano fill the air around us. Grady steps closer to me, bringing his torso inches from mine, then adjusts his hold so his fingers curl around my hand. His other arm circles my waist and slowly, he pulls my body flush with his. I lay my cheek on his shirt and inhale, our feet beginning to move to the music. It's a beautiful, haunting melody.

I have never done this.

Never taken this time with anyone.

Never danced with anyone.

Never been . . . held like this by anyone.

I smile to myself, savoring the foreign feeling.

"What song is this?" I ask, enjoying the warmth of his body so close to mine.

His voice rumbles against my ear. "'Draw Your Swords,' by Angus & Julia Stone."

"It's sad," I reflect.

"I feel it's appropriate," he states, then continues, "The man is pleading with her to understand that she's the only one for him, but she doesn't believe him, or she doesn't care. Either way, he's asking her to draw her swords, to challenge him so she can truly understand how much she means to him. He's telling her they are meant for each other and to stop wasting time fucking around. At least, that's my take on it. It probably means something else, but whenever I've heard it, I've thought of you, always drawing your swords. Still do."

I lift my head, meeting his eyes, and grin. "Well, if nothing else, I'm definitely challenging."

He smiles back at me and winks. "Nothing I can't handle. I'm always up for a good challenge."

My grin widens tenfold and I surprise myself with my bluntness. "Are you saying I'm the one for you, Grady Bennett?"

"The only one," he answers, right along with the man singing. His tone is full of conviction, and the sincerity in his returning stare stops my feet from moving.

And in the strength of that gaze, I find courage to ask him the one question that's been plaguing me since our time earlier at the gym. "You really think I'm a fighter?"

Grady releases my hand to trail his knuckles gently down my cheek. "I do. I see it in your eyes. Your fire still burns, sweetheart, whether you can feel it or not."

I will myself not to become sad with his words, because I know it's there. I feel it sometimes, flickering somewhere within the depths of my past, but I'm too scared to approach it. The fight that lies before me is one that threatens to take me into complete nothingness. I'm not sure my fire will ever burn brightly enough to protect me from that.

Grady speaks, interrupting me from my thoughts. "Do you trust me yet?"

I release a tiny laugh as I answer honestly, "I'm getting there."

He grins and moves closer to resume our dance, but I have something else in mind. I may not be the best at discussing my thoughts or vocalizing my feelings, but I do know how to use my body to communicate. And I want to show him exactly what *getting there* means for me. It may seem crazy to anyone else, but to me it makes perfect sense. Because in learning to trust Grady, in order to be able do so wholly, I need to bare myself to him. This isn't about sex for me. It's about my body, my most protected vulnerability. It's about the control associated with it, in how I use it and how I allow it to be used, as I readily hand that power over to him.

I lower my arms, tucking my fingers under the hem of my tank, and drag it slowly up and over my head. It hangs in between my clutched fingers before finally dropping to the floor.

He holds my stare, his eyes drifting nowhere else as they desperately search mine, seeking motive. I can't explain it to him, not yet. I'm not at the point where I can discuss why this is so important, but I know in my heart, this is what I need to do. So, with my voice so soft, it's barely heard above the music, I whisper, "Touch me."

Seconds pass, our stares impenetrable, before he finally relents, lifting his hand and trailing his fingers down the skin covering my stomach. The muscles quiver below his feather-light touch, but instead of going lower, they circle around my waist and then run lightly up my back. My lids drift closed from the sensation of his stroking fingers along my skin, and with each pass, my ever-present guard slowly begins to lower.

Swallowing deeply, my gaze returns to his. I reach behind me with both hands to unclasp my bra, leaving the straps hanging from my shoulders as he watches.

He shuts his eyes, drawing in a long breath and clenching his jaw. I know it's restraint on his part, and in this moment as I watch his reaction, I breathe an inward sigh of relief. In some odd way, even though I've never told him of my past, he *understands* me. Something I never thought I would be lucky enough to experience again.

But as he looks deeply into my eyes, that same strange pull happens for a third time.

I feel our interweaving connection as it laces. It tightens, securing us together, and I begin to feel lighter as I offer him yet another piece of me. I want so badly to give him everything that has weighed on me since I was eight years old, but I know if I were to do just that, I could lose him. So I give him what I can.

Eyes never leaving mine, he lifts his hands and slides the pads of his fingers over the straps of my bra, then hooks them, gradually sliding them over my shoulders and down my arms. Heat trails his touch as it glides down my skin until the fabric lands on the carpet below us. My hands find the bottom of his shirt, seeking permission before he nods, and I lift it upward. The sight of his muscles flexing mesmerizes me as he takes over, arms crossing in front of his toned stomach before he yanks the shirt over his head and discards it to the floor. We remain fixed where we stand, neither of us moving, but taking the time to absorb the sight of our bare flesh as it's exposed.

I become intoxicated in a way I've never experienced.

My fingers itch to touch—no, devour his gorgeous body. Feel the warmth of his skin beneath my fingers. Scrape my nails down the ripples of his abs. Hear him moan as they inch their way downward.

I want all of that with him.

Under his scrutiny, I don't feel embarrassed. I don't feel dirty or thoroughly repulsed by what we're doing. There is just the beauty of this moment, of two people introducing their vulnerabilities, as we both stand bare-chested in the center of his living room.

I feel completely comfortable in my own skin as desire builds. It rushes me, a surging swell of fire that ignites every cell in its wake. My body is an endless sea of tingles as it comes alive beneath his gaze.

His eyes rake over me, the blistering heat in them evident, but he takes no step in my direction. He stands, unmoving, allowing this time for us both to savor the sight of each other's bodies. I peruse his muscled shoulders, then down his defined chest and chiseled abs before finally drifting up to his face.

His mouth quirks at the side, forming a crooked smile as he whispers, "Perfection. All of you."

The ideal of flawlessness stands in front of me, and *he* thinks *I'm* perfection?

Speechless.

I can't fight the smile as it forms on my lips. Grady simply shakes his head, pleased grin still on his face. "That smile. There it is. And just when I thought you couldn't get any more beautiful."

This earns an even wider smile, and I step closer to him, instigating our movement. He closes the distance, and as another song begins to play, he takes my hand and gently tugs me, my naked breasts connecting with the heat of his skin.

I suck in a breath, the sensation overwhelming me. My nipples harden and stiffen with every brush of his chest against mine. He lowers his arm, wrapping it around my waist, and fastens me to his body as we continue our dance.

Wow. I was sorely mistaken before.

This *is heaven.*

His fingers trace lightly along my lower back, and mine stroke along the hollow of the muscles lining his. Grady lowers his head and I feel the scorch of his lips caress my temple. His heated breaths soothe me as he makes his way down my cheek to the corner of my mouth.

I turn my head slightly, and when those lips land on mine, a hungry moan escapes me, finding exit into his open mouth. Our tongues touch, stroking and caressing. His hand disappears, finding the elastic band at the back of my head. My hair tumbles with its release, falling across my shoulders and grazing my midback. Strong fingers are lodged where it lines the nape of my neck, sifting through the strands and hooking them tightly. My body arches in his hold as I'm lowered, held by his strength and my fingers curl around his biceps, for touch alone, nothing else.

I place in him my ultimate trust as I surrender my weight in his arms, and he doesn't disappoint. He lowers me away from his body until his eyes find mine. "Fucking phenomenal."

Keeping his hold firm, he lowers his mouth to trail kisses along my collarbone and between my breasts. Each of his kisses is gentle—reverent, as he takes his time—as though worshipping my body. His tongue laps gently along the swell of my breast, alternating with open-mouthed kisses before crossing to find my nipple.

Slick warmth envelops it, spurring my whimper. His tongue works mercilessly, flattening over its hardness before flicking it lightly. My hands find his head, fiercely wrenching his hair free before clutching my fingers tightly through its silky strands. Teeth playfully nibble my skin, and my body jolts in pleasure. I tug the hair wound within my grasp.

A growl erupts from Grady's chest before he ceases his relentless assault, but only to redirect to the other breast, which has been excitedly waiting its turn. I remain suspended in his arms, allowing the sensations of passion and need to flood me. Feelings I have never allowed myself to experience, their enjoyment never before possible. I smile and bite my lip, desire overtaking me with each lap of his tongue.

His lips seal around my breast, and he presses a kiss on its surface before pulling me closer and lifting me to his chest. He rises, taking me with him, and as soon as I'm standing, he bends, taking my mouth with his. I open for him and he moans deeply. His warm tongue sweeps along mine, deeply and languidly with each stroke, tasting me. Our mouths are perfectly aligned, sealed together, nothing able to break us apart.

I've never felt worshipped before.

Savored.

Tasted.

Cherished.

I'm in dangerous territory here, because when he gives up trying to find me . . . When his patience eventually ceases . . .

As though reinforcing my worry, his phone vibrates on the coffee table beside our legs.

Slowly, his tongue traces the seal of my mouth before his teeth nip my bottom lip, then he ends the kiss with a sweet peck. As he steps back, our gazes remain unbreakable and our heavy breaths alternate with vibrations of his cell as both fill the air.

"I need to get this. I'm sorry."

His expression is one of apology, and I shake my head.

"Go ahead. I'm not going anywhere."

A contented smile crosses his face when he lifts his hand, curling his fingers at the base of my neck and stroking my cheek with his thumb. "Good thing, sweetheart, because neither am I."

I jerk my head in the direction of the table, indicating for him to answer the call. Grin still present, he leans to kiss my forehead, then bends to retrieve his phone. While leaning, his fingers hook my bra and he tosses it clear across the room. Then, he snakes my tank top off the floor, impishly waggling his eyebrows. Smiling openly, I accept the shirt and he releases me with a wink then turns, answering the phone on his way out of the room.

I just stand there, watching the muscles of his back work as he walks away, thinking that Grady Bennett is indeed a very *decent* man. And along with that thought circle many other unrelenting assertions.

I'm in danger.

I'm beginning to trust this man.

I can no longer deny it.

I'm falling for Grady.

And all I can think when he shuts the door behind him is, Will he leave me too?

Chapter 17

Paths

Lying in Grady's bed, I inhale deeply, listening to the sound of his bare feet cross the floor. As his scent fills my nostrils, my entire body relaxes and I nestle comfortably into the warmth of the cotton sheets draped around me.

This isn't the first time I've spent the night in this room. Over the past couple weeks, this sleeping-over nonsense has become a very dangerous habit. One I seem incapable of breaking.

The mattress dips as he slides in next to me, and with the magnetism of his presence, my body turns on its side, pulled in his direction to face him. I tuck my hands under my cheek and lock eyes with his as he turns, positioning our faces inches apart.

His mouth curls into a satisfied grin and he lifts his hand, pressing the hair off my forehead before trailing the tips of his fingers along my cheek.

"Hi."

Laughter bubbles through my nose with my response. "Hi."

He makes no move to kiss me. His gentle stare remains on my face, and I bask in the silence of the moment. I still can't get over the oddity of sleeping with someone without feeling forced to have sex. The innocence of being in someone's presence without the pressure of doing anything other than to simply remain.

Moonlight filters through the room, illuminating the silhouette of his bare shoulder and highlighting the loose strands of hair alongside his face. This man, this wonderfully patient man who lies next to me, watching me tenderly, is still such a mystery to me. Yet, I'm drawn to him. Pulled by a force beyond my own comprehension.

Grady's calm tone pulls me from thoughts. "What's going on in that head of yours?"

My lips twitch as I answer honestly, "You."

"Really?" His eyes light with humor. "Do tell."

"Well," I begin, "I don't really know much about you. I mean, we've spent plenty of time discussing me, what you see and what you've observed. I've even shared some things on my own. But we haven't really talked about you. About your life." I shrug. "I would like to know more."

Grady chuckles, and an amused grin settles into his features. "All you have to do is ask, Cass."

My stomach flips, and I breathe in deeply as I eye his confident expression. What I wouldn't give to be an open book. To be freed from the need to keep my secrets buried. To be able to offer the story of my past openly, without fear of judgment.

Stay quiet, little girl.

No one will ever look at you the same if you tell them.

Your past is disgusting.

Vile like you.

I clear my throat then inquire, "For starters, how old are you? I don't even know your age."

Grady's smile widens with his answer. "Twenty-nine."

I grin in return. "Cradle-robber. You're *six* years older than me."

Laughter escapes me as Grady waggles his eyebrows, clearly not at all offended by my jest. "Age is irrelevant, sweetheart. Plus, I'm pretty sure this old man owned you at Crow's last night."

He did. He totally kicked my ass sparring yesterday.

Jerk.

But then he made up for it by kissing me senseless on the mats when we were through.

A shiver goes through me with the memory. Our slick, sweaty bodies melded together as his mouth claimed mine. Definitely worth the ass-kicking.

"Moving on," I segue, garnering more laughter from Grady. "How long have you been a cop?"

"Since I was about your age. Graduated with a criminal justice degree, headed to the police academy the very next day, been on the same path ever since."

Path.

My mind recalls something he said our first night together.

Went down a path I'm not proud of, but eventually I made peace with her death and moved forward.

"You weren't always on that path though?" I inquire.

The shake of his head is subtle. "No. I wasn't. After Ashley was killed, I was angry. Hurt. I couldn't understand why she was murdered. I didn't deal well with her loss. In fact, I didn't really deal at all, at first."

Grady exhales. "I was piss drunk almost every night for years. Barely graduated high school. And I stumbled along that same drunken path for a long while after that. I picked fights because I was pissed, yelled at my parents because I was angry. When they packed up her room, I fucking lost it. I couldn't understand how they could just move on with their lives."

I reach forward and lace his fingers with mine, squeezing his hand for encouragement. He gifts me a small grin before he continues. "I know now they needed to move on. They went through their grieving process, came to terms with her death. It would be many years before I would be able to do the same."

Bringing my hand to his mouth, he tenderly places a warm kiss on my skin then watches the movement of his thumb as it grazes along my knuckles. "One day, I'd just had enough. I was so fucking tired of being pissed all the time. I was selfish, wasting my life when Ashley no longer had hers to live. Once I came to terms with that fact, I got my shit together. I stopped drinking, started therapy, eventually went to college. After a couple years, I knew I wanted to be in the force. I wanted to do my part to protect people, help keep them safe. They never found her murderer, did I ever tell you that?"

My mouth dips, weighted with sorrow, and I shake my head. "No."

His shoulders lift then fall. "Well, I guess that was part of the reason I made the decision to enter the Fuller Police Force. To catch the bad guys. Another way for me to make some sort of peace with her death, I guess."

Grady tightens his grip on my hand and fixes his stare on mine. "You're tired too, sweetheart. I see the same exhaustion clouding those eyes when you look at me, holding hostage that beautiful smile of yours. Maintaining your guard isn't easy. It takes its toll, physically, emotionally. I know because I've been there. But if I was able to find my way, make my peace, I know you can too." He winks. "We'll get ya there."

I wish.

I wish.

I wish.

I want.

I swallow the boulder clogging my throat and nod, releasing Grady's hand to lift my arm and capture a tear before it escapes. A response I'm becoming quite used to when around Grady. It's almost as though he's somehow able to reach inside me and touch those pieces of my soul I thought long dead, bringing them back to life. And as they're revived, I'm left with no choice but to weep, flooded with the repressed emotions resurrected right along with them.

The old Cassie Cooper would have run for the hills before the first tear even hit the ground.

But this *new* Cassie, the one Grady seems to draw forth, finds it refreshing. Cathartic.

It's freeing, in a way, to be able to *feel* and *express* the emotion he elicits.

His fingers curl around the back of my neck and he urges me closer, bringing my head into his chest. I allow his arms to curl around me, encasing me protectively within his frame. My cheek rests comfortably against his soft skin as I listen to the sound of his heart beating and his calming breaths pass through his chest.

You're not going anywhere, little girl.

You're ours.

Not his to take.

Grady's words resound in my head, drowning out the whispers of my voices.

I was able to find my way . . . I know you can too.

As he holds me in his arms, I find myself astounded that this man of absolute perfection once traveled a darkened, angry path very similar to mine.

My walls begin to tremble with force from the realization, and gaping cracks tear along their surface.

I'm so fucking tired.
Grady understands that.
He understands me.
Maybe I'm not alone after all.

Willing them to be true, I replay those thoughts, effectually blocking my voices from reentry. Soon after, my relaxed eyes drift shut. Enveloped in warmth and the strength of Grady's presence, an unfamiliar feeling soothes my insides as it coats the exposed wounds hidden beneath my breast. And as it spreads, my heart fills, brimming with a feeling I haven't truly experienced since early childhood.

I feel happy.

Chapter 18

Redo

"Cass. I'm going to Mom's. Want to go with me?"

With a spoonful of peanut butter, I turn in the direction of Spencer's room, eyeing it with abhorrence. I haven't set foot anywhere near my parents' house since the second I turned eighteen.

Carrying the spoon with me, I tread toward Spencer's room, missing Grady's cooking immensely. We've now spent a solid month together, and I've become extremely spoiled by several flawlessly cooked meals, as well as tremendously horny due to the many hot make-out sessions at his apartment.

Jesus, but that man can kiss.

A flush warms my face with the thought of his mouth on mine. Of the weight of his body pressed against my chest. Of our naked skin gliding frictionless under his sheets.

And yet, we *still* haven't had sex. The bottom halves of our bodies have remained clothed, the pure innocence of exploring bringing sensuality to a level I've never experienced.

I have no doubt that sex with Grady Bennett will be . . . *fucking phenomenal*. But the buildup, the journey toward getting to that point, is one I wanted to take slowly. Especially with him, because I want it to mean something when we do. I want it to be special.

But it's been a month, and honestly, I feel I'm ready to take that step. I want to share that with him, to watch his reaction as I give him that part of me. I'm excited for it, actually.

I sigh a surprisingly girly sigh as I walk, then stand in Spencer's doorway, bringing myself back into the conversation. "Across the street from *my* parents' house?"

Spencer nods.

I pinch my face as though she's crazy and shake my head. "Oh hell no. Mom found my diary from eighth grade when she was cleaning out my bedroom. I won't be going back over there . . . ever."

All truth, especially the last sentence. Man, I miss that diary. It was highly entertaining.

Cocking my hip, I relax my body into the wood framing her doorway and ask, "Do you think you can sneak in my window and grab it? There were some really inventive positions I practiced with Pete Johnson noted in there." I waggle my brow for effect and Spencer rolls her eyes, but I spy a grin on her face as she does it.

"Your parents put an alarm on that window the summer of our senior year, remember?"

My face falls straight to the floor when she points out the obvious. I meant it when I told Grady I would never be able to forgive them for that. And I won't.

I lose myself in my hatred for them, before finally snapping out of it. Bringing my eyes to Spencer's, I lie, "Yeah, I forgot. Man," I add a whine, "that sucks. I was gearing up for the big night with Grady."

I grin at her, cementing the decision in my mind. Tonight.

"You haven't had sex with Grady yet?" she inquires, not surprisingly taken aback by this information.

I shake my head. "No, just good ol' fooling around and spooning. Nothing else . . . *yet*."

This elicits a truly happy smile from my best friend as she responds, "Good."

I give her a wink, then follow it up with, "You?"

"With Grady? Eww." She gags mockingly and I narrow my stare. "No, hooker. With Dalton."

She smiles the same goofy smile she always has when it comes to Dalton. "No, not yet."

Thinking on this, I lick the spoon clean then point it in her direction. "He owes you another birthday night. Like, complete redo."

And he does.

She gave her virginity to him on the night of her eighteenth birthday.

He disappeared the same evening.

It was heart-wrenching to watch my best friend crumble under the absolute devastation of giving her most precious gift to the one person in this world she deemed worthy to receive it.

I can't begin to imagine the torture and agony she felt after she realized he was gone. Especially since her biggest fear was abandonment from those she loved. It was hard enough to watch her experience it, but to actually *feel* that amount of pain, I wouldn't wish that on my worst enemy. I gave my virginity away so thoughtlessly, and I hated myself for it. But to have that purity to offer, the gift of doing so with the utmost trust and love, only to have that person take off afterward . . . such a tragedy. For both of them.

She laughs, the idea clearly rooting its way into her mind as she grabs her purse and blatantly asks, "Are you going to be at Grady's tonight?"

I grin, catching onto her game. "Why, yes. Yes, I am. Looks like we're both doing the dirty tonight."

I hope.

Spencer laughs upon exiting her room, passing me on the way. I chuckle to myself, then offer her my best instruction before she leaves the apartment. "Make sure he wraps it before he taps it. Safety first."

I can hear her laughter as she shuts the door, then I make a mental note to follow my own brilliant advice. Flicking off her light, I hit the kitchen and toss the empty spoon in the sink. Just as it clatters against the stainless steel, my cell sounds from my room.

My feet carry me quickly, and I grab the phone on my way to landing on the bed.

"'Sup?"

Grady's responding chuckle warms my insides. "Plans today?"

Today? No, tonight . . . hopefully.

I grin into the receiver and answer honestly, "Nope."

I can hear the smile in Grady's voice when he speaks. "Well, you do now. If you're free, that is."

"It's Sunday. You know I'm free."

"I do. So I've taken the liberty of planning something fun for us to do together today. If you trust me enough, that is."

My mind goes straight to sex, of course, then I reel it back to consider his statement.

More silence ensues, and Grady, being Grady, waits patiently for my answer. I relive the last month, the times he's pushed me to see the good in myself, the tender moments we've shared as I opened myself up to him in a painstakingly slow manner, and his caring in waiting for me to do so. I know without a doubt, I trust this man.

"I trust you," I answer.

Grady exhales into the phone. "Good, because you're going to need to for this."

My brows hit the ceiling with that cryptic revelation. "What exactly *are* we doing?"

More laughter fills my ear before he evades, "I have a couple errands to run, so meet me here at two. We'll go together from my apartment."

"Grady," I draw suspiciously and repeat, "what are we doing?"

Grady answers in a very Grady-like manner, "Wouldn't be a surprise if I told you, now would it?"

I say nothing. My mind is lost, searching the list of infinite possibilities.

Grady chuckles once more, then concludes, "See ya at two. Don't be late."

"Grady," I screech into the phone, but there's no answer.

My mouth pinches to the side as I look at the time on the screen. He has given me exactly one hour to get ready for a date in which I have no idea what we're doing. How in the hell am I supposed to dress?

I growl, tossing my cell onto my comforter, then stand and walk to my closet. Knowing Grady, it's not going to be something as simple as dinner. Hanging out at his apartment is one thing, but the couple times we've gone anywhere, it's been something completely crazy.

Case in point, skating. And sparring.

I narrow my eyes at my various outfits.

If it's rock-climbing, I'm going to kill him.

I hate heights.

Yanking a pair of jeans off the hanger, I hold them firmly within my grasp, eyeing the several sleek dresses hanging off to the side. I look back down at the jeans, then sigh in resignation.

After apologizing to my heels, and promising to wear them soon, I grab the only pair of tennis shoes I own—a pair of black Chuck Taylors—and rummage through my drawers until I find the perfect T-shirt.

I laugh out loud then tug it on before yanking on my jeans and tying my Chucks. Heading into the bathroom, I do make a decent attempt on my hair, curling the ends until the brown tousled waves are perfectly imperfect. After applying a light, shimmery shadow to my lids, I add a coat of mascara to my eyes, and a subtle beige gloss to my lips. Looking at my reflection, I grin, surprised by my approval of the understated appearance I'm donning this afternoon. For the first time in as long as I can remember, I'm comfortable, relaxed in my own skin.

The feeling is . . . *immeasurable*.

And I owe it all to Grady.

His perseverance. His persistence.

His . . . everything.

Noting I now have exactly twenty minutes to get to Grady's, I grab my phone and purse, fingering blindly for my keys, before setting the alarm and locking the apartment. Eagerness begins a flurry in my stomach as I head to my Jeep, and by the time I'm pulling in to Grady's, I'm practically bouncing in my seat.

Grinning the entire way up the cement steps, I land myself right in front of Grady's door.

Knocking twice, I wait for him to answer, stubborn smile still on my face.

The locks click over and Grady whips the door open, the excitement in those blue eyes rivaling my own. Then, his stare drifts to my shirt, which reads, *Wanna See My Ninja?*

His shoulders bob and he shakes his head, a breathtaking smile overtaking his features. "Dare I ask?"

My brows lift expectedly as I respond, "Would you *like* to see my ninja?"

His eyes rise to meet mine and a dip of his head is all it takes. My smile widens. "All right, but remember, you asked for it."

I lift the front of my shirt and hook it over the top of my head, displaying what's printed on the inside: a ninja mask that slides down over my face. Then, I step back, lowering into a crouching position and swipe through the air, performing multiple karate chops just in case he missed the joke.

Which, judging by the sound of his laughter, he did not.

A warm arm snags me by the waist, pulling my body into a very hard chest—which smells delicious by the way—and hauls me safely into Grady's apartment.

His voice is full of amusement as he states for the umpteenth time since knowing me, "I cannot believe you just did that."

I grin into the safety of my ninja mask before it's whipped back over my head. My shirt falls to my waist and fresh air hits my face. Meeting Grady's laughter-filled expression, he adds, "Sweetheart, as much as I love your tits, I gotta say, I'm loving that smile even more."

Had it really been a month since he'd said those words?

I want to know what makes you smile, how to make you smile, and how to keep that smile a permanent fixture on that gorgeous face of yours.

Does he realize he *has* achieved his goal?

The usual murmurs of doubt and whispers of self-loathing rush forth, but I capture them and shove them aside with strength I never thought possible.

They quiet immediately and I grin inwardly, then, with a sense of pride, outwardly too.

Grady bends, planting a tender kiss on the corner of my mouth, and releases me. "Still love the tits though; do not mistake what I'm saying. I'll make sure to show them how much later, but for now, we've got to go."

"'Kay," I concede, laughing.

As always when I'm with Grady, I'm blown away by my natural ease when in his presence. I've never felt so carefree, so able to have fun and smile without worry of how I will be perceived.

I watch the returning smile on his face as he so effortlessly affirms and actually compliments this ridiculous behavior, and I can't help but grin even wider.

His eyes fall to my mouth and he winks in response, then hooks my finger with his, leading us out of the apartment.

Forty-five minutes later, I'm no longer smiling.

I'm petrified.

My fingers are clearly demonstrating this as they dig into the leather of Grady's seat when we finally park.

I turn to him, eyes wide. "You're fucking crazy."

He grins, then retorts, "Ah, but crazy is such a subjective term."

"This isn't funny, Grady. There is nothing humorous about this, at all."

"I beg to differ," he declares, then laughs outright when my eyes narrow into a threatening stare. "Cass—"

"There is absolutely *no fucking way* I am jumping out of an airplane with you," I shriek.

Grady shifts in his seat, bringing his face closer to mine. Void of humor he asks, "Do you trust me?"

I scoff, trying to buy more time with my nonanswer. "What?"

He cocks a brow and angles his head. "If you jump, you will be jumping tandem with me. So I need to know, do you trust that I will land you safely? Because, Cass, on my life, I will guide you to safety, and we will land together. But you have to trust I can do that, that I *will* do that."

My mouth shifts to the side, and I nibble my bottom lip, pondering my answer. "You said, 'if I jump,' so I have a choice?"

His expression is one of determination as he replies, "You *always* have a choice. It's up to you. You can take this jump with me, a jump that has the potential to change your life, or you can say the word and I'll take you back to the apartment."

He raises his hand, brushing my hair away from my face, then cups my chin with his fingers. "But sometimes, Cass, you have to find the courage to take that leap. The fall may be scary as hell, but the landing is what really matters. Once your feet hit the ground, you know that no matter how afraid you were, you landed. You survived. You faced that fear, and you fucking conquered it. And in that moment, you're awarded a sense of peace in knowing there's absolutely nothing that can be thrown at you that you can't handle."

His mouth quirks at the side as he concludes, "I want that for you, and I want to help you do that. But I need your trust to get you there."

My lips curl into themselves and I inhale a long, deep breath. I hold his unwavering gaze as he watches me closely.

My eyes flick to a plane as it takes off into the air. I think about my past, about the nights spent in absolute terror, about how I would have given anything to be free from the chains bound upon me at such a young age. And here, Grady is offering me a way—albeit a fucking insane one—to possibly break free from them forever.

And for the first time since my childhood, the voices remain silent without my interference. I feel renewed, inundated in strength with the awareness of their nonexistence.

Minutes pass, then finally I slide my eyes back in Grady's direction. I exhale at length, releasing my breath as I surrender to his request, knowing he's making progress with me and praying he will continue with his plight.

"Get me there, Grady."

Chapter 19

The Landing

Wind is whipping through my hair, mercilessly slapping me in the face, most likely trying to knock some sense into me. I can't tear my eyes away from the drop we're about to make as Grady and I stand at the open door of the plane, harnessed together. I imagine his face though, beautifully stoic, completely unaffected by the fact we're . . . how high?

"Um, how high are we, exactly?" I yell over my shoulder. The sound of the plane's engine and the massive gusts of wind make it practically impossible to hear myself speak. Grady's lips hit my ear and his strong voice booms as he responds, "About ten thousand feet."

"Oh, is that all?" I mutter under my breath, then swallow the anxiety churning in my stomach as it makes its way up my throat.

Grady's arm envelops my waist, strong and firm as he tugs me into his body. "It's time. Ready to jump?"

Tremors wreak havoc on my entire body as the words leave his mouth. My eyes slam shut and I inhale deeply in an attempt to control the quaking. Thank God I'm bound to Grady right now, because I'm pretty sure he's holding every ounce of my weight. My legs have officially checked right the fuck out of this situation. And as I open my eyes, taking another look out of the plane, I'm pretty sure my mind is right behind them.

Nerves constrict my throat, and the edges of my vision begin to darken. Just when I thought it couldn't get any worse, Grady instructs, "Cross your arms over your chest and lift your feet. You will be hanging from me and I might need to lean out of the plane to view the ground. Go ahead and rest your head back onto my shoulder if you don't want to look."

Fuck. This. Insanity.

My legs snap to attention and fly to my chest at the invitation to get the hell off this ride. I cross my arms right above them, gripping the straps of my harness so tightly I can no longer feel my fingers. With my eyes cemented shut, I force my head back, feeling the rustle of Grady's body behind me. Together, we dip forward, and I squeal in anticipation for the jump, but it never comes.

Grady leans us back into the plane, and my heart is racing so fast, I'm certain I'm having a full-on heart attack. Just as I'm about to communicate this information, we shift forward, and once again I'm hanging out of the plane, tethered to Grady's chest. Another high-pitched shriek escapes my throat, but as before, there is no jump.

Frustration builds as my poor heart hammers, pounding so hard I feel each beat in my throat. As we slink our way back into the plane, I bite through clenched teeth, "One more time, Grady. One more time and I swear to God I will die of a heart attack before we hit the ground."

If I didn't know better, I'd swear I could hear his laughter. But that would be impossible, because my heart has now jumped its way clear into my ears, its *whoosh* drowning out all other sounds around us.

Grady's voice is muffled. "Ready?"

"Ready." I respond immediately, because honestly, I want to get the hell off this plane. This leaning in and out shit *has* to be worse than the jump itself. My poor body can't take much more.

After a few seconds, our bodies dip downward, and Grady yells, "Here we go."

And then we leap.

Roaring wind is the first thing I notice. It assaults me from below, muting everything around me. I hear nothing. Just pure silence.

Time seems to slow as we fall. But strangely enough, it doesn't feel as though we're falling. There is no drop in my stomach, as I anticipated. It's a smooth transition, so smooth, it's peaceful. Serene.

I force myself to open my eyes, seeing nothing but the radiance and clarity of the blue sky surrounding us.

It's breathtaking.

Pure joy and tranquility fill me as I take in the openness, the freedom laid out right in front of me.

I'm not falling . . .

I'm flying.

I'm weightless.

I'm *free*.

And in this moment, my shackles no longer remain.

I release my hold on the harness and extend my arms to the sides as though they were wings. I smile against the rushing wind, fascinated by the feeling of pure, unadulterated freedom and the associated weightlessness. Masculine hands soon cover my own, interlacing our fingers as they curl between mine, and I know as we fly together, Grady Bennett has taken me somewhere within myself I never imagined I would have the courage to go.

Fear no longer exists in this place. There is just calming peace and resounding strength. They wash through me, bathing and cleansing as they flow. My eyes shut peacefully from the overwhelming relief provided.

With his arms overlaying mine, Grady squeezes my hands, and in turn, I tighten my grip around his fingers, offering him a silent *thank you* for the absolute beauty of this moment.

Shortly after, I lose the weight of his arms. They disappear and I bring my own across my chest, preparing for the jolt of the chute. Then, we're upright.

I focus my stare on the patches of brown and green below us as we drift toward the ground. The smile on my face is cemented, unbreakable as we continue our glide through the air. The next sixty seconds are some of the most beautiful I have ever experienced. They're filled with calm silence as I reflect on my life, knowing that the strength Grady sees in me does in fact exist. *I* was wronged. I have suffered because of that, but I don't have to suffer forever. I can choose to let that darkness go. I can choose to live without its vicious talons attempting to repeatedly rip at my flesh—at the flesh of my soul.

I. Can. Live.

I feel it, vigorous and lively as it surges through my soul, clearing the previous darkness with its resilient light. The process warms me through and through, and I feel its heat rising, encompassing my heart.

This must be what love feels like, I surmise.

And I know, as we continue our downward approach toward the vast earth below us, I've landed before my feet have even touched the ground.

The warmth of full-fledged joy spreads, further heating my insides with the stark realization I have indeed completed the fall. And with this newfound freedom, with this landing, I am no longer afraid to acknowledge what I've been denying myself for so long.

I am in love with Grady Bennett.

Minutes later, Grady offers instruction in my ear about landing, and I do as I'm told. Bringing my knees back up into the safety of my chest, I hold on for dear life as I watch the terrain coming at us at what seems like a million miles an hour.

I squeal loudly with its fast approach, but we land softly, Grady's legs absorbing the majority of the impact. As soon as I'm unhooked from the harness, I turn, my body still shaking from adrenalin overload, and jump into his expectant arms.

He wraps them tightly around my body and my legs circle his waist. I grin into his neck, inhaling his scent, then press my quivering lips against his skin and murmur excitedly between repeated kisses, "I did it. I jumped out of a fucking plane!"

His cheek presses against my temple with his grin, and with my arms still hooked around his neck, I lift myself away from his body to take in his beauty.

The sun shines down like a beacon of light made just for us. His eyes gleam just as brightly, wild with his own rush, and his smile one of unmistakable pride.

"You did it. I knew you could."

My cheeks ache from the constant smiling, but I don't care.

He holds me tightly in his arms then sinks his teeth into that bottom lip, shaking his head. "Beautiful."

And just when I didn't think I could grin any wider, I do.

Beautiful.

For once, I actually believe him. And with that belief, the light of pure happiness floods me. Like Spencer's light.

Maybe this is what love feels like.

Can I love . . . *can I love myself?*

My heart is pounding, each beat a fresh rush of life and energy. I feel alive.

I feel capable.

I feel strong.

Fear no longer reigns as I secure myself into his beautiful, riveting stare.

Beautiful.

There are no more walls between us as he continues to hold me. There is just an unrivaled sensation of liveliness as my heart continues pumping wildly within my chest.

Every cell inside my body flares to life as I bring my hands to frame his face and give him yet another piece of me. Moisture lines my eyes, and I swallow my emotions as best I can before I speak. "I love you, Grady Bennett. I do. I love you."

I shake my head, refusing to let my past taint the innocence of this moment. "I want to give you every part of me, share things with you that need to be shared, and I will. But tonight, it's about us. No one or nothing else. Can you give me that, please?"

Grady's stare tightens on my pleading eyes, still threatening unshed tears. He lowers his forehead to mine, pulling my body as close as he can within his arms, then whispers, "I love you too, Cass. *All* of you. I need you to know that. Understand that. Hear me when I say, I love every single piece of you, broken or not. Can you *trust* me in that, sweetheart?"

He loves me.

Grady Bennett, badass cop, sensational cook, sexy-as-fuck incredible man, LOVES me. What in the hell could I have possibly done to ever deserve *that?*

I love every single piece of you, broken or not.

Is it only possible because I'm learning to love me too?

My throat wells with unspoken sentiment, and I nod my head, because I do trust him, completely. With my heart. With my past. With my secrets. I know with absolute certainty, as I live and breathe, as I remain held in his arms with his own eyes glistening back at mine, I do.

Grady grins, then lessens his hold to set me on my feet as he repeats the very thing he said to me on our first date.

"Then let's get the fuck out of here."

I laugh as he presses his lips firmly against my forehead, linking his finger with mine to lead the way.

I couldn't agree more.

Chapter 20

Binding

The ride back to Grady's apartment is one of silence, filled with implicit looks of longing and gentle caresses of our joined hands. Strong fingers remain threaded between mine, woven tightly with the unspoken promise of what awaits us. His thumb casually strokes the soft flesh of my palm, sending a zing of warmth straight to my lower stomach in anticipation. Across the cab of the car, we join passionate stares, our eyes blistering with both want and need. The fire in my belly plummets, sending waves of pulsating heat between my thighs when his tongue darts between the seal of his lips. He redirects his gaze to the road in front of us, then lifts my hand, opening it widely so he can press his open mouth to the center of my palm. Blood warms my cheeks, and I clear my throat before shifting in my seat in an attempt to lessen the urgent ache each throb brings.

Grady releases my hand, but I keep it raised, placing it tenderly against the stubble of his cheek. From the side, my eyes take in his strong profile as he drives, embedding the sight in my mind. The slight curl of his rounded, full lips due to my blatant stare. The way his jaw tightens and how the muscle lining it ticks as he forces himself to keep his eyes on the road. The rise of his chest when I creep over the console separating us to press a soft kiss in the crook of his corded neck. And as his scent fills my lungs, I run my nose along his skin, creating forever memories of this moment. Parting my lips, I drag them upward until they land and seal around the bottom of his earlobe.

A low growl breaks the silence, and I grin before gripping his ear with my teeth.

"Sweetheart, at this rate we're not going to make it to the apartment."

My smile extends, delightfully satisfied with the effect I have on him, before I lower my head and ease my body back into my seat. Just as before, his hand reaches for mine, and I willingly comply, joy filling my heart with the knowledge that he longs for my touch as much as I do his. His fingers curl into mine, resuming his firm grip, and I tear my eyes away, redirecting them toward the windshield.

After what seems like an eternity, we finally make it to his apartment. Grady parks, pulls the keys from the ignition, and twists to face me. He lifts his hand, tracing the pads of his fingers along my forehead and down my cheek. The air grows heavy, coated with hunger and anticipation as he draws his fingers along my lips. My mouth opens slightly, and my tongue grazes his fingers with their pass. As it makes contact, Grady's nostrils flare, and the pooling heat blossoms into an inferno as I watch his reaction.

His voice is raspy, gruff, and low as he drops his hand and directs, "Come here."

No "please" is necessary this time. My body voluntarily rises and crosses the space between us, propelling me forward until I can go no farther. Our slick mouths meet, opening immediately upon impact. I angle my head, sealing my lips against his, and our tongues graze with each hungry sweep. A moan is pulled from my throat, and Grady swallows it as he continues devouring my mouth, tilting his head in the opposite direction for better access. The kiss becomes frenzied and urgent, deepening until our teeth clash and our tongues wage their own war.

"God, Grady," I moan against his lips, "I need you."

Grady tears his mouth away from mine, face flushed and eyes wild, feverish with desire. He maintains his stare, lowering his arm and yanking the handle to his door. Only when it's open do his eyes break from mine. He swiftly removes himself from the car, leaving me alone when he shuts the door behind him. My heavy pants are all I hear as I watch his deliberate steps. He rounds the front and makes his way to my door, whipping it open once he arrives. A muscular hand reaches inside the car, waiting for me to take hold. As soon as

I make contact, I'm tugged from my seat and the door is shut. I grin up at him, his obvious hurry making me giggle.

His face relaxes with my smile and his movements slow as he steps forward. His forearms hit the window behind me, pinning me inside his frame. "As much as I want to be a gentleman tonight, I make no promises."

It's been a month for me, waaaay too long.

I definitely don't want a gentleman tonight.

He wedges his thigh between my knees, opening my stance. Then his warm body closes around me, and he presses his hardened erection into the seam of my jeans. Fiery sensations rush through my body, and my fingers fist the back of his shirt, pulling him close as I grind against his hardened cock. His chest heaves against mine. My lips find his ear and I whisper headily, "I trust you, Grady. I'll take it however you want to give it to me."

Grady's mouth finds my neck and his hips roll into my center, temporarily relieving the ache, only for it to be replaced with a more heightened, undulating surge of need. I whimper with the feeling just as Grady lifts his head, his eyes landing on mine as he states, "*Rock-fucking-hard* for a solid month, sweetheart."

I release his shirt and lower my hand, curling my fingers and gripping his bulge between our bodies. "Then do something about it," I challenge.

His jaw clenches with my brazen hold, and he presses his weight off his arms, his warmth disappearing as he rises. Taking my hand into his, he whirls on his heel, his feet on a mission as he pulls me behind him. I fight the urge to giggle, excitement and giddiness flooding me with his insistent strides.

As soon as we make it up the steps, I'm whipped upward and cradled against his chest as his steps strengthen. The laughter breaks free as I wrap my arms around his neck, nestling my forehead into his warmth as I inquire, "In a hurry?"

"To get you inside the apartment, yes."

I grin into his shirt. "And after we're inside?"

My body is jostled as he works his key into the lock of his door. "Then I'll no longer be in a hurry, because I plan on taking my sweet fucking time with that body of yours."

Another pang strikes right between my legs, and I open my mouth on his skin, nipping him lightly with my teeth, signaling my approval.

"Jesus Christ, Cass," he groans, throwing the door open and kicking it closed behind him. His keys hit the floor just as the click of his turned lock sounds. I toe off my shoes and Grady's body shifts as he does the same. Then, more purposeful strides until I find myself in the familiar darkness of Grady's bedroom. I'm lowered to my feet, but Grady's hands remain on my waist, guiding me with each of his forward steps. The backs of my knees hit the side of his bed, and I willingly lower myself onto its surface.

"Stay there." Grady's tone is insistent.

My brows hit my hairline with his instruction, and I watch as he crosses the room in three wide strides. He flicks on the light then turns to face me.

"Eyes on me, sweetheart. I want to see you."

I do as I'm told, surprisingly compliant to his demands. Every single time I've had sex, since the very beginning, I have always ensured *I* was the one in complete control. I dictated everything from kissing, to foreplay, to entry, to coming. There was nothing about the act that brought about any sensation of desire for me. It was always about the control.

But as I lie here, watching Grady's arm extend over his back to tug his shirt over his head, I want nothing more than to surrender. I'm tired of not feeling, of not experiencing all that sex has to offer. I want him to show me, to teach me, to guide me in how to be physically intimate with someone I care about, in a way that doesn't end in complete and demeaning hatred for myself.

I trust him to do that and to care for me and treat me with the utmost of respect while he does it.

So as I lift my arms above my head, submissively crossing them at the wrist, I deliver into his hands the very last piece of me: complete control over my body.

Grady's eyes are molten as they take in my offering. They slide slowly along the length of my body, clear in their understanding of exactly what I'm giving him. His throat works a swallow, then he steps closer and leans his weight onto the bed. My stare holds his as he moves to straddle my waist, his knees pressing down on each side of me. He sits back on his heels, sparing me of his weight, his eyes locked on mine.

"So goddamn beautiful, Cass, I can hardly breathe."

Everything within me wants to weep for the beauty of this moment. A moment that could have been—that *should* have been— had I not so thoughtlessly given it to someone who didn't matter. Someone who hadn't cared.

Yet, as our stares remain bound, I know this is a *new* moment, one that can be re-created. Redone. This isn't about sex. This isn't about control. This is about the demonstration of love in a physical sense. An action I've never known, never had the pleasure of understanding, but as I willingly offer myself to him, I know he can teach me.

So, in essence, as I openly give myself, I'm also relinquishing my virginity . . .

Restored for the sole purpose of being taken just so I can experience *him*.

I inhale contently when his fingers brush just under the hem of my shirt, blazing as they graze upward along the line of my stomach. His touch lingers just under my bra and is feather-light with its descent. My mouth opens and I lick my lips, breaking away from his stare to watch his hands trace their path downward underneath the cotton of my shirt. As soon as they hit the ridge of my jeans, his hands grip the bottom and my upper body rises as my shirt is tugged over my head. After its removal, I resume my position on the bed, lying back and overlapping my wrists.

Grady lowers his chest and the warmth of his bare flesh hovers above me, just before his mouth hits the rounded top of my breast. The pads of his fingers dance along my ribs, tracing their way toward my back. The center of my body rises, giving him the access he needs to remove my bra, which he does deftly.

His mouth works its way downward, lapping a heated trail between my breasts, along my sternum, and down my stomach. After a deep sweep of his tongue into my bellybutton, he lifts his body off mine and shifts lower. My skin blisters with each touch of his parted lips, and when their path lingers slowly along my waistline, my back arches off the bed, greedy for his mouth to relieve the throbbing ache between my legs.

As soon as it strikes, my moan rips through the air. Fire erupts with the sealing of his mouth over my core, its heat penetrating through the denim.

"Oh God," I mutter incoherently.

All warmth is lost when Grady's body slides off the bed. His feet hit the floor, and I tilt my neck to watch his fingers work the top of my jeans, first the button then the zipper.

"Look at me, Cass."

I look up, and the stare I receive in return sets my insides ablaze. With his teeth grazing his bottom lip, Grady hooks his fingers into the waistline of my jeans and panties, tugging gently. I press my back against the bed, lifting my lower body to aid in their removal, and moan with the feel of his knuckles as they slide down my legs, gasping as cool air strikes my heated center.

Grady stands with his waist parting my legs, and I lie on the mattress, completely bared to him. My lips lift into a shy smile, the vulnerability of my naked body on display making my cheeks warm with Grady's passionate gaze.

His mouth quirks up on the side, forming a crooked grin. Slowly, his head moves back and forth, his expression one of pained reverence. "I wish you could understand how fucking beautiful you are right now. I would give anything for you to be able to see yourself through my eyes."

My throat constricts and tears burn as they surface, the sincerity and pleading in his tone hitting me square in the chest. I close my eyes and inhale deeply, opening myself and allowing his words to strike where I need it the most, my heart. Slowly my lids drift open and I raise my hips off the bed, insistence flooding my tone when I demand, "Then show me."

I need him like I need my next breath.

His touch.

His everything.

Him.

Determination flashes through Grady's eyes with my request, then he shifts his body forward and his knees hit the bed. Slowly, he lowers his hand and curls his fingers around my calf muscle, lifting it to his mouth. His lips are warm as they linger, pressed tenderly against my skin, before he gently hooks my left leg over his bare shoulder. His other arm lowers to grasp the right, kissing it reverently before placing it over his other shoulder.

Never before have I felt like this, unapologetic and bold—yet so exposed. But with Grady everything is different. There is no shame. No need to hide or be embarrassed. *No need to rush and achieve the quick, mindless orgasm.* His hungry, intense look fuels my confidence.

Our locked gazes remain unbroken as he angles forward, extending his arm underneath my raised body to guide me to his mouth. Both thighs slide over his shoulders with the movement, and he lowers his lips to brush over the apex between my legs.

My body scorches as soon as his talented mouth begins to work my core. *Unabashedly.* It feels so fucking good, an urgent whimper finds its way through my lips. "*Grady.*"

His returning growl sounds in the air and the vibrations released are almost too much for me to handle. With my forearms flat against the bed, my fingers lace together and tightly curl into themselves. My entire body seizes with the sensation and I'm forced to suck in a deep breath. Encouraged by my response, Grady's mouth works me harder, the suction of his heated lips and the glide of his slick tongue bringing me to the brink of a maddened frenzy.

My weight is completely suspended within Grady's arms as he devours me. His mouth alternates between tortuous, languid licks and deep, delving dives of his tongue. The contrast of the two sensations is almost too much for me to handle. I cry out in ecstasy, my entire body covered in sweat and tingling with pleasure as I rock my hips against his mouth. He moans into my core and more vibrations from his lips send another jolt of fiery need throughout my lower body. Every single muscle it hits tightens, driving more tremors of pleasure to build with each stroke of his greedy mouth.

"Grady," I whimper. "I—"

My heady words are cut off as Grady adjusts his hold, yanking me closer, his tongue removed and changing direction with one long lick. His darkened eyes watch my reaction as his warm lips seal around my pulsing center, and then with one more flick of his tongue, my stomach clenches and I'm gone, lost to the throes of my orgasm. My legs clasp tightly against the side of his head as he coaxes me with his mouth, waves lurching and reeling throughout my lower body.

All words escape me, not that I was really able to articulate much to begin with. My grip is still strong, my nails still digging, and all I can hear are my own heavy pants as they fill the room. Grady's gaze remains on me, hooded yet commanding as he presses his lips against the soft skin of my inner thigh. He lifts my body and gently lowers my legs to the bed, his body following suit. His weight is glorious as his chest lands between my legs and my sensitive body bucks against him with the added pressure.

"Beautiful," he moans into my skin.

Beautiful?

I can barely breathe. I can barely move.

I've never known sensations like the ones I just experienced. I've never known an orgasm to be so intense, so incredible, so . . . earth-shattering. I've read about them but never believed they were true.

The man is a god.

Stunning.

Magnificent.

And he thinks *I'm* beautiful?

He's absolute perfection.

Sexy perfection.

Lazy kisses patter my stomach before he works his way upward, and I fight the urge to tug his hair free and weave my fingers through the strands. He presses his lips to the side of my breast then smiles, clearly satisfied with my response.

I grin back, because who the hell wouldn't after that?

He makes his way to my neck, his mouth tickling as it grazes. "Fucking hottest thing I've ever seen, you comin' from my mouth."

My face splits into a beaming smile. "Fucking hottest thing I've ever experienced, you watching me while I'm comin' from your mouth."

His body shakes with silent laughter, then he raises his head. "Got an answer for everything, don't you, sweetheart?"

"I do," I retort, which makes him chuckle more. His eyes fall to my mouth when I add, "Maybe you should just shut me up then?"

His brow rises with my suggestion, and I lift my head, touching my lips to his.

"Tempting," he replies, then sweeps his tongue between my lips. My arms finally unlock, folding around his neck and pulling him closer as I deepen the kiss. After a few tangled caresses of his tongue with mine, he pulls back, his head cocked as he regards me. With his fingers sifting through my hair, his probing eyes assess me, and I answer the question before he even has to ask.

"You wanted me to be there with you, Grady. And I am. Right now. Tomorrow. Forever. I am *with* you. No one or nothing else between us."

My fingers drift over his back, flitting lightly over the pocket of his jeans, before sinking into it and pulling his wallet free. Bringing it into view, I open it and snag the condom I spied weeks ago before tossing the leather to the ground.

For the first time tonight, Grady's eyes briefly break away to look at the foil pinched between my fingers before bringing them back to mine.

My tone is unyielding as I repeat, "I'm with *you*, Grady."

His eyes flare, filled with pure animalistic desire. "Then show me."

Grady leans to kiss me, and as he does, the condom disappears from my grip. With nothing else to do with my hands, I reach forward and unbutton his jeans, pushing them slowly over his hips. As he shifts helpfully, his cock springs free from its confines. I raise my brows and redirect my gaze to his, met with an unapologetic grin.

I fight my own smile, then feast my eyes on Grady's erection and when I do, all amusement disappears, churned into need to feel him inside me. I lift my hand, curling my fingers and fisting him at the base. I notice his mouth fall slightly open with his intake of air. Then it's his mouth that snags my attention. His tongue drags leisurely across his lips when I pump my hand, his hips jutting forward in sync with the motion. I'm hypnotized, unable to see anything other than how fucking sexy Grady Bennett looks when he grinds into my grip. *I need to see his eyes.* Muscles flexed to capacity, sensual expression with half-lidded eyes gazing at me, his teeth sinking into his bottom lip with each stroke of my hand.

And just when I thought he couldn't look any sexier, his hand covers mine, tightening around my grip and directing my movements.

On the downward stroke, he leans his upper body, snatching the condom and ripping it open with his teeth. He releases his grip on my hand to pinch the top and roll it over the head of his cock, then brings his eyes to mine. I take his silent instruction, circling my thumb and forefinger around his massive girth and rolling it until I hit the base.

"Eyes on me, sweetheart."

As if I could look anywhere else. This man is consuming me.

I hold his stare as he shifts between my legs. He lowers his body, pressing his weight on his forearms as he places them on either side of my head and covers me with his chest.

The head of his cock sits at my entrance, his eyes are locked on mine, and his thumbs stroke my cheeks as he confirms, "You with me?"

I raise my head, press my lips to his, and mumble against his mouth, "Right. Here."

My body lowers to the bed and I wrap my legs around his waist. He slides into me, drawing deep groans from us both. His cock continues to claim me, slowly pressing forward and filling me until it can go no farther. My fingers dig into the skin of his back as he rolls his hips, deepening his thrust and circling until he finds the spot he's looking for. My entire body bucks underneath him, and once satisfied, he pulls out just as slowly, then repeats the motion.

"Jesus, Cass," he groans, his breathing labored. "Fucking—"

"*Phenomenal,*" I finish for him.

His stare intensifies and I squeeze my thighs, the tension building inside me as I rock my hips against him. His arm curls around my waist, lifting me as he continues stroking, each deep plunge not meant for his own pleasure but for mine.

I have never felt more treasured than this moment, right now. This isn't fucking. This isn't lust. This isn't even just sex.

This is *real* love as demonstrated in a physical sense. A true gift that Grady Bennett has unknowingly provided me, and one that I will never forget. No, not unknowingly. *He does know. He is giving me this gift willingly. Generously. Selflessly.*

He continues to rock forward, deliberate and measured in his movement, and my body is overcome with every emotion possible.

Relief.

Gratitude.

Desire.

Need.

Love.

He retreats and my body seems to follow him. When he slams back into me, I feel complete. His hard against my smooth. His strength against my soft. Our hearts beating as one.

My skin is alive.

My breathing erratic.

I don't want this to end.

It's *never* felt like this. Control has been so vital for so long, until this man. With him, my submission is being rewarded with his ardent, flawless loving.

How? How can he simply know how to love me? Emotionally. Physically.

He breathes against my neck, "So warm, Cass. Feels. So. Fucking. Amazing."

I'm speechless. As his body covers mine there's nowhere else I ever want to be. *Ever.*

My fingers cling to him, but then I can no longer resist moving them down his back. His skin is hot, slick with sweat.

Mine.

Another groan is released when my hands find his ass. Tight. Muscular. Flexing as he thrusts inside me.

I'm so close.

His hot breath.

His skin.

The feel of his muscle beneath my hands.

Too much.

Can't hold on.

"So. Good. Wanted you for so fucking long. Cass. My beautiful Cass. Fuck me. So fucking—"

His words are my undoing. Pure ecstasy as every muscle contracts around him. I bite down on my lip as he pumps faster into me.

With every push, my taut nipples rub against his smooth chest, and it feels so fucking good. More hot breaths in my ear. More words of love, adoration, worship.

"So incredible."

"Waited so long."

"My Cass. My beautiful Cass."

A guttural growl rips from Grady's chest.

I did that . . . to him. This ridiculously glorious man who loves me.

We hold each other's eyes with our release, and not until we're through does Grady lower my body to the bed. He remains inside me, his head nestled in the crook of my neck, heavy breaths tickling as they fan across my skin.

And I hold him, silently thanking him for loving me. For thinking me worthy and strong. For believing in me. And for giving me such an unbelievable, unforgettable gift.

One for which I will be eternally grateful.

"I love you, Grady," I whisper.

He smiles into my neck before he answers, "Love you, Cass. I'm glad we finally got ya there."

I giggle a ridiculous giggle, then sigh, still holding him in my arms. "Yeah, me too."

And then I show him exactly how grateful I am . . .

Three more *phenomenal* times that night.

Chapter 21

Ever After

"What?" I screech, hauling myself into upright position in Grady's bed—a bed I've become quite accustomed to sleeping in. My phone is pressed securely to my ear as my legs fly out from underneath the warmth of the covers.

My feet hit the floor with a *thunk* and I pull on some leggings beside them, listening to Grady's muffled instructions, panic and anger fueling my hurried movements as I tug one of his old sweat shirts over my head.

"Got it. I'm on my way," I yell before ending the call and whirling madly on my socked feet, snatching my purse off the floor on my way out the door.

"Shit!"

Dashing back into the apartment, I grab my pair of Chucks, gripping them tightly between my fingers, then haul ass out of the apartment and down the steps.

Heavy breaths escape me just as I yank open the door to my Jeep, and I mentally remind myself that I really need to work out more before climbing inside and slamming the keys in the ignition. After haphazardly cramming my feet in my shoes, I throw it into reverse and ram my foot on the gas, then brake, shifting into drive and watching as a thick plume of smoke is left behind when I peel out of the parking lot.

Twenty minutes later, I'm storming into the doors of St. Andrew's Hospital. My face is flushed and my heart is beating just as fast as my swift steps hit the linoleum flooring. Running up to the nurses' station, I slam my hand on the counter repeatedly, inquiring in a raised voice, "Spencer Locke! I need to see Spencer Locke! Where's her room?"

The eyes of a chestnut-haired, mousy nurse with huge black-rimmed glasses glare at me from behind the lenses. I narrow my stare, because I am *so* not up for backing down or playing nice when I've been alerted that my friend is in the hospital at three o'clock in the morning.

Fuck. That. Shit.

She opens her mouth to speak, but it's Grady's smooth, low tone that hits my ears. "She's this way."

"I'm sorry, sir," the nurse begins, flabbergasted with our blatant disregard for her authority.

Grady strides right up beside me, then flashes his badge. "Police business, ma'am."

Her mouth clamps shut, but her eyes tighten in my direction. I grin up at Grady, then offer her a smirk as he drapes his arm around my shoulder. She narrows her stare at the both of us, but before I'm able to leer further, Grady turns our bodies away and leads me in the opposite direction.

"Bitch," I mutter under my breath, solely for the benefit of having the last word.

Grady chuckles next to me. "They have rules to follow, sweetheart."

"Bitch," I state louder, again, for my own benefit.

More laughter from Grady as we turn down a long hallway. Despite his chuckles, I can feel the tension in his arm. To anyone else, it may look as though it is casually draped across my shoulder. But I know this man. I *love* this man. He has held me close, night after night, loved me in ways I never thought possible. Right now, that man is stretched. Tense. Yet somehow calm. He knows I just need to get to my girl. His calm is for me.

Twenty more paces and Grady gestures at room 211. He removes his arm to pull down on the handle, opening it wide for my entrance. I rush into the room, my feet almost sliding out from underneath me when they come to a screeching halt.

Because in front of me is not *Spencer* groggy and heavily medicated in the bed as I expected.

It's Dalton Greer.

I frantically search the room for her. Standing right beside him at the side of his bed, Spencer's tear-stricken face stokes the burn of anger to the fire of my rage. My eyes fall to her hands, gripping the railing so tightly her knuckles are white. The look of complete shock is all I can register on her face, her vacant stare locked intensely on Dalton. The sight alone tears my heart to shreds.

Immediately, Grady releases me and I race over to Spencer, enveloping her safely in my arms. Her tiny body folds into mine, and I tenderly stroke her hair as I glare at the people around me.

"Please," I make sure to look at every single man standing in the room, including Grady, "tell me someone shot that motherfucker, because I swear on all that is holy, I will gladly remove a fucking Glock from one of you and bust a cap in his ass by my own damn hand. I'll take care of this shit myself if I have to."

A sea of muffled laughter fills the room, only furthering my fury. "I kid you the fuck not."

My rage begins to churn. There is nothing even remotely fucking funny about this situation. My best friend is in danger of losing the love of her life, and they're laughing?

My expression is filled with ferocity and my eyes wild. All males in the room sober immediately, drawing their faces tight in attempt to hide their amusement, but I'm beyond caring at the moment. I eye them all and as I do, realization strikes. *It's April 23rd. Fuck.*

And just when I thought I couldn't get angrier, I experience a whole new level of wrath.

As Spencer's tears bleed onto my shoulder, I see no one else but Grady as I continue my rant. "Five years, to the day, people. Spencer's birthday. Five years ago exactly, when Dalton disappeared into oblivion, out from underneath Silas's control, and *none* of you thought to have more protection on her? On Dalton? Who in the hell is leading this farce of an investigation?"

My eyes narrow. "Tell me it's not you, Grady. Please tell me that's not the case, because if it is, you and I are going to have some serious fucking words."

I hear the sound of shuffling feet then turn, looking over my shoulder as a few part the way for Detective Kirk Lawson to enter the room.

"That would be me." His tone is somber, his caring brown eyes weighted with grief. He looks to Spencer. "You okay, kiddo?"

She sniffles from within my hold, nods her head, and releases me. I step out of the way as Lawson's feet carry him wordlessly to her side. He tucks her securely into his body, muting her sobs within the safety of his chest. He squeezes her tightly then turns his attention to me. "We had a mole. One of our own took out the rest of the unit assigned to Spencer's detail. Kincaid took that opportunity to grab her, but Greer tracked her location. Took a bullet in the back when Kincaid fired at her, but not before getting in the kill shot to take him out."

Lawson's tone lowers, as does his stare, both for emphasis. "Silas Kincaid is dead."

A breath escapes my lips. A breath that I just realized I've been holding for five long years. A breath that unleashes a wave of emotion as tears pool in my eyes and my voice softens with the knowledge that Dalton Greer just laid his life down for not only Spencer, but Rat as well. "Is he going to be okay?"

Lawson's tortured eyes meet my own. "Yeah. He has some swelling, fluid buildup in the spine, but they were able to remove the fragments without causing any permanent damage. Might need a wheelchair for a bit, but he'll be up and around in no time."

With that, he looks back down at Spencer, her blonde hair falling over her shoulder as she meets his gaze. "Couldn't ask for a better man to take care of my girl."

I take in the scene in front of me, thankful Spencer was given another father figure in her life. A man who loves her completely with unrivaled affection and adoration.

With the sound of Lawson's words, Spencer's face crumbles, and he tugs her again into his body, placing a tender kiss on the crown of her head as he embraces her. Moisture seeps down my cheeks, and as I raise my hand to clear the tears, a strong arm curls around my waist and the soothing feel of Grady's warmth envelops me. Relief with the knowledge Dalton will be okay replaces my previous anger and anxiety. I release another breath and with my eyes still brimming with tears, I look up at Grady and offer him a half smile as I inquire, "Do people really still say *mole*?"

He meets my stare with amused eyes and leans down to whisper in my ear, "Probably the same people that say 'bust a cap.'"

I pinch my mouth tightly to hide my smile, because he has a point. I should probably stop listening to early '90s gangsta rap. Then I laugh to myself as I draw the obvious conclusion, that yeah . . . that's never going to happen.

My arms circle Grady's waist and I squeeze him tight before releasing my hold and taking the few necessary steps to reach Dalton's side. His clear blue eyes flicker open and he grins a droopy grin.

"Made it right, Daisy Mae," he whispers, and it takes everything in me not to break down and cry. Or laugh. I'm so overwhelmed with emotion, it could really go either way at this point.

Teetering on the side of bawling, I lean into him and whisper back, "You did, and you got the girl. In fact, if your life were a book right now, your story would end here. But it's not. So I need you to dig deep for our heroine over there." I look over at Spencer and smile before returning to his ear. "And continue with an amazing, forever epilogue, just for the two of you." I grin back down at him. "Keep on living your happily-ever-after, Dalton, you both deserve it."

Then a smile crosses my face and I shift closer to relay, "And by the way, I feel I should tell you that Rat, in the utmost of confidence, shared something I think he would like you to know."

Dalton's face takes on a concerned expression, but I shake my head as I say, "Those made-up words he used to say, the ones that used to piss you off so much? He totally did that to fuck with you." I shift away, taking in his appreciative expression as his eyes are coated with fresh tears. "I just thought you should know."

He grins, white teeth on full display as he laughs. "That fucker."

I smile back and reach to cup his cheek. "You made it right, Dalton. Now you get yourself better so you can take care of her."

"Epilogue," he whispers, his tone laced with sleep.

I nod, then affectionately tug the hair of his overgrown beard with my fingers before rising off the bed.

"Kirk! Kirk Lawson!" Spencer's mother's voice booms from the hallway, and the fear that flashes in Lawson's brown eyes clearly indicates she's been in the dark about a lot of whatever has been happening.

His expression falls to one of defeat, and something tells me Detective Kirk Lawson is going to be sleeping on the couch for a while. I stifle a smile as he carefully leads Spencer to the chair next to Dalton's bed, sighs upon releasing her, and heads toward the door. As he passes me by, he leans and whispers, "Seeing as Greer is out, if you would like to 'bust a cap' in someone's ass, let me know. We have a temporary opening."

His eyes are full of amusement, but as he looks to Grady's, his are *not*. At all. He watches Grady's reaction, then laughs to himself before resigning to his fate, walking out the door to meet Mrs. Locke and quite possibly his death.

I frown.

Poor guy.

After the door shuts, I head over to Spencer, forcibly nudging her with my foot until she scoots over, then land myself right next to her. Pulling her into my arms, I hold her while she tucks her head into my chest, then I stare at everyone still in the room.

What the hell are they all here for anyway?

With a flick of my hand, I announce, "You are all dismissed."

They look to Grady, who dips his head, a smile creeping on his face as he ushers them out of the room. Before exiting, he turns to face me and winks. "I feel an epilogue coming on. I'm going to go write one."

"You do that," I remark, soothing Spencer's hair as I speak. "And make it good."

Grady smiles. "It'll be fucking phenomenal."

And with that crooked grin that so often renders me breathless, he leaves me to console my friend, thinking we had both finally found our happily-ever-after.

Turns out, much more of my story would need to be written first.

Chapter 22 ✦
Blindsided

"Cass, wake up, sweetheart."

Grady's soothing voice rouses me. Slowly, my lids flutter open to find his warm gaze. I smile sleepily back at him, then look over his shoulder to see Spencer sleeping next to Dalton in his hospital bed. She no longer looks worried, but peaceful as she lies next to him, her hand on his chest, his curled over hers. I watch their joined hands rise and fall with his deep breaths, both finding the comfort they need in the presence of each other. A truly beautiful sight.

Bringing my arms above my head, I stretch silently then look back to Grady.

My whispering voice is still laced with sleep when I inquire, "What time is it?"

"Around eight in the morning." He lifts his hand, stroking my cheek lightly with his knuckles. "Wanted to wake you, in case you needed to get to work. Plus, that chair can't be too comfortable."

"It's not," I concur, then stretch my neck from side to side. My brain clicks on, recalling Grady's reasoning for waking me up. I narrow my eyes, but my mouth contradicts my glare as it quirks upward at the corners. "You know I never schedule appointments before eleven."

Grady releases a breath of laughter. "I do. I also know I missed your mouth."

"Ew, Grady, no." My nose crinkles and I shake my head. "I need to brush my teeth first."

"You have a toothbrush here I don't know about?"

"No," I admit with a huff.

Grady gives a slight shrug of his shoulders. "Damn, that's too bad."

He grins, then rises off his haunches, extending a helpful hand in my direction. As soon as my palm hits his, I'm hauled out of the chair and into his arms. His muscled chest brushes against mine as he angles his head, lightly touching his mouth to mine.

I grin against his lips, feeling his voice vibrate in his chest as he states, "I guess that'll have to do, for now."

He winks, then releases me before relaying, "I have to run to the station, but I won't be long. Meet me at the apartment. I'll cook breakfast."

My eyes widen with pure elation, and I grin back at him. My smile falls when he adds, "Then we can talk, finally."

I force the corners of my mouth to rise and nod as though this is the best idea ever. Anxiety roots itself in my gut, but I maintain my façade by leaning into him and placing my lips against the scruff on his cheek. "Meet ya there."

He considers my words, but I say nothing else. I just toss him an adorable smile—a measly attempt to distract him—then turn on my heel, whisking my purse off the table. I look back over my shoulder to where Spencer and Dalton lie, and joy fills my heart that they will indeed be given their happily-ever-after. My mouth curves into a relieved grin before I turn toward the door and make my exit before Grady can say anything else.

Weeks ago, I promised Grady I would share my secrets, but we've yet to make time to discuss them. It's not entirely my fault though. I just didn't bring it up.

Our time together lately has been extremely sporadic, with Grady often popping in and out when he can. I didn't want the precious moments we *could* spend together to be anything other than that. I didn't want to taint them with my past, or relive parts of my life filled with sickening memories. I wanted that time to be purely about us.

In light of recent events, I'm sure the heightened activity of his schedule was due to increased interest in Silas and his whereabouts. But seeing as Silas is now dead, I'm pretty sure Grady's schedule is wide open, for a while at least.

And now he's ready to talk.

Me? Not so much.

Just thinking about it makes me want to hurl as I exit the hospital.

Cool morning air hits my face, the sensation a welcome relief. I inhale deeply, willing the breath to calm my racing heart.

I can do this.

I need to do this.

I want to do this.

Silent variations of the mantra repeat as I make my way to my car. Just as I reach for the handle of my door, my cell rings. I dig into the bag and blindly attempt to locate it. Once it's in my grasp, I pull it out and glance at the screen.

My mother?

Trying to remember the last time she called me, I draw a blank. It's been months.

Leisurely, I drag my finger across the screen then bring the phone to my ear. "Mother."

"Cassie?"

My eyes roll into the back of my head, my tolerance for her already waning with one word spoken. "Uh, yeah? Who else would it be?"

She releases a long, exasperated breath, a clear demonstration that her patience is as thin as mine. Sounds of rustling followed by muffled voices fill my ear, and I clear my throat loudly, irritation probably kicking up my blood pressure.

"I'm on with her now," I hear before she finally returns her attention to me. "Cassie, I need to talk to you."

I snort into the phone. "I gathered as much, seeing as you called me."

"Can you please cool it with the attitude for one second?"

"One," I fire back, laughter building in my chest.

A grin breaks free as I grab my keys, and open my door.

"Damn it, Cassie. This is serious. I need to tell you something. It's about . . ." She stalls, then blurts, "Uncle Alan."

With the mention of a name that has so long remained unspoken, my heart explodes beneath my chest and my fingers splay with the impact. My keys fall to the pavement below me, their clatter barely audible over the thrumming between my ears. Everything around me slows. My entire body begins to tremble and my knees threaten to buckle. With the phone somehow still glued to my ear,

I lift my eyes, watching an ambulance pass the emergency room entrance from which I just left. The sirens probably wail, but I don't hear them. There is only the sound of pure terror as it overwhelms my entire system.

My mother's voice is a mere murmur in my ear as my stare locks on the lights on top of the van. They circle, going round and round and round, their reflection dancing off the white of the vehicle.

I try to speak, but there is no voice.

I try to breathe, but there is no air.

There is nothing.

Just those fucking lights.

Fear worms its way through my body as they continue to endlessly revolve, and I finally lose my grip on the phone, barely registering when it falls to the ground. I try to break my stare, but I'm unable.

You're not strong enough, child.

We will never let you go.

I'm too weak.

The lights reel me in, refusing to let go, clearing my barriers with each turn so the suppressed recollections of my childhood can take root. My memories are furious, clawing as they etch themselves prominently in my mind again, my refusal to acknowledge their existence driving their anger. No longer will they remain unseen.

I try to fight them, but I can't.

I'm just so weak.

So eventually, I just give up.

Tears fill my eyes as I succumb and allow them to pull me straight into their darkness. They easily overpower me, upheaving any semblance of strength I thought I could ever possess.

Be a good little girl.

Don't make a sound.

That's my beautiful Cassandra.

Their snickers echo as they delightedly take hold, drawing me downward and releasing me only when they've delivered me into nothingness.

Except I'm not alone.

I'm *never* alone.

Because *he's* always there.

Chapter 23 ✳

Fairies

Past—Eight Years Old

My sheets are warm and clean, fresh from the dryer. I turn my head and breathe deeply, smiling into my pillow because I love the smell when Mommy washes them. I feel loved. I feel happy.

My long brown hair falls into my eyes when I rest my cheek on my pillow, and I giggle because it tickles. I quietly watch the lights from the box turning on my nightstand move slowly across my white wall. I imagine them as little fairies sent here to protect me while I sleep. Sometimes I have bad dreams about the monsters from Sesame Street, and Mommy says my fairies are there to protect me when I feel scared. I love my fairies. My mouth curves into another happy smile, and as I watch my fairies dance all around me, my eyelids slowly begin to shut.

Sometime during the night, I hear my door opening.

Did Mommy want to give me another kiss goodnight?

I love her kisses.

I open my eyes, but the box on my table is no longer spinning, and my fairies are no longer dancing. I squint when a tiny bit of light enters my room, then disappears just as quickly. I can see nothing but darkness as I listen to the sound of footsteps crossing my room.

"Mommy?" I ask. My voice sounds rough as I rub my eyes and start to sit up.

A hand softly touches my shoulder before it presses me back down. My eyebrows dip down, confused when fingertips brush lightly down my cheek, then across my lips. I open my mouth to ask again but stop when I hear him whisper, "Shh, Cassandra."

Uncle Alan.

I love my Uncle Alan. He makes me laugh when he makes the girly voices for my stuffed animals.

Uncle Alan doesn't say anything. He kisses my forehead, then slowly tugs down my sheets, leaving my legs cold because my nightgown isn't long enough to cover them. I begin to pull them back up, but he takes hold of both my wrists with his much bigger hand. His other one is clammy, shaking as it touches the skin of my neck. It lowers to my chest then runs down my stomach. I keep hoping he'll stop there, but he keeps going. His fingers touch me lightly through my nightgown, tracing over my panties. I bite my lip, trying not to scream, and begin to cry softly to myself. Then suddenly, I turn cold and begin to shake when he lifts my gown.

I'm so scared.

What do I do?

What am I supposed to do?

The tips of his fingers feel like ice on the inside of my leg. I open my mouth to speak, but Uncle Alan leans in closer, whispering, "Shh, Cassandra. It's our little secret. You trust me, don't you?"

I think so?

I don't know.

I know I don't like this.

I feel scared.

But I do as I'm told. I say nothing.

I say nothing as warm tears fall down my cheek.

I say nothing as I look helplessly to the walls for my dancing fairies and their protection.

I say nothing when he tells me he's sorry and that he loves me, then asks me not to cry.

And I say nothing when he's finally through and leaves me alone in the darkness.

I keep our secret. I have no choice because he tells me good little girls do what they're told, and if I tell our secret, that means I'm bad. And if I'm bad, Mommy and Daddy won't love me anymore.

He tells me the same thing the next time.

And the next time.

And the next.

And each time, I'm a good girl . . .

Because I never say a word.

Chapter 24 ✳

Numb

Honestly, I don't remember much of what happened after my mother's call. I don't remember grabbing my keys or my phone off the ground. I don't remember climbing into my Jeep and driving away. I don't even remember in which direction I traveled, how long I drove, or how I actually ended up at *my* apartment, bypassing Grady's completely.

I do, however, remember what my mother said just before I dropped the phone.

Uncle Alan is dead.

Found dead from a drug overdose, his body has been brought back to Fuller to be buried with the remainder of his deceased family, and the funeral is tomorrow. I've been ordered home to attend and instructed to be on my best behavior as I am to greet various family members who have come to offer their condolences.

I inhale at length. I guess I should feel some sort of relief with the news of his death, the ability for him to hurt me further no longer a possibility. Physically, anyway.

But the emotional pain and scarring will always be there. Just like the memory of him.

It's a sad reality, I admit. I will never be rid of him or his revolting existence. Disgust will forever remain, hollowing me from the inside out. His presence will always loom, a blackened, overbearing figure of cold and darkness whose strength will forever surpass my own.

So no, I don't feel any respite or reprieve.

I feel nothing, because I *am* nothing.

That's right, Cassie.

You are nothing.

You were a stupid girl to think you would ever escape us.

You will never be free.

The voices are right. I will forever remain his prisoner.

From the first night he entered my bedroom, Uncle Alan stole everything. He took my innocence, suffocated my spirit, and drained me of every ounce of strength that had once so vigorously flowed through my veins. I was no longer the same Cassie after Uncle Alan's brief stay. I was forever changed, weak and pitiful, drifting through life with absolutely no direction or goal other than numbing the constant pain.

It's who I am. What I do.

I was a fool to believe otherwise.

I was stupid.

A naïve creature to allow Grady Bennett anywhere near me, with his promises of love and happily-ever-afters. His ridiculous belief that I ever possessed any strength or resolve. His false sparks of hope and courage, since replaced with the coldness accompanying my surrender.

Because once Grady Bennett placed me on that extremely high, undeserving pedestal, it was inevitable I would eventually face my reality and be thrown off. *To fall.* I know now it was completely unavoidable that he would break his promise, and not in the way I thought.

Because now I'm falling.

Really falling.

And when I land, all I have done to protect myself, every single one of my walls and barriers that I foolishly gave up to be with him, will be long gone.

I will shatter.

And it is exactly what I deserve.

My phone rings. *Grady.*

I don't answer. I can't bring myself to. I'm too exhausted to pretend, and honestly, I can't have anything to do with him anymore.

How could I?

His voice, his eyes, his smile—all serve as reminders of what will never be.

I can no longer live in a fabricated, fairy tale world, where love blossoms and hope heals. Those things don't exist in my realm. In my reality.

I decline the call, then my fingers fire off a responding text, letting him know that I had a family emergency. And when he asks if I need him, I tell him no, then advise I'll be out of contact for a while.

With that done, I also text Spencer, apologizing for my departure and letting her know I'll call her in a couple days. Her worry is evident with her response, but as with Grady, I decline the invitation for help, telling her to focus on Dalton and repeating that I will call her soon.

Will I?

Spencer is finally living her happily-ever-after. Our paths are going in different directions.

She doesn't need my darkness.

I stare at my phone when I'm done, sadness clawing my throat. Because I always knew the fork in our road would come, and although it has, in a way, and she has started traveling down her own path, I had no idea I would be the one to forever sever the conduit between the two.

Tears begin to form but I quickly toss my phone onto my bed, cementing my decision. Turning away, I approach my closet and grab an overnight bag. After stuffing some clothes into it, I peruse my wardrobe, picking out the perfect outfit to attend the funeral. I throw in a pair of heels, then head to the bathroom to grab my necessities. Once I'm packed, I grab the bag and turn to give a long glance at my room. I don't know why really. It feels as though I'm saying good-bye, but how can I be, because I was never really here.

A cold, foreboding sensation washes over me as I flick off the light, then exit my apartment. With my mind detached, I head to my car, fling the bag inside, and wearily slide into the driver's seat, suddenly so tired. Defeated. Numb.

On my way, I make a quick call to have my appointments rescheduled for the next few days, briefly explaining there was a death in the family before assuring them I would be back next week. The rest of the drive to my parents' house is a blur and my arrival on their doorstep awkward as usual.

"Cassie." My mother's tone is stern. Her hair, the same shade of brown as mine, is perfectly coiffed on top of her head, and her style is much the same as I remember. Conservative trouser slacks with a perfectly pressed light-blue poplin tucked in at the waist. Her blue eyes narrow on my appearance, still dressed in what I wore to the hospital.

I lift my brows, challenging her to say something. When she says nothing, I mutter my hello, my tone just as unforgiving as hers. "Mother."

My father trudges behind her, placing his hands on her shoulders. His face has aged since I've last seen him. His brown eyes are no longer warm, but tired as he offers me a small smile. "Your room is as we left it."

I snicker. "Right. And fully armed, I assume."

Both bodies stiffen at the mention of the alarm, but they say nothing. I brush past them without another word, heading down the hall until I find my room. My fingers graze the knob, sudden unease and anxiety overwhelming me. Twenty-three years old, and I'm still scared to death to sleep in this room.

Whirling on my heel, I dash into the living room and rummage through my father's liquor cabinet. I spy a bottle of scotch, Uncle Alan's favorite. The smell of it filled my room the nights he would visit me. To this day, I cannot smell its stench without feeling as though I'm going to vomit. Just thinking about it makes me ill. My gag reflex kicks in, and my eyes water in response. I blink rapidly, clearing the tears before I find what I'm looking for. An unopened bottle of Patrón hidden in the back, screaming my name.

I clear a path, then whisk it out of the cabinet, feeling my parents' disapproving eyes follow me as I make my exit. Now equipped with my weapon of choice, I fling open my door and enter my room, fear controlled.

My bag hits the floor and I grip the bottle with both hands, unsealing it and popping the rounded cork free from its neck. Lifting it to my mouth, I take a long draw and attempt to avoid the urge to throw it back up.

I force the contents into my stomach and close my eyes, allowing the soothing burn to work its way into my system. With the bottle still gripped tightly in my hand, I toss the cork into the trashcan on my way to closing my door as I seal myself inside my own tomb.

Landing on my bed, I reach for the remote and turn on my TV for distraction. I don't really pay attention to what's on, but the noise is nice. It lulls me with each draw I take from the bottle. On my third drink, my phone rings and I decline Grady's call. Then take a shot.

Another half hour, it rings again. Decline and shot.

Again after another hour. Decline and shot.

I can no longer feel my face when it rings again. I giggle and hiccup, very much enthralled with my new game, then down another one.

It rings again, and I laugh. And I keep laughing.

I laugh.

And laugh.

And laugh.

I laugh until tears stream down my face. But they're no longer tears from the onslaught of drunken laughter, they're tears coming from within my anguished soul. It weeps uncontrollably, sobbing so violently, its wails tear wildly through my mind. Crying out for the little girl held hostage, demanding her freedom. Screaming helplessly, frantically, as it searches for a way to release her from the restraints that bind her here. Raging against the chains when he approaches, his dampened skin brushing along hers as he tightens her shackles, refusing to let her go. Yowling in defeat as he walks away, leaving her alone in this darkened room that is my mind.

I'm alone.

Alone.

Alone.

Alone.

Hours later, just as I lay my head on my pillow while my world continues to spin with my fall, my phone rings again.

Grady.

I feel absolutely nothing as I reach for it.

I simply turn it off.

Chapter 25

Cold

"You're drunk." My mother leans against the wall of my bathroom, crossing her arms over her chest, her eyes scrutinizing my every move in the mirror. As always, she's impeccably dressed. A black pencil skirt hits her knees, and the matching blazer is buttoned at her waist, laced with the collar of a dark-gray button-up as it peeks out from the top.

"And you're perceptive," I fire back, sarcasm weaved masterfully through my tone.

I woke up inebriated, and I sure as hell plan on staying that way through this ordeal. I press one of my palms flat on the counter, using it for balance while trying to line my eyes with the other hand. Once through, I step away, assessing my appearance.

Not bad. All things considered, I guess.

My long brown hair is wound into a tight bun at the base of my neck, because there is no way I trust myself with a curling iron right now. The whites of my eyes are no longer white, but reddened by the expanse of the vessels lining them, and with the exception of the alcohol-infused blood lining the tops of my cheeks, my skin is pallid and grossly pale. My hands tremble as I smooth the front of my red dress—tight and short—against the upper part of my thighs. Five-inch, straight-up hooker heels complete the look.

My mother shifts her stance, bringing my attention back to her. She holds my gaze, then breaks away to rake over my dress. "What you're wearing is completely inappropriate, Cassie."

I laugh, my words slurred. "Appropriateness is a matter of opinion, *Mother*. And I happen to find this dress extremely appropriate to attend Uncle Alan's funeral. I mean," more self-induced laughter, "no one knew him like I did, and trust me when I say, I know without a doubt, he would have *loved this dress*."

My eyes bore into hers, and I watch as she swallows deeply, her voice affected as she states, "We leave in thirty."

"My own designated drivers. Everyone should be so lucky."

I throw her a condescending smile, which she rebounds with a familiar glare, then finally turns to leave.

Leaning down, I grab the near-empty bottle of Patrón I stashed in the cabinet below and take a swig. Its warmth pricks my throat, and I revel in the feeling before placing it safely behind the doors.

As soon as I hit the living room, tension and unspoken irritation radiates from both my parents. Lucky for me, I don't feel either as I breeze through to the kitchen.

Just as I'm finishing a reheated slice of pizza, my father announces, "It's time. Let's go."

We pile into their car, my mother rambling incessantly about something I couldn't care less about and my father replying with his typical courteous nods and gestures. I tune them out as usual, focusing on the blur of terrain as it passes by on the way to the church.

As soon as we arrive and park, anxiety rears its ugly head through my drunken haze. From behind the safety of the window, my eyes stubbornly lock on to the front door of the church. I vaguely recognize some family members, a herd of black as I watch them enter. My teeth find my bottom lip, nibbling nervously, and I force myself to take in a breath before reaching for the handle.

My parents don't even bother to wait for me. Without a word, they link arms and stride into the church, leaving me alone to face the devil himself. I shouldn't be surprised really. But yet, somewhere, I'm sure a part of me hurts with the ease of their dismissal.

For years, I longed for them to know. To care. To listen.

To fucking pay attention.

Instead, they dismissed.

Ignored.

Turned away.

As I pull the handle to the door, it registers from the quick flashing lights that my dad didn't neglect to lock his car though.

Neglect me? Yes.

His car? No.

Fucking typical.

My steadiness teeters on the heels of my shoes as I exit, the trembling of my legs not really helping with my balance. A long breath passes in and out of my lungs, and I close my eyes, my lips quivering as I arch my neck toward the sky. Warm tears leak into the sides of my hair, and I continue my deep breathing, trying to garner the courage necessary to take the first step. After another couple of breaths, my burning eyes open, and I lift my hands to clear the moisture from my temples before lowering my stare. Shakily, I force my legs to obey, finally taking the first of many difficult strides until finally reaching the front of the church.

The wooden doors are closed and I extend my arms, pressing my palms against their grain and leaning forward. All my weight shifts onto their sturdiness, and my trembling muscles breathe a sigh of relief with the reprieve. After a couple minutes alone, escalating voices from behind alert me to another influx of people. Saddened, I lean away from the temporary quiet provided by the wood and hook my fingers around the metal handle of the door. I pull it open.

It takes a couple seconds for my eyes to adjust. As I begin to make my way down the center aisle, harsh whispers filter in and out of my ears, my choice of apparel most likely the main topic of discussion. I don't bother to meet their eyes. My stare remains bound to the black casket on display at the front of the sanctuary. Fear spikes my blood, sending a wave of anxiety through my body as I continue the long trek. My parents are seated in the second pew, and with my eyes remaining on the casket, I continue my strides until I land myself right next to them. They shift over, making room for me to sit. *Reluctantly.*

As soon as my ass hits the pew, I open the stylish clutch brought not for its appearance, but for its concealment. The silver flask is cold against the pads of my fingers as they take hold and extract the container, bringing it into the view of my parents.

"Cassie!" my mother snarls.

My shoulders lift into an indifferent shrug, then I unscrew the top and tilt it upward, the clear liquid hitting my throat as I swallow. Just as I lower the flask, my eyes land on the minister, taking his place behind the pulpit as people begin to find their seats. His warning stare lands on me and he offers a slight shake of his head.

An audible snort passes through my nose, and I lift the flask for an even longer draw before finally screwing the top back on and sliding it back into my clutch. Once it has disappeared, the minister clears his throat and begins the service.

The tequila works its magic, numbing me further as his voice carries through the sanctuary, endlessly droning on and on and on about Alan Cooper and all of his endearing qualities. Unable to hide my disgust, I offer my own commentary as he speaks, earning me several annoyed glares from the people surrounding me, including my parents.

"Alan Cooper was a man of great character."

"Riiiiight."

"He will always be remembered."

"No matter how hard we try to forget."

"Always a wanderer, Alan has finally found his place with the Lord."

"Or Satan. But hey, at least he finally found his place."

By the time the service is over, my flask is empty and I'm wiping tears of repressed laughter from my eyes. I'm so beyond caring what anyone thinks at this point.

Fuck them.

And fuck *him*.

Our entire row stands, and I'm last in line as we shuffle our way into the aisle for Uncle Alan's final viewing. All humor is lost when I finally step out from behind the safety of the pew. I stand painfully patient, watching the line of people in front of me slowly decreasing in length. My entire body begins to shake uncontrollably as I get closer to him with each person concluding their good-bye.

When only my mother remains, her body the only barrier between the casket and me, my heart is thudding so hard, it threatens to rip apart my ribcage with each beat. I clench my hands into fists, my nails digging into my skin, as I try to control their trembling. My throat swells when my mother disappears, and my steps are wobbly with my slow approach to the side of the casket.

I focus on the shiny black surface, promising myself I won't look. But my traitorous eyes have a mind of their own. They disobey my orders, breaking from the slick surface and sliding over the top. I try to draw them away, but they're on a mission and force their way to his prone body, dressed in a black suit, his hands resting at his sides.

Clammy hands.

My mouth pinches with disgust as I fight the urge to wipe their touch from my skin. I swallow back the bile rising in my throat with the vivid recollection. My throat burns, and I tell myself that the burning is what brings tears to my eyes as they continue onward. Once they land on his face, my memories, in all their horror, assault me, relentless as they strike my mind over and over again.

His dark hair flopping over his eyes as he leans over me.

His eyes half-lidded, heavy with desire.

His mouth parted, releasing erratic, heavy breaths.

A cold torrent of absolute terror floods me. Fear my mind somehow managed to temporarily disallow roars to life and seizes my body. I gasp out loud, unable to control my reaction. Both trembling hands fly upward to cover my mouth. The clutch looped safely around my wrist bounces off my chest as I stare, my eyes glued to his face. Tears run in a continuous stream down my cheeks, their suppression impossible. My feet are cemented to the floor as I stare, completely comatose with the insistent memories looping over and over, bringing fresh waves of anguish with each repetition.

My sobs stifled as I tried to remain quiet.

His cold, clammy hands all over me. Touching me.

The sated smile when he was through.

And the isolation that swallowed me every single time he left my room.

I have no idea how long I remain. It's not until the person behind me clears their throat that my trance is broken and I'm finally able to tear my eyes away from Uncle Alan. Driving them to the carpeted floor beneath my feet, I step away and dazedly make my way back to the pew.

No matter how hard I try, I cannot contain my tears.

Cold emptiness fills me while blackness hollows my mind.

To others it may look as though I'm merely mourning the loss of a loved one.

And maybe that's the case.

Because as my mind goes blank, worn to the point of complete exhaustion as it shuts down, I find myself so lost, I wouldn't even begin to know where to look to find myself.

Not that I will be looking.

I'm no longer afraid to be trapped here.

Because here—in the darkness—I don't have to pretend.

There is no pain, no fear.

There is only comfort.

So here I plan to stay, as long as it will house me.

Even if it's for all eternity.

Chapter 26

Open Wounds

I somehow manage to stay awake through the influx of family that gathers at our house after we lay Uncle Alan to rest. I ignore the openly aghast stares and accusatory glares, as though I should be of sound mind and body to help my father through this difficult time.

Right.

So I continue my binge, content in my numbness, thankful for the blur of vaguely familiar faces. My father's liquor cabinet is pretty decimated by dinnertime, the only traces of alcohol remaining a bottle of scotch and a liter of vodka, which I totally would have downed as well, could I stomach either.

The thing about being completely wasted for hours on end is that sleep is inevitable. I fight it as long as I can but it eventually overpowers me.

I trudge to my room with weighty legs and even heavier lids, my cumbersome body uncooperative as I attempt to guide myself to bed. As soon as I hit the side, exhaustion claims me. My strength wanes, my body succumbs, and my eyes seal shut before my head even hits the pillow.

What's also inevitable is the fact that I have no control over my dreams. I can successfully numb the pain and tame the fear while awake, but in sleep, it's open season for my nightmares.

One after another they find me: the image of Uncle Alan's face, the feel of his trembling hands on my body, the sound of my stifled sobs as they echo around my darkened room. My eyes remain sealed shut, locking me inside my terror-filled dreams with no available escape. For hours, his menacing whispers invade my mind. Only when the feel of his touch along my skin becomes painfully distinctive am I able to break free. As it travels along my inner thigh, I cry out, startling myself awake.

And as I enter my realm of consciousness, I am no longer a twenty-three-year-old woman, but a terrified eight-year-old little girl. My hands are curled into my sheets, fisting them tightly as they tremble uncontrollably, and the familiar scent of fresh urine assaults my nostrils.

"God," I sob into the air. "Why? Why me?"

My throat is constricted with such agony; I can barely breathe. Sorrow and shame blanket me as I continue trying to catch my breath between cries. I begin to quake underneath the sheets cooling rapidly against my skin. I throw off my comforter and another sob wracks my entire body when the stench wafts through the air.

Quietly, I set my feet on the ground then scurry to the dresser, my fingers working frantically as they search for dry clothing. I pull out a pair of recently unpacked shorts and a shirt, peel the drenched dress from my body, and tug on its replacements before turning and yanking the sheets off my bed.

Gathering them against my chest, tears leak from my eyes as I exit my room, crossing the now soundless house as quietly and quickly as I can. In the dark, my fingers find the knob to the door leading to the basement, and I inhale my courage before opening it and stepping onto the first step.

One.

Two.

Three.

I count each one silently to fill my mind, and once at the bottom, I race to the washer and throw the sheets in with a cup of detergent. Lowering the lid, I turn, repeating the counting sequence with each upward step, then make a mad dash to the bathroom. Stripping the shorts and shirt from my body, I step out of them and place a clean towel on the side of the bathtub's cold porcelain before taking a seat. I lean, turning the water on and running my fingers underneath the stream until it's warm.

As soon as it hits the right level, I turn it off and step in, sliding my legs just under the surface of the water. Reaching for the bar of soap, I scrub furiously. My nails scrape the skin of my stomach, my chest, my arms, my thighs—everywhere the disgust of his touch remains—shame-filled tears running along my cheeks the entire time.

I hate this.

I hate him.

I hate this.

Hate.

Hate.

Hate.

The water cools quickly and goose bumps line my reddened skin when I finally stand. Grabbing the towel, I wrap it carefully around my sensitive body before opening the door. Making my escape into the hallway, the balls of my feet are quiet as I pad back to my room.

The window catches my eye and I tiptoe over, seeking the solace of Spencer's light across the street. Only then does my mind snap back to the present.

Darkness.

No light.

Of course she's not there.

I'm alone.

In the darkness.

She's on her new path now.

Content and happy.

In the light.

And I'm alone.

Achingly alone.

In the darkness.

I shake my head, exhausted and defeated.

The dulling sensation of alcohol in my blood has long since been absorbed during my sleep. With no barrier to protect me, pain and humiliation have been allowed free rein, of which they take full advantage with their continuous slaps to my face.

I'm twenty-three years old and I just fucking pissed my own bed.

Mortification squeezes my chest as I dress myself. I glance over my shoulder in the direction of the living room, anger rising as it overshadows embarrassment.

Fuck.

You.

No longer caring to hide being awake, I stomp my bare feet out of my bedroom and follow the trail to my father's cabinet. Flinging the door open, I grab the bottle of scotch, fisting it so tightly I'm surprised the glass doesn't fracture in my hand.

Snaking my keys off the kitchen table, I head to the front door and throw it open.

Ten minutes later, in a pair of sleeping shorts, a thin cami, and no shoes covering my feet, I navigate my way through the cemetery. The sun is rising just above the horizon, providing me the light I need to find my destination.

I find his headstone in a matter of minutes, the freshly dug soil darkened as it lines his grave. I glance down at the bottle still clenched in my hand, grinding my teeth before I unscrew the top and tip it upward, the smell alone causing my mouth to clamp shut and my face to pinch tightly. As soon as it hits my throat, my body rejects it, vomiting it onto the ground. It leeches into the soil, as though trying to find its way to the body underneath where it belongs.

"There you go, you sick motherfucker!" I scream at the ground. "You like that?"

I raise the bottle again and try to force the liquid down my throat, attempting to punish myself for what I've become. This pitiful creature who allows the fear of a dead man to rule her life. But again, it's immediately spewed and seeps into the ground. I shake my head and relent, pouring some more onto the grave while focusing my attention instead on the corpse within it.

"I fucking hate you," I cry through clenched teeth. My tortured throat closes, but I force my voice through its constriction. "Why?" A cry breaks free. "Why me, Uncle Alan? What did I do to deserve what you did to me? I was such a happy little girl. A strong and fierce child, who knew nothing about the horrors that existed in the world. I was innocent and naïve. I was brave. I was . . . *happy* . . ."

The word steals my breath.

I was happy. I loved my parents. I loved life. The world was mine to be had. I could have been anything I wanted to be. Anything I wanted to do, I knew I could have done it.

"But you stole my happiness." Another sob. "You stole it and I want it back!"

I drop the bottle and fall to the ground, exhausted. "I'm so tired of hating myself for what you did to me. I'm so tired of feeling empty inside. I'm so tired of being ashamed. I'm so tired. So *tired*, Uncle Alan. Why can't you just leave me alone? Please . . ."

I rise to my knees and fold my hands, crying, pleading. "Please just leave me alone. I paid the price for your sins. I lived with the consequences of your actions. I kept your secrets. I was a good girl."

I press my trembling lips to my knitted fingers, tears overflowing as I mutter, "Please, please, please . . . just leave me alone and let me have my happiness."

I don't know what I expect to happen. I don't know if I expect the tremendous weight of the burden carried to be lifted in this pleading moment, or if I expect the clouds to miraculously part and allow a ray of sun to shine down, filling my empty soul with peace and comfort, or if I expect happiness to suddenly rain down upon me, soothing the open wounds exposed by this conversation. But *none* of that happens.

There is no ray of sunshine. *I'll forever be in darkness.*

There is no peace and comfort. *I'll forever be empty.*

There is no happiness. *I'll forever know sadness.*

In the end, there is just silence.

Just as I was silent for him, his *silence seals my fate among the shadows.*

Reaching to the side, I grip the bottle and throw it as hard as I can against the granite headstone. The bottle explodes upon impact, the amber liquid coating the surface as it trails to where it belongs. *With him. Fucking with him.*

"I hope you rot in hell."

I wipe my swollen eyes and rise to my feet, frigid and deadened from the cold dew lining the grass. The sensation rises and spreads through my body.

I feel absolutely nothing as I turn and walk away.

Just empty.

Always empty.

Chapter 27 ✴

Lies

I don't bother going back to my parents' house after that.

I continue right on past, driving for a long while before finally arriving at my apartment. I'm chilled to the bone as I trudge to the front door. My shorts are still damp from sitting on the ground and my toes still reddened as they continue to thaw.

The apartment is as I left it: a blanket haphazardly thrown over the back of the couch and my cereal bowl still on the kitchen counter. Both of which tell me Spencer has not been home since my departure, or if she has, she didn't stay long.

I trek sluggishly across the living room, nudging my bedroom door open with the tips of my fingers. As it swings open, my eyes land on a pair of navy-blue irises staring right back at me.

I don't even experience a jolt of surprise seeing Grady sitting on my bed, waiting patiently with his elbows on his knees, hands interlaced and dangling toward the floor. Not a shred of remorse passes through my heart at the sight of his tightened expression, brows furrowed and channels of worry etched into his forehead.

I feel absolutely nothing.

I'm just . . . empty. Void of emotion. Deflated and exhausted.

"Where have you been?" Grady's tone is clipped, his voice firm.

I disengage from his confronting stare and enter the room fully with no answer. I head to the dresser, pulling out a pair of yoga pants, a pullover, and a pair of socks. The sight of his sister's borrowed clothes catches my eye, washed and folded for their safekeeping. I grab them and set them on top of the wooden surface, my fingers gently brushing along the fabrics in apology for ever wearing them.

My back remains to Grady, and when I refuse to meet the scrutiny of his stare or answer his question, he clears his throat, demanding to be heard. I turn, my gaze rising from the floor to narrow on his face, but still say nothing. His demeanor changes with my continued silence. His features harden and the anger in his voice surpasses his attempt to restrain it. "Family emergency, was it?"

When I shrug my answer, his fury spikes. "Emergency enough you couldn't be bothered to answer my calls, or to provide something as simple as common fucking courtesy by letting me know you were okay?"

I hold his stare, finally relenting when I respond, "I was at my parents' house."

His eyes rake over me, then he inquires, "No bag?"

"It was a quick visit." My tone is hollow.

"Two days is not a quick visit, Cassie. Your bag?" he repeats, his patience steadily declining.

"Left everything." My shoulders lift again. "Just needed to come home."

Grady angles his head, brows lifted. "Want to talk about it?"

"No. I don't. I want you to leave because I'm too fucking exhausted to discuss anything right now."

His head bobs up and down and his mouth curves toward the floor, considering my answer before he goes dangerously still, his eyes piercing right through me. He holds my stare as he rises off my bed and with deliberate, calculated steps, makes his way to where I stand. "You were never there with me, were ya, Cass?" Absolutely no humor is in his expression when he laughs and shakes his head. "You lied. Plain and simple."

It's my turn to laugh. My returning stare tightens on the condescending grin still present on his face. "Yeah," I admit. "Well, you lied too."

Grady's smile disappears as his neck jerks backward. "What? I never lied to you."

I swallow the rapidly escalating emotion. "You promised to *never* let me fall, Grady." My hand forms into a fist and I pound it once against my chest. "Well, I'm fucking falling. I'm falling so fast, so out of control, I don't even know which way is right side up anymore."

I lean into him and whisper, my anger finally provoked and rising to the surface. "I tried to be there with you, Grady, but the place where you reside is unattainable for someone like me. I foolishly tried to reach you though. I climbed and climbed and climbed, only to become too high, too unsteady, when I allowed myself to believe what you saw in me. I lost my balance because I trusted you. I believed you, I reached for you, and *you let me fall.*"

His eyes grow wild, blazing back at me as he slams his open palm against my dresser. "Because you're giving me no choice! No other option! You've completely shut me out and now, you're so fucking holed up in that head of yours, there's no way I can reach you. You're too far gone."

His heavy breaths are all I hear as he tries to gather his composure. He breaks his stare, forcing it to the carpet and inhales deeply. Once his breathing has returned to normal, he looks back at me, the *pain* in his expression . . . "I love you, Cass. I do. But I can't love you enough for the both of us. I don't understand why you feel as though being *there with me* is so impossible for you. For the life of me, I will never be able to comprehend how or why you devalue yourself so much."

I try to look away, but he lifts his hand to my face, gently pinching my chin and forcing my attention to remain solely on him. "And it kills me to have to say this, but you're right. You're *forcing* me to break that promise, because now I have to let you keep falling, sweetheart. It's the only way for you to learn how to right yourself."

His throat works a deep swallow. "But so help me, I do intend on keeping another very important promise I made. I *will* guide you to safety. Help you land. Because, Cass, you may be falling, but remember, it's the landing that counts. And when you land, I need you to land strong. Safe. This is me ensuring that promise is kept."

With his other hand, he reaches into his back pocket and pulls out a business card. He flashes it in front of my face, and I jerk my chin out of his hold before taking it from him.

I read the inscription and scoff. "A fucking shrink?"

"A *friend,*" he counters. Then he adds, "You won't let me in, you don't want to talk to me, fine. But when you reach that point, when you've had enough, you call her. She will help you land safe when you're tired of the free fall. And more importantly, she will help get you where *you* need to be. Whether or not that's with me doesn't matter now."

His words pierce the numbness, and just when I thought I couldn't hurt any more, my heart is sliced wide open. I choke back the tears and clench his sister's clothes in my hand, forcing them into his chest. Venom erupts from within me, the taste so bitter, it turns my stomach as soon it's spit from my mouth.

"I'm broken, Grady. I tried to explain this to you. There's no reason, I just *am*. So if you're looking for a cause, or some sort of vindication to right the wrongs that occur in this life, look somewhere else. I'm *not* your sister, I'm *not* your purpose, and I sure as hell don't need your help."

Tears fill my eyes and my chin quivers. His expression is impassive. He simply shakes his head, disappointment tinged in his low register when he finally speaks. "That one just might have been a lethal strike, sweetheart."

Up until now, Grady hasn't ever raised his voice in anger toward me. In fact, quite the opposite. He has been exceedingly patient with me.

That one just might have been a lethal strike.

Can't blame him though. I don't have the energy to care right now anyway.

With his sister's garments cradled against his chest, he turns away from me and leaves my room, closing the door quietly behind him. Tears find their release, seeping out the corners of my eyes. My arms wrap around my midsection, searching for some source of warmth. To try to find some sort of comfort as I watch the only man I've ever truly loved walk right out of my life.

I breathe in a deep breath, trying to convince myself that it's for the best.

I'm poison.

I have nothing to offer him, not anymore.

Not that I ever did, really.

He simply deserves, whereas I do not.

I keep repeating the words, encouraging them to solidify in an effort to stop the bleeding of my shattered heart. But no matter how many times I say them, it doesn't work.

The pain is still very much present when I crawl into bed an hour later. I pull my comforter over my head, and only then do I release my desolation. Tears drench the sheets and my muffled wails are securely released into the pillows. I scream until I have no voice left. I cry until there are no tears remaining. And only then, worn to the point of complete exhaustion, do I find sleep.

When I wake and am staring at my blinds, I wish the sun could encompass me and give me some sort of warmth. It's so cold here.

You don't deserve warmth, Cassie.

You're trapped here forever, with us.

Get used to the cold, little girl.

You're not going anywhere.

Eventually I roll over. My overnight bag and purse are directly in front of me, safe and secure. Did Grady extract them from my parents' house? *Why would he bother?*

Why would he bother? Because he is kind. He is so many things. Deliciously cooked breakfasts. *Thoughtful.* Warm arms wrapped around me when I felt sad or had an awful client. *Kind.* Sharing his memories of his sister with me. *Funny.* Taking me to my favorite ice cream shop just because. *Generous.* Teaching me self-defense tirelessly. *Selfless.*

Why would he bother? Because he is Grady Bennett. And now he's gone.

My mouth pinches in thought as I eye the bag with wariness.

Perched on top are two things.

One is a note written in Grady's unmistakable scrawl that reads only two words: *Land strong.*

The other item is a little more vague. It's a green, plastic paratrooper with a string looped through the holes in the shoulders, binding him to a white vinyl parachute as it hangs open from his back.

Another wave of agony pours through me at this kind gesture, especially after having spoken to him the way I did, but I don't cry. I'm officially wrung dry.

I slide out of bed and onto the floor in front of the figurine. Crossing my legs in front of me, I pinch it between my fingers, instantly recalling the feel from when I was a little girl. I had a ton of these guys.

"I shall name you Roger, roger?"

I snicker, feeling a bit absurd quoting *Airplane* movie lines and joking at a time when everything around me has gone to absolute shit.

Chalking it up to delirium, I give it a whirl and fling Roger high into the air. I watch as he glides slowly downward, eventually landing himself within the safety of my lap. I do it again, and again, and again.

Each toss is different, some much harsher than the others. I do this for what seems like hours because all of a sudden, I'm obsessed with forcing poor Roger into a crash landing.

But no matter how hard I throw him, no matter the angle or the velocity, the bastard *will not* crash. He catches air every single time, hovering down gently and landing on my floor unscathed.

It would take me months to be in the right frame of mind to accept what Grady was telling me with Roger.

But once I finally understood, I would never forget it.

Chapter 28

Free Fall

It's been six weeks since Grady walked out of my apartment. Six weeks of Roger sitting on my bedside table, judging me with his plastic, beady little eyes. Six weeks since I began my fall, and six weeks that I've continued to plummet into absolute nothingness.

I tried to escape it, in the beginning. I spent the first three weeks getting obliterated with old *friends*, trying to numb the constant ache in my chest, but the gaping hole refused to be sealed with the familiar aid of alcohol. I tried to pretend, to smile when Spencer would pop into the apartment, sharing news about Dalton's recovery, excitedly chattering about how rapidly he was healing, overjoyed and smiling from ear to ear when he finally took his first step. I tried to move on, as though I wasn't completely enveloped in darkness, but each step forward was nothing more than me blindly trying to find my way back to where I used to be.

But even the low place where I used to stand is unreachable for me now. It's too far above me, the ground on which I took those steps no longer. There is only the blackened blur of where it used to remain as I continue falling with no new ground in sight.

I thought I was broken before, but I had no idea what broken really was.

I do now.

For the past three weeks, I've done nothing but go to work, come home, cover my head with my comforter, and sleep for hours on end. I've distanced myself from Spencer, often explaining to her that I don't feel well when she pokes her head in my room. I refuse to talk when she stubbornly sits on my bed, and I cannot even seem to gather the strength necessary to provide a fake laugh when she pulls the covers off me and does something Spencer-like, slapping my ass or trying to stick her finger in my ear and/or nose.

I'm just too tired to do anything anymore.

My bones ache and my skin hurts as the reality of being truly alone and shattered sets in, pulverizing me from the inside out. It's so draining being here, endlessly drifting through the coldness of oblivion.

My thoughts wander, and memories of my early youth somehow manage to seep into my mind. Arm in arm with Spencer as we visited the zoo with Mrs. Locke, laughing so hard we cried when that stupid bird pooped in my hair. Giggling while playing tag in my front yard, with Spencer calling me out every time I cheated by changing the location of the base.

Everything was so simple then. Before Uncle Alan.

"*I was* . . . happy . . ."

The words I spoke at Uncle Alan's graveside circle my mind as I lie in bed.

Happy.

God, I *was* happy.

Grady's soothing tone enters my mind, and with it, a jolt of surprise. It seeps through me, a salve of relief from the constant ache.

"Are you going to let your fears reign over you, allow them to keep you from really living? Or are you going to dig deep, face them head on, and fight for yourself to have a better life? A happier one? The one you *deserve."*

I *do* want to be happy again.

I want to feel warmth.

I want to smile.

I want to laugh.

I want to love.

He speaks again, stronger this time. *"The choice is yours."*

It's not that simple, I argue internally.

"The choice is yours."

I shake my head. *It's not that simple*, I repeat.

I expect to hear it again, but instead, Spencer's angelic laughter fills my ears. The memory of us lying side by side in my bed just mere months ago follows close behind, her holding my hand, giving it an encouraging squeeze.

"It's a new day, Cass."

What I wouldn't give for it to be a new day.

Just as I begin to consider her words, I feel a slither of fear strike at the memory. It dissipates like a cloud of smoke, and tears crawl up my throat with the loss as it's replaced by the ever-present blur of darkness.

You are nothing.

You are disgusting.

No one wants you.

You are alone because you deserve to be.

You will never be happy.

Pain creeps back and settles into its usual places, my bones feeling brittle and weak under its weight.

I'm so tired.

I'm tired of feeling this way.

I'm tired of missing the people I love.

I'm tired of the constant, overbearing agony.

Grady's words are like a finger, tapping repeatedly on the outskirts of my mind, reminding me that it's *my* choice. I can let the darkness drag me further, or jump off and hope to hell I find something to grab on to with my exit.

My eyes narrow at the comforter shielding me from the sun, and slowly, I drag it over my face until it pools onto my chest. I inhale deeply with the gust of fresh air and blink my eyes until they finally adjust. Light rushes me, the warmth from the rays leeching through my window, blanketing me. With the sun shining into my room, it's as though my eyes have been opened for the first time in six weeks. Everything around me is vivid and bright with colors I haven't bothered to notice in a long while.

I take a peek at Roger.

"Stop looking at me like that," I mutter, then rise, my comforter falling across my waist as I stretch widely before swinging my legs off the side of the bed. Unsteadily, I make my way to the bathroom and flick on the light.

I look at my reflection and tears gather as I attempt to find my focus. I clear them away and take in another long breath, staring back at myself.

Sometimes, if you're lucky enough, there comes a point in your life when you stop cowering and somehow muster the courage to raise your head to take a good, hard look at your reflection, and in turn, at your life. A point in time when you finally rise above your manufactured walls to observe exactly where the road you've chosen has landed you. And when you see everything at once, all the missed opportunities and numerous broken relationships, the sight is enough to shatter an already broken heart.

Some people quit. They willingly accept the fate they've dealt themselves and shrink back into the nothingness from which they briefly emerged.

Others are stubborn. They choose to keep their eyes open, not just to look, but to *see*. The need to survive strengthens them as they come face to face with their own worst enemy:

Themselves.

I level my stare at the reflection in front of me. My hair is messy and tangled and my skin is pale and ashen, but what really draws my attention is the dull haze cloaking my once-spirited brown eyes. Its presence is a stark reminder of how truly lifeless I've allowed myself to become.

And for the first time in years, I acknowledge why.

In avoiding my past, I've cut off any chance I've ever had to really live.

Because the truth is, the past is an extension of one's self. It's an integral part of who you are, and if you refuse to acknowledge it, if you refuse to nurture and heal its wounds, that part will eventually dwindle to nothing and its death will spread like a frenzied virus. Before you know it, any remnants of the person you were will no longer exist. One day, you'll wake up and take a long look in the mirror, with absolutely no recognition of the person standing in front of you.

Even worse, you will loathe them.

Anger and disappointment flood me, their weight so heavy I'm forced to rest my palms on the counter for balance. My chin trembles and tears strike the laminate below me.

Without a doubt, I know this is it. My time to choose. I can slink back into the shelter of numbness and allow it to dull the absolute agony ripping through my chest, *or* I can search deep within myself and try to find my strength to help me weather the pain.

Shaking my head, my mind teeters back and forth, and continues to do so until I'm finally able to brave another look in the mirror.

And that's when I see it.

It's dim but it's there.

Buried deep, a tiny glimmer of hope somehow remains, safely preserved within the memories of a dark-haired little girl. The girl who one day excitedly skipped her way across the street to meet her new best friend. The girl who loved and trusted so easily, and who even vowed to protect those who meant the most to her.

The same girl who later experienced the most horrific of tragedies and understandably lost herself in the darkness as she tried to navigate the nightmares left behind. Alone.

But now, as I stare back as my reflection, I know I will find my way.

I take hold of that hope and allow it to tether me as I find footing in my newfound focus.

I *refuse* to allow myself to feel like a victim any longer.

I am a survivor.

It runs through my mind on replay over, and over, and over again. With each revolution, strength churns and resolve steels itself inside me.

I dip my head at the mirror, my mouth set with determination. My legs already feel lighter as I exit the bathroom and head to the top drawer of my dresser. I hook my fingers around the handle, then tug it open and reach for the wadded-up card stashed underneath my clothes.

As soon as it's extracted, I unfold its crinkled edges and smooth it in my hands.

Thank you, I whisper silently to Grady before grabbing my phone and dialing the number on the card before I lose my nerve. Two rings later, I've hopefully found someone to help guide me off this fucking hell ride.

"Hi, um, Dr. Miller?"

Chapter 29

Dr. Miller

I was extremely surprised by Dr. Miller's youthful voice when she answered her phone. Her tone was cheery and welcoming, not at all uppity or stiff as I had imagined it would be. To my surprise, she knew exactly who I was, and even more shocking, she insisted we meet immediately. On a weekend. At her house.

So I accepted her invitation, jumping in my Jeep before I had a chance to second-guess my actions. Which brings me to now, pulling up to the curb, in front of a red-brick, two-story house. A single red wagon sits on the porch, filled with a multitude of stuffed animals, some hanging off the sides as though seeking help.

The sight brings a small grin to my face, in spite of the herd of elephants running amuck in my stomach. Taking a deep breath, I tear my gaze away from the porch and pull my rearview mirror down to examine my face.

I clear yesterday's eyeliner that has drifted below my lashes with the tips of my fingers, the only makeup on my face. After one final look, I give up on bettering my appearance and tug on the handle, finally stepping onto the asphalt of the street. My ponytail blows in the breeze as I shut the door, and I steal another calming breath before beginning the trek toward the porch. I pass by the two cars in the driveway, one a black Chevy Z71 truck and the other a bright-yellow MINI Cooper, my brows lifting in appreciation for the latter.

Another slight smile plays on my lips, but falls with my slowed steps as I approach the front door. I'm not sure if it's anxiety due to my recent decision to contact and potentially trust this random person, or if it's fear that the underlying hope motivating me to keep walking will be crushed if I made the wrong choice in doing so.

I don't even have time to ponder the answer to my own question before the door swings open and I'm met with two sky-blue eyes and a huge beaming smile. My eyes widen in surprise, only to break from hers to take a quick glance behind me, making sure I have the right address.

There is no way this is Dr. Miller.

She's absolutely stunning. Her light-blonde hair is formed into an angular bob that perfectly frames her face, highlighting her amused stare complete with dimpled grin. She steps onto the porch and my gaze falls to a very worn concert tee with a few bands' names on the front. Some I recognize, some I don't.

My brows form a crease as I read them all in their entirety before inquiring, "Who's Poe?"

Finished with the shirt, I'm surprised at her appalled expression as she wordlessly stares back at me. After a few seconds, she closes her mouth, shakes her head, and clears her throat before announcing, "I'm going to pretend you didn't ask me that."

The sun illuminates her face as she takes another step toward me and extends her hand in greeting. "Dr. Miller. But please, call me Aubrey. And you're Cassie?"

I nod and my eyes flit briefly over several remnant piercings in her face before they disappear into her dimples when she smiles again. I breathe a sigh of relief and clasp her hand with mine.

I don't know why seeing the practically sealed holes calms my nerves, but it does. Maybe it's because I know she's not perfect, that she won't pass judgment on me because perhaps she's made some mistakes of her own at a particularly low point in her life. I really can't explain it, but as she turns to head into her house, I no longer feel anxious.

I follow her lead, closing the door behind me, and as soon as it's shut, she turns to face me, gesturing widely. "I apologize for having to meet at my home, but my office is being renovated at the moment. I have another one here, so I figured we could use it in the meantime, if that's okay with you?"

My face splits into a smile. "I prefer it actually. I feel more . . . comfortable here, I think."

She grins back at me. "Excellent. Then let's get to know each other."

I watch her feet as she pivots around. Her frayed bell-bottom jeans cover the top of her feet, leaving her painted-black toenails on clear display as she walks.

Yeah, I think we will get along just fine.

Together, we maneuver over many more stuffed animals strewn along the hallway as she apologizes over her shoulder. "It's a wreck in here, sorry. My office is down this way, just off the hall."

"No worries," I state, stepping over a koala.

A burst of giggles and baritone laughter come from the other side of the house, and I can't help but smile at the sound. Aubrey shakes her head in front of me. "They're ridiculous, those two."

"You're married?" I inquire as she opens a door, then reaches to turn on the light before we enter.

"For five blissful years."

More giggles sound. She grins back at me, her face beaming with the sound.

She offers no more and I don't ask, unsure of proper protocol in this situation. Of this *whole* situation, in fact. I'm not sure how many patients actually visit their therapist's homes.

As though reading my mind, Aubrey offers, "I normally don't meet people here, in case you're wondering. I do have a temporary office downtown, but I've been waiting on your call for a while, and I didn't want to lose the chance to chat with you before you changed your mind."

Right then, I know, and I breathe out a sigh of relief.

She understands. She understands how terrifying this is for me.

She gestures for me to have a seat in one of the leather chairs while she sits in the other. My body folds into the seat and I watch as she tucks her legs underneath her body, getting comfortable. My eyes land on the wall behind her, taking in the radiance of the mural filling the entire space. Brilliant shades of yellows, oranges, and reds are masterfully woven together, painted along its length to form an image of a burning sun.

Aubrey follows my stare, looking over her shoulder, and brings her eyes back to mine. "Sometimes even the smallest bit of light can lead you through the darkness. All you need is a spark."

She grins back at me, and tears surface as I ingest the beauty of her words. Hope blossoms with her sentiment, warming me as it grows, because for the first time in all my blackened years, I feel as though maybe there's someone else besides me who understands the meaning of *true* darkness. I can only nod in agreement, overcome with emotion.

She holds my stare and winks. "We'll get ya there."

The gesture and the words, both so familiar, steal the air from my lungs.

Her expression turns curious, and she angles her head to the side in question.

"I'm sorry." I inhale deeply. "Grady used to say that to me. And he winked. A lot."

Laughter bubbles through her nose and I smile a wobbly smile with her.

She narrows her eyes. "Grady cares for you very deeply, Cassie. You should know that. Remember that. Keep hold of that as we move through this process."

I clear my throat before asking, "How is it that you know him?"

"We've done some casework together; that's really all I can say." She smiles apologetically, then adds, "But Grady isn't why we are here, is he? Let's focus on you."

She inhales deeply and locks her gaze with mine before starting. "Now I want to preface by saying, I wanted to meet today in order for us to get to know each other. But the more you open up, the more questions I will ask. We will take this at *your* speed. If at any time you're uncomfortable with providing an answer, just let me know and we can move on to something else."

My smile is weak, but accepting of her offer.

She continues. "Now that we've established that Grady isn't the reason we're here, would you mind sharing why *you* are here?"

My throat works a swallow before I answer. "I'm lost. I feel lost, I guess I should say. Out of control, out of focus, like I can't get my bearings." I sigh. "I don't even know where to start." My shoulders lift into a shrug.

Aubrey continues to hold my eyes carefully with hers. "Let's start with when you began feeling this way."

"Well," I begin, "I, uh . . . it started when I was eight really. That's when I started to lose my grasp on the person I was. My world was tilted, throwing me off balance as it spun out of control. Everything became a blur, but after time, I found comfort in the haze. It made the pain more manageable, you know?"

She nods in understanding, so I continue. "But then I met Grady and everything slowed, bringing everything back into focus and forcing me to see what I had been missing. I just started wanting more. Wanting to be happy. Wanting to find love. Wanting things I never thought I could have." I swallow deeply. "And then six weeks ago, I was reminded of why I should never have hoped for those things. My world sped up, and everything became distorted and unclear. I lost my focus. And with it, I lost that hope. I lost him. And I lost myself. Again."

Aubrey dips her head again, then asks, "What happened six weeks ago that made you lose all of those things?"

"My uncle Alan died," I respond, surprised by the ease of my answer, knowing exactly where this conversation is heading.

"You were close?" Her eyebrows depress with the question.

I snicker to myself. "We used to be, I guess."

"And what changed within your relationship that distanced you from him?"

I have always been so preoccupied about the division between Spencer's road and mine, I've never really thought about my own. But as she asks that one question, I know I'm reaching the proverbial fork in my own path.

Aubrey's pushing me. Not aggressively, not so I feel threatened or fearful, but she's testing the boundaries. Seeing how much I'm willing to give as she presses for information.

I get it. I see what she's doing. And I want to provide her the information she seeks, because I'm so fucking tired of bearing the weight of my secrets alone. Neither my mind nor my body can handle them anymore. I want to pass them over to her, praying she's someone who can help me shoulder their pain.

My stare breaks from hers, glancing over her shoulder at the sun and its symbolism. Can she help me find my way out of the darkness? Is there any spark even left in me?

I don't know. I really don't.

But I pray there is.

"He molested me when I was eight."

I hold her stare, surprised when there's no recoil. No surprise. No judgment or pity.

It's as if she experiences relief; her mouth curves up slightly with her nod. Almost as though she expected it. "Wow, Cassie, I'm *very* proud of you. Very proud. I'm sure that wasn't easy."

She's proud of me.

No, she's very proud of me.

Wow.

Just hearing the words pass from her mouth lights a fire in my soul. My desolate, aching heart is soothed by their warmth and a tiny, encouraged grin dances on my lips.

Aubrey's face breaks into a prideful smile. "That spark of yours is still there. I see it in your eyes, your fight to heal. And mark my words, we will get you there, and we will do it together."

"I hope so," I breathe. "Because honestly, I'm exhausted. I feel as though I'm constantly trying to breathe, but can't. I feel smothered, slowly suffocating under the weight of the secrets I've kept. I just want to be free of them. To live without continuously fighting back the memories and the fear I experienced when I was a child. It's ever-present, you know? Always there."

"I completely understand, Cassie. Nothing you're saying is out of the norm for someone who has experienced the trauma you have, especially at such a young age." Her mouth tightens a smidge before she asks, "Now, you mentioned secrets. You've told no one about this? Not even your parents?"

I shake my head, my throat tightening with the admission. "No. When I was young, when it would happen, he would tell me that my parents would be angry if I told them. That they would be upset with me for disobeying his orders, and if I did so, they wouldn't want me anymore because that would make me a bad girl. I was so scared, Aubrey." My voice begins to tremble. "I know now that he was manipulating me. But then, I didn't know what to do."

A tear breaks free, rolling down my cheek.

"I believed everything he told me. And then after a while, even after he left and I knew better, so much time had passed, I didn't want to bring it up. It was easier for me to pretend. I just acted as though it didn't happen, so I would never have to explain to them what actually *did*. I was scared of the way they would look at me, that they would blame me for letting it happen. I just . . . couldn't."

"What happened wasn't your fault, Cassie. You need to understand that."

I swallow and offer her a slight dip of my head.

"Cassie, I need you to look at me." Aubrey's tone is firm and demanding.

Tearing my eyes from the view of the carpet, I raise them to meet hers, equally as unwavering as her voice. She leans forward and repeats, "It wasn't your fault."

Aubrey's face is blurry through my tears. "I know."

She cocks her head. "Do you?"

"I do," I assure her. "I mean, I get that there was nothing I could do at that age to stop him. The only thing I could do was what I was told, so that's what I did, what I've been doing, for the past fifteen years. But even with that knowledge, it doesn't seem to make it any easier. It still happened. I still feel him touching me. I still feel the disgust and humiliation that followed once I realized what had actually happened. Because I didn't know."

My head bobs from side to side. It's so surreal, so strangely freeing, to be saying these things aloud. Words and thoughts I've had ruminating in my head for years.

More tears surface, replacing the ones escaping my eyes as I decide to give her everything. Because Uncle Alan's secret wasn't the only one I've been keeping. I've also been hiding the shame felt with my own. The words tumble from my mouth, for fear I will never find the courage to release them again.

"I didn't know what he was doing was wrong. I trusted him when he told me it wasn't. I didn't recognize it then, but when I grew older and finally understood . . . I was no longer innocent. I felt dirty. I felt sick. Grotesque. It *had* been wrong. It changed me." I take a deep breath. Aubrey waits patiently. "So I did my best to cope with those feelings by taking ownership of my own body. Sex, and any feelings of pleasure associated with it, were *given* by me, not taken. And each time it happened, I felt empowered, relieved I still had some sort of control. But soon after would come the loathing and self-hatred, overshadowing my relief. It was an endless, whirling cycle that dictated my life for many years."

Aubrey's expression is thoughtful as she takes in my account, then she gives me an encouraging nod. "Again. A completely normal response. Nothing you have done, Cassie, is wrong. Like you said, you did the best to cope in the only way you knew how. It's how you survived. And I think now that you're older, we can work on finding different ways to deal with your past. With the anger. With the remorse. With the violation of both your body and your trust."

She smiles and adds, "With a healthier, more healing approach, we can help you move past the pain, instead of simply masking it. It won't be easy. Some days will be more difficult than others, but I'm willing to lead you, if you're ready."

She looks at me intently. "Your willingness is the key to your healing. You have to want to travel that path with me. I can't help you unless you *want* to be helped."

I look at her, her expression filled with determination and strength, and I know that if anyone can help guide me to where I want to be, it's Dr. Aubrey Miller.

"I'm ready." My voice is strong and resolute with my answer.

"Good," she replies. "Then I have a homework assignment for you. When you're ready." Her mouth lifts at the corners. "The first step toward healing is the most difficult, and it may seem a little crazy, but you have to trust me on this."

I love the way she calmly assesses my reaction. I remain silent, unfazed by her statement, because I'm ready to do whatever it takes.

Presumably after gauging that in my expression, she explains, "You need to look inward and make peace with that eight-year-old little girl inside of you. Find her and say the things that need to be said, whatever they may be, so she may be released from her own pain. It's *her* agony and terror that you feel, not twenty-three-year-old Cassie's. Twenty-three-year-old Cassie knows what happened and has created coping strategies, some not as helpful as others, but eight-year-old Cassie is still bound by her fears, unable to break through because of the uncertainty of what she has experienced. *You are the only one who can reach her, who can soothe her, and ultimately, who can free her. Once you do that, then your true healing can begin."*

Aubrey grins and laughs under her breath. "Sounds crazy, doesn't it?"

My own smile breaks free and I shake my head. "No, I've seen her," I admit. "I just couldn't get to her."

I wouldn't even know what to say to her.

I feel so guilty.

Another reassuring grin from Aubrey. "That's because you weren't *ready* then. Now you are. And I'll help you find the right words she needs to hear."

The meaning of her words, and her unwavering belief in them as she speaks, furthers the fledgling sensation of hope. *Could I do this?* Reclining into my seat, I reflect on the ease of her statement. I look over her shoulder at the magnificent image of the burning sun.

I know it won't be easy, but I refuse to live like this any longer.

Focusing on that sun, everything slows and I find I'm no longer falling.

My feet hit the ground, strong and steady, and as though landing on a piece of flint, a spark is ignited by the strength of their impact. It twists upward, carrying with it a glimmer of light, and as I watch it float in front of my eyes, power surges and clarity sharpens my mind.

I am stronger than *him*.

I will find the Cassie of my youth, and *I* will free her.

I will heal us both.

And after that, I will forever emerge from the darkened hollows of my mind . . .

My *own* victor.

And I won't have to do it alone.

I'm no longer alone.

Chapter 30

Reconnection

Courage can be such a fleeting emotion. One moment, you feel it rising in your blood, strengthening your resolve as it prepares you to face your greatest fears. The next, it recedes like the tide of the ocean, leaving you bereft, uncertain of its existence in the first place.

I head home the first day after meeting with Aubrey, convinced I will find that little girl inside me and set her free. But as soon as I step into my apartment, cold fear slithers its way into my mind, weakening me to the point that I don't even try.

What will I say when I find her?

Will she decline my offer and choose to stay in the darkness forever, thereby locking me in with her?

Will she be able to forgive me?

Will she hate me?

This last question seals the deal, and I find myself absolutely petrified to learn the answer. So I choose not to ask. I do it the first time, the second, the third . . .

It takes me five sessions with Aubrey to finally lock on to that courage and manage to keep hold.

She never pushes me, though. Each time she asks if I've made my peace, only to receive a negative shake of my head as my answer, she simply offers an encouraging dimpled smile and states with full certainty, "She will forgive you, Cassie. She wants to be set free just as much as you want her to be free. That little girl needs and wants you. Her little hands are eager to hold on to you, to reach you, be held by you. You can tell her it was wrong. *He* was wrong. She was a good little girl. Always."

Well, I'm there now.

Literally.

I'm in my bathroom, courage piqued and pumping through my veins as I stare at my own reflection, searching for the little girl lost inside me. My breaths are deep in attempt to calm myself, to relax to the point that I can focus my energy where it needs to be in order to find her.

Much to my surprise, it doesn't take long.

I watch, transfixed, as my face morphs in the mirror. The bones in my cheeks are no longer angular and drawn, but hidden behind the rounded flesh of my youth. My eyes are the same deep brown as they stare back at me, but they are no longer lifeless. They're filled with vigor and excitement. Joy. Following suit, my mouth is curved slightly upward at its edges, lifting into a meek smile as we make our reacquaintance.

I lift my arm, splaying my fingers on the coolness of the glass just to touch her face. To remember her as she should be. Full of joy and strength. Not shackled in the darkness, terrified and alone.

Her smile remains, but mine falls and moisture begins to build along the base of my lashes.

"I just left you there."

Guilt consumes me, washing over me completely, and my chin quivers violently with the admission. I remove my hand and look to the counter below me.

"I should have protected you. I just . . . I wasn't strong enough. I didn't know what to do. I felt so helpless. I'm so sorry. I'm so sorry. I'm so sorry."

The whispers turn into chants as I focus on the Formica. Tears of remorse stream down my face, falling from my cheeks and striking the tops of my hands as they continue to steady me.

And just when I'm about to give up, when I've convinced myself of my inability to completely free her from the chains of fear and sorrow, a gentle rush of warmth fills my chest. It spreads slowly, blissfully sealing the open gash carved into my heart by my own guilt and blame long ago. I gasp, the sensation startling, and bring my eyes back to the mirror.

My eight-year-old self stares back at me, a lilting smile on her face and her eyes as bright as I remember. "It's not your fault."

Tears stream down my cheeks as she continues.

"I didn't like what he did to me. I was scared. My fairies . . . my fairies didn't protect me. But . . . but you're here with me now."

Another wave of peace rolls through me, her words resounding as they cauterize my gaping wounds. I've allowed myself to think them, to hear Aubrey state them, but coming from the child in front of me, I finally accept them.

Her grin widens, displaying the new teeth she hasn't yet grown into. "*You* survived while you kept *me* hidden. Don't you see? You *did* protect me from him. And now that you've found me again, I'm not scared anymore. I'm ready to leave this place and go play. I can be happy now."

I dip my head at my reflection and exhale. Through the tears, a relieved smile crosses my face and I jerk my head to the side, signaling for her to go. She giggles, infusing me with comfort. It sweeps through me, mending anything the previous two passes might have missed, and as it continues to expand, I breathe in deeply.

I'm no longer broken, the tattered pieces of my former self now mended.

I'm whole, as her soul weaves in between and fuses with mine, completing the first of many steps toward healing. Her essence interlaces with mine, lifting me with her strength, relieving the weight I've carried for so long.

Her image fades, leaving me staring back at my own reflection, but I'm not alone. Her vivacious spirit flows powerfully through my veins.

And her smile, well, she left that with me.

I silently thank her for the beauty of her gift, then practically skip my way out of the bathroom, settled on beginning the next phase of healing as planned with Aubrey just earlier today.

My love for reading has come up in several of our discussions. I was surprised to find that we have read many of the same authors. Often we find ourselves comparing our favorite books, debating the strengths and weaknesses of different heroes and heroines, and quoting the lines read so often they're etched forever in our minds.

Grady was right.

She's not only my psychiatrist.

In Dr. Miller, in Aubrey, I feel as though I've found a friend.

And because of those friendly conversations, I'm following her suggestion to write down how I feel, describe how I felt at particular times in my life. Her idea being that if I put my feelings on paper, it will help me sift through the feelings, making them easier to address.

But I've decided to take a different approach.

There are things that need to be said.

Explanations provided.

Apologies given.

And reasons demanded.

This part of my healing will consist of four separate letters, delivered to the recipients in the same order written.

I open the bag sitting on my dresser and pull out both the stationery and new pen I bought before I came home. The tips of my fingers graze the plastic encasing as I set it down, knowing that this step, once taken, cannot be undone. After I reveal my darkness, it's out there and there's no taking it back.

I'm surprisingly okay with that knowledge, because in sharing my past, I know I will only become stronger as I acknowledge what happened, the repercussions, *and* the aftermath.

I will heal.

Next I remove four lavender-scented candles from the bag, lighting each one and placing them randomly around my room. The closest is on my bedside table, right next to Roger. I pat his head and apologize, because something tells me the fragrance is just too girly for a manly man such as himself.

I imagine his beady eyes rolling into his head, and I chuckle as I take a seat on my bed, stationery now in hand. After opening it, I set the pile of paper in front of me and prepare to unleash my heart on paper.

With my legs bent at the knees, I lean to grab the first sheet, place it to fit perfectly onto the magazine sticking to my thighs, and then . . .

I write.

Chapter 31

The First Letter

Dear Spencer,

First, I would like to apologize for the amount of distance I've put between us lately. I'm sure you've noticed, but that didn't stop you from incessantly checking on me and trying to make me laugh. Just one of the reasons I love you like mad.

I'm back now, though. Fully present for the first time in a really long time. And I thank you for having the patience to stick by my side while giving me the time I needed to sort through my life.

You may be wondering at this point why I'm writing you a letter instead of telling you what I'm about to tell you in person. Part of the reason is I made a very important decision this week that will forever change me and my course in life, and this letter is a crucial part in helping me do just that.

The other part isn't as easy to admit, however, because the truth is, I'm scared. I'm scared of what your reaction will be to what I'm about to share with you. I'm scared you will look at me differently, or that it will change our relationship. Our friendship.

Yet, as fearful as I am of that happening, I need to do this, not only for me, but for you as well. You deserve my honesty. You deserve to know the truth. You told me the day we met that friends don't keep secrets, and I feel I've failed you in doing that. Because in keeping certain parts of my past hidden, I feel I've misled you. I've allowed you to believe you were friends with a person who didn't really exist, and I'm sincerely sorry for that.

You have always been truthful with me, upfront about your own past and fears. I have admired you for possessing that incredible amount of confidence and strength for so long. It shines like a beacon, on clear display for everyone around you to see. So often I would look at you and wish I could be more like you. You didn't cower; you didn't hide. You faced your fears head on, while I pushed mine to the side, pretending they didn't exist or masking the pain they inflicted. Smiling to hide my tears. Laughing so I wouldn't scream. Talking to avoid the silence. Having random sex with countless partners for nothing other than validation.

But I refuse to do that, to *be* that, anymore. And in writing this letter, I am taking my first step toward that goal. By the end of this, you will know everything. You will know my secrets. My darkness. And it will be your decision, as it should have been all along, whether or not you still want to be my friend.

So, here goes . . .

I'm not sure if you remember my uncle Alan, but he stayed with my family briefly when you and I were around eight years old, just after your dad died. I'm sure I mentioned his name at some point because I was completely enchanted by him when we first met. He was one of my favorite people, until he wasn't.

Uncle Alan molested me, Spence. For the six months he resided in our basement, he would visit me often in the middle of the night. I won't go into specifics, because they are unnecessary and well, it's pretty obvious what happened.

One day he up and left with no explanation, and I never saw him again. His presence, though, was inescapable. Everywhere I looked, he was there. Every time I shut my eyes, he appeared.

God, Spence. The dreams. They were so vivid, so real, so unavoidable. Even though he was gone, he wasn't, and even though the abuse had stopped, it hadn't. Not in my mind, not in my nightmares. It would happen over and over and over again, for years.

I'm sure you noticed the changes in me. I'm sure you wondered why I started showing up in the middle of the night, knocking at your window. But as always with you, you just accepted it, accepted *me*, without question. Your light is what drew me, but it was your friendship that made me feel safe, truly safe, on those nights when I would come over, searching for some sort of haven from the terror. You could have had no way of knowing at that time that you, your friendship, was the only thing keeping me sane.

You never passed judgment on me, or my extremely questionable actions. You never pushed me to explain why I made the choices I made, that I continued to make, for years. You loved me for me being me, even though I had no idea who I even was, and you did this for years. I cannot begin to thank you enough for that.

A little over two months ago—on your birthday, actually, when Dalton was shot—I received a call from my mother telling me that Uncle Alan had died and his body had been brought back to Fuller to be buried. That was the "family emergency" I told you about. I was forced to attend his funeral, and let's just say, I lost it. I completely shut down after that. I did a lot that I'm not proud of over the next several weeks, including pushing you away. The only explanation I have is that I wasn't in a good place, and I was so scared I would somehow drag you into my own darkness. I would never be able to forgive myself for doing that to you. So, I hope you understand and can forgive me for making that choice.

I eventually found my way out though. Something I never thought I would be able to do. It turns out that the strength I envied in you, I already possessed. I'm proud to be able to say that.

It's funny, for so long, I knew our paths were not to be the same. I imagined yours breaking from mine when you found your own happiness one day. It would be full of light and happiness, and Dalton would be by your side. Mine, however, would be the exact opposite, lined in darkness and flooded with my own demons.

I couldn't have been more mistaken.

Now, I'm on the path I should have been on all along. I found my way to a path of *my* choosing, not one forced upon me. A path of healing, full of warmth and courage. And I'm happy here.

Did our paths diverge? Yes. As they were supposed to do. We can't grow into the people we're supposed to be if we stay in the same place, traveling the same road, going nowhere new or unexplored. We have to brave the unknown and allow our feet to carry us where we're destined to be.

That's exactly what growth is, and that's what I'm doing.

I realize now that we don't have to be traveling through life side by side to remain friends. Our bond, our friendship, will secure us for the rest of our lives, no matter where we go.

I just hope I didn't sever that bond. That I didn't push you so far away that it snapped apart. That I didn't slice right through it by not telling you about my past.

But like I said, the choice is yours, now that you know everything.

That's it.

That's all of me, my story, my past.

I really hope you can forgive me for not sharing it with you sooner.

Love you, times two.

Cass

My nerves are at an all-time high when I hear the front door shut, announcing Spencer's arrival. I left her letter on her dresser, then hauled ass to my room, where I've been hiding since waiting for her to get home. Ten minutes pass with no sound or movement stemming from the other side of the apartment, but just as I toss Roger above my head for the forty-seventh time, I hear her door softly click shut.

Roger drifts through the air as I listen to footsteps cross the living room, and he lands on my carpet just as there's a gentle knock on my door. I swallow deeply, rising from the floor, and wipe my sweaty palms along my thighs.

My steps are hesitant and slow, and my hands tremble slightly as I reach for the knob. I breathe in a large gulp of air, then release it before tugging the door open.

I barely have time to register Spencer's glistening eyes and reddened nose before she hauls into me, wrapping her arms around my shoulders to embrace me tightly. Not at all prepared, I clumsily stumble backward with her excessive momentum, and together, we fall to the carpet.

As she rolls off me, her entire body shakes from either laughing or crying, I can't tell. Her long blonde hair is covering her face when she lands on her back, and I reach toward her to hook a section with my index finger and slide it toward me to better assess her reaction. A huge smile takes up the lower part of her face but fat droplets continue to stream across her temples.

Great. She's laugh-crying.

I turn on my side and she does the same, both of us landing on our shoulders with smiles on our faces and moisture lining our eyes.

"Well, that was embarrassing," Spencer wipes a tear as it crosses the bridge of her freckled nose before adding, "and not at all what I had planned."

I grin and sniffle. "For us, it's about standard."

She lifts her arm, running her hand along my hair. The smile disappears and her face crumbles right in front of my eyes. My chest splits in two as my heart breaks. I hate seeing her cry.

"Spence—"

She cuts me off, blubbering, "I wish you would have told me, Cass. I could have done something. Helped you in some way."

Emotion clogs my throat making speech impossible, and I clear it before speaking. "This is why I didn't tell you, Spence. At the time, I didn't believe I could tell you. I didn't understand that I needed help. As I got older and understood more, I certainly didn't want to tell you and then only see pity in your eyes when you looked at me. I didn't want to become a project for you, someone for you to fix. I just wanted to be your friend, like I was before it happened. That's the only thing I had to hang on to, and I was so scared I would lose it. Lose you. I couldn't have handled that if it happened."

She reaches forward and takes my hand into hers, interlacing our fingers and locking our stares. "Love you." Nothing more needs to be said.

The tears break free from my eyes as I respond, "Love you, times two."

Both of our mouths lift into simultaneous smiles with the words, then Spencer laughs under her breath. "I'm officially renouncing my birthday. It's bad luck."

My bottom lip pokes out as I pout, "But you lost your virginity to Dalton on your birthday."

"He disappeared the same night. It cancels out," Spencer counters.

"But you had a birthday redo, so it doesn't. It's back on the table," I reason.

She shakes her head. "That wasn't on my birthday, it was two weeks prior. Doesn't count. Plus, this time around, I was kidnapped, Dalton was shot, and your uncle reappeared after years. All on my birthday." I open my mouth to challenge that Alan was dead, therefore it doesn't count, but she states firmly, "It counts."

I consider her argument, then nod. "Yes, I think that would be for the best. No more birthdays for Spencer."

As we fall into our typical banter, I wrack my brain.

Why had I been worried about her reaction?

This is Spencer, my beautiful, brave, funny friend. Always forgiving. Always finding and distributing her light.

I never should've doubted her.

My mouth twists to the side as I remember. "Hey . . . I didn't get you anything this year."

Spencer's face forms into contented expression, and she lifts her hand once again to stroke my hair. "You heal, Cass. That's the *only* present I want from you."

My hand curls over hers against my head, and I squeeze tight. As we hold each other's eyes, I don't see pity. If anything, I see admiration and pride.

My chest tightens as the familiar tug forms between us, reinforcing the bond whose integrity should have never been put into question.

We might be on different paths, but there's nothing that can ever keep us apart.

That's just how our friendship works.

Chapter 32

The Second Letter

Mom and Dad,

I'm writing you this letter to inform you of something you already know, but have refused to admit to yourselves. So, I will be the adult in this situation and bring it out into the open for us to discuss.

Uncle Alan sexually abused me when he lived at this house.

What Uncle Alan did was inexcusable, but the ease of your dismissal, your refusal to acknowledge the psychological damage incurred because of his actions, well . . . those things are far worse. They're deplorable. Unforgivable.

When it happened, *every time* it happened, Uncle Alan told me I couldn't tell you, so I didn't. I kept his secret. I was a good girl. But I kept thinking, kept hoping, that one of you would ask what was wrong with me, because in my simplistic mind, if you asked and I told you because I was simply responding, then I wouldn't be breaking my word to Uncle Alan. I would still be a good girl.

But the fucked-up thing is, you never asked.

Not once.

Not when I started jumping anytime anyone entered my room.

Not when I started flinching every time someone would touch me.

Not when your usually rambunctious, inquisitive, outspoken little girl went practically mute, too frightened to speak.

Not even when I couldn't make eye contact with my own father, his face too similar to the man who haunted my dreams. Who destroyed my happiness.

And definitely not when I would wake in the middle of the night after experiencing those terrifying dreams, forced to wash my own urine-soaked sheets before washing the stench from my body.

I know you heard me those nights.

Yet, you never asked.

So I never told.

I lived with the repercussions of his actions, while you both lived in denial. You took the easy road, while your daughter paid the price.

Your eight-year-old daughter.

Where the fuck were you?

Why didn't you protect me?

Why didn't you get me help?

How could you just sit there, day in and day out, with all these visible changes happening, and never fucking ask? You just sat by, playing ignorant while waiting for the eight-year-old of the house to come to you, to admit the most horrifying thing ever that could happen to a child, just so you wouldn't have to say the words.

And quite possibly worst of all, you made me go to his funeral. You knew what he had done to me, but you forced me to attend the bastard's funeral, regardless of the pain you knew I'd feel in seeing him again.

Un-fucking-forgivable.

I'm washing my hands of both of you, until you can choose me over your own goddamn pride.

I refuse to waste my energy being angry with the two of you anymore.

When or if you choose to acknowledge what happened, when you're open to discussion and willing to take the steps necessary for this family to heal, I will be there to hear what you have to say.

But until that day comes, I'm done.

I cannot, and will not, ruin my chance to move forward and mend the damage done.

I suffered in silence, but I will heal vocally.

And this letter is my vocalization to you, as my parents, as those who were supposed to protect me. You failed miserably.

What Alan did didn't destroy this family, you did.

I will no longer allow you to destroy me along with it.

I will heal.

And I will do it with or without you.

Because this letter is just another step, taken by me, for me, as I bring myself closer to doing that.

There are only so many steps I can take until I'm forced to leave you behind.

The ball is in your court now; the decision is yours to make.

Your daughter or your pride.

Cassie

Unlike with Spencer, I did *not* give my parents room to digest their letter without my presence. I wanted to see their reactions, watch their faces, as they read my words. I know what I wrote was harsh, severe, unsympathetic. But there was just too much suppressed anger and disappointment to say anything other than what I did. I needed to express exactly how I felt, without regret or worry regarding their reaction.

I've known for years that they suspected something happened when Alan entered my life. It doesn't take a rocket scientist to figure it out, and they're not oblivious people. For a long time, we all existed within the comfort of denial. I made excuses for their lack of interest, of worry, and they . . . well, they did nothing.

It is what it is.

The damage is done.

I watch my father's face fall, his entire expression weighted with sorrow as he sobs silently to himself before heading out of the room, leaving me alone with my mother.

He only made it to the second paragraph. I figured as much.

The sad thing is, I don't even know the real reason he's crying.

Is it because the truth was finally spelled out for him?

Or because of the atrocities committed by his own brother?

Or is it simply because he misses the piece of shit?

Who knows?

Who cares?

His inability to comfort me during this time pretty much tells me all I need to know about our relationship, or lack thereof. *He used to mean the world to me.*

My mother, as usual, remains indifferent as she reads on, her slacks impeccable, creased along the length of her crossed legs and hitting her ankle as her agitated foot swings back and forth. Her brown hair is in a tight bun, the slivers of gray strands woven expertly with the rest. I watch, standing in the middle of the living room until she finishes the letter, then her eyes rise to meet mine. They narrow on my face, but I give nothing away.

I remain emotionless as she dissects me from afar, then with a careless fling, she tosses the letter on the coffee table in front of her.

"I find it surprising that you're making these accusations when Alan is no longer here to defend himself."

Her tone is haughty, condescending.

I laugh, unabashedly, then shake my head. "I'm sure you do; I would expect nothing less."

Leaving her in the living room, I grab my purse off the kitchen table, then turn to her after opening the door. She's standing with her arms crossed over her chest, mouth pinched tightly, watching my exit.

Fresh air and sunlight surround me, and I breathe it in deeply and feel warmed. My tone is calm and even as I state, "I should hate you for making me attend his funeral. For watching me break right in front of your eyes while you did nothing but cast judgment, but I don't. Actually, I thank you for it. I thought I was weak, but taking so long to finally shatter, to reach the point where facing my fears was better than the agony felt once every piece of me finally disintegrated, well . . . I'm stronger than I thought. It took fifteen years for me to break. Thank you for forcing me to find and finally realize my own strength."

She says nothing as I wheel around and step into the awaiting sunshine, leaving her behind.

Just as I unlock my Jeep, I hear a screen door slap shut in the distance. I smile at the driveway, then lift my eyes to find Spencer's mother watching me warily from across the street. My feet carry me across the very worn path between the two houses, until I'm racing up the familiar steps to find myself enveloped in her waiting arms.

I know she knows what happened. I gave Spencer permission to tell her when she asked, knowing I would do it eventually anyway.

And I'm so glad her arms are here to hold me. A mother's arms to provide the comfort I have so needed.

Mrs. Locke's shoulders shudder against mine as she cries. Her touch is soft as her hand tenderly strokes my back in a familiar circular fashion, the gesture reminiscent of the hugs so often received when at this house.

"Oh, Cassie. My sweet, sweet Cassie," she sobs into my ear.

I can't fight the grin as I press away to reassure her. "I'm okay, Mrs. Locke. I promise."

She nods, then sniffs back her tears. "I know, I know."

Her other hand lifts, cupping my cheek. "I wish I would have said something. All those nights you came over to sleep in Spencer's room, and I never asked. I should've asked."

I want to laugh at the fact that neither Spencer nor I had any idea her mom knew about my late-night excursions, yet I'm not surprised.

My mouth forms a watery smile as I reply, "It wasn't you who should have been asking the questions, Mrs. Locke. And besides, I wouldn't have said anything, not then anyway. But you, you welcomed me into your home without question, providing me comfort and safety when I needed it the most. I wouldn't have made it without that."

Mrs. Locke's chin trembles as I speak, and I wipe the warmth from my cheeks with my fingertips before adding, "Thank you."

Her head dips toward the wooden porch beneath our feet as she collects herself before she lifts her face, gracing me with a relieved smile as she nods. Her light-brown eyes hold my dark ones before she pulls me into her body, practically suffocating me as her arms fold tightly around my upper body. I would laugh, but I only have a small amount of air available, so I use the rest within my lungs to state, "Mrs. Locke, I'm fine. I promise."

"Love you, Cassie, so very much." I can't help the swift breath in. *I needed those words. Needed* these *hugs.*

She squeezes me tighter, and just when I begin to feel faint she finally releases me. Her warm hands glide tenderly down my arms and as they do, I catch a glimmer out of the corner of my eye. My stare homes in on her hand as it lowers and I gasp when I see a sizable diamond sitting atop her left ring finger.

"OH MY GOD!" I squeal. "YOU'RE ENGAGED!"

Mrs. Locke's smile breaks across her face before she leans into me. "It just happened this morning."

"I'm assuming this means he's no longer in trouble then, not sleeping on the couch anymore?" I consider the last time I heard her—blazing into the ER looking for Detective Kirk Lawson. "The makeup sex must have been astounding," I add.

She waggles her eyebrows and opens her mouth, but I cover my ears. "Too much, Mrs. Locke. Forget I said anything."

She throws her head back in laughter before lowering her eyes to mine. She sobers, bringing her hand to my face and stroking my cheek gently with her thumb, clearing the moisture from my previously shed tears. "You're going to be okay," she states, more for her benefit than mine. Her eyes hold my stare with the strength and ferocity that I've seen so often in Spencer's.

I nod, lean into her, and allow her to hold me in her arms, determining that family isn't necessarily something you can only be born into. Mrs. Locke adopted Spencer, but as different as the color of their eyes may be, they still share the many of the same characteristics.

Both are loyal.

Loving.

Determined.

Fierce.

Although some of those features may be inherent, it's clear that Spencer acquired much of her personality from the woman holding me right now.

Love isn't an obligation. In fact, it's when you find it so willingly offered in the most unexpected places that you should hold on to it and never let go, because *that* love is real, unconditional.

I can't help but wonder how much of Mrs. Locke's strength I was lucky enough to capture along the way, because as she tightens her hold, and I once again find myself unable to breathe, I know without a doubt . . .

I'm lucky enough to be a part of their family too.

Unconditionally.

Chapter 33

The Third Letter

Grady,

It's been almost three months since we've seen each other, and there hasn't been a day that has gone by that I haven't thought about you. But as much as I longed to reach for you, to wrap myself around you and allow your arms to carry me when I thought I had no strength left, I couldn't. Wouldn't.

I had to stop my own fall. It was necessary for me bear my own weight through this journey so I could finally see what you saw in me all along. I needed to finally realize my strength and discover my worth, on my own.

You told me once that you couldn't love me enough for the both of us. I get it now. I understand what you meant, because then, at the time, I didn't really understand how to love myself. Even though I was beginning to learn, I think deep down I still couldn't believe myself worthy of such a truly extraordinary gift.

I never really knew what love was because, up until that point, love was a word used to manipulate. It was a term used to mask certain indiscretions. An expression used for the purpose of pacification.

It was a word that for years I had identified only with the sexual abuse that ripped apart my childhood. Each time it was spoken, I lost another fragment of my youth. My innocence. I heard it so often, one day, the child inside me just vanished. She was gone, retreating into the safety of my mind . . .

Until I met you.

You helped me find her.

Something about you called to her the instant your insightful blue eyes met mine. She was intrigued by the strength, the confidence portrayed in them as they assessed her from across the room. Because you weren't just looking at me, you were seeing her.

Little by little, you coaxed her out of the darkness, allowing her to experience the wonders of a childhood missed. You gave her butterflies and made her stupid-giddy. You took her skating and made her laugh. You held her pinky with your finger and played Twister with her. You jumped out of a plane with her, giving her the very first taste of freedom she'd had in years. You made her nervous, but in a good way. A youthful and innocent way. A way she so often longed to experience when she read her books.

You gave her her first real kiss. A kiss that she will remember forever.

But you also pushed her to see what you saw. The strength she thought she lacked. The life she was missing by remaining hidden. You gave her the courage to step into the light, allowing her to display her vulnerability while taking the first of many steps toward learning to trust. Toward learning what love really is.

And once she understood, she loved you in return, wholly and completely.

As did I.

She came out of the darkness for you, and because of that, I was able to find her when I needed her most.

I need you to know, if nothing else, that I was there with you, Grady. I was there. I did not lie about that. I gave myself to you in a way that I had never offered myself to anyone before, because I trusted you implicitly. I never want you to doubt where my head was in those very special moments shared between us.

I loved you.

I still love you.

I know I said some things that I had no right to say. I hurt you with my words because I was scared. So scared. I was falling fast, spinning so out of control, and I couldn't focus. I couldn't see you. I couldn't find your eyes.

Without them to tether me, I was so afraid I would be lost forever in the darkness.

But I wasn't.

Somehow, I found the strength to get my bearings and slow my world.

I landed the fall.

I found my focus.

I found myself.

I found that little eight-year-old girl inside me along the way, and I helped her too.

I don't know what the future holds for us, if anything at all after how I treated you, but if nothing else, I needed to tell you why.

Why I felt unworthy.

Why I rarely smiled.

Why I was so guarded.

I wanted you to understand, to finally know part of me, of my past.

And I wanted to say thank you.

It sounds so trite, so insufficient for the amount of gratitude I hold in my heart for you, but still, it needs to be said.

I will forever be grateful.

And so will she.

Thank you, Grady, for showing us what real love is.

Cass

I'm a wreck. I must have changed twenty times before finally landing on the pair of dark-blue skinny jeans hugging my curves, an oversized black sweater that hangs loosely off my shoulders, and of course, my kick-ass black patent-leather Mary Janes (four inches, not my standard five or six). My brown hair is loose, curled in tousled sections as it falls over my shoulders, tickling my skin. And my makeup is minimal, fresh and light on my eyes, with no blush necessary. The nervous flush warming the tops of my cheeks is enough. My teeth graze my lower lip, no longer coated with gloss because of the repeated action. I inhale, raise my arm, and knock three times on Grady's apartment door.

As I wait for him to answer, I agitatedly fan my face with the envelope concealing his letter. I chose to come in person to deliver it, not because I wanted to see his response, but because I have something to show him when he's done.

Then it's up to him whether I leave or stay.

It hurts knowing there's a very good chance he may ask me to go, and honestly, I wouldn't blame him if he did. But I pray that doesn't happen. That he still feels the same way. That he still loves me.

I hope.

I hope.

I hope.

The door swings open and I pause midfan. I don't think I will ever get used to my initial reaction when seeing Grady Bennett. His hair is loose, light-brown waves framing his face as they gently brush against the shoulders of the white polo covering them. It pulls taut across his chest as he presses his elbow against the frame of the door and leans against it, the sleeves fully stretched around his bicep with its support of his shifted weight.

The corner of his mouth lifts into a half smile and the edges of his familiar blue eyes crinkle as they drift downward to take in my appearance. The other side of his mouth finally rises along with his stare, forming a knowing smile as his right brow arches.

"Miss me?"

My lips pinch tightly against the laughter, but I'm pretty sure he spied the beginnings of my smile before my measly attempt to hide it.

I lift my bare shoulder and offer in a nonchalant voice, "Maybe."

His smile widens and he steps to the side, allowing my entrance. The door closes behind me, and even though Grady's standing three feet away, his presence engulfs me. Warmth races through my veins, and my cheeks heat as he passes. I breathe in the familiar smell, revel silently in its aftermath, then follow him to the kitchen.

As he opens his cabinet, I eye his perfectly shaped ass, beautifully accentuated by the designs on the back pockets of his jeans. My view only gets better when he lifts his arm, inquiring over his shoulder, "Wine?"

I bite down on my bottom lip to keep from drooling, then shake my head even though he can't see me. "Nah, water would be great though. Thanks."

Grady twists his body, smile still present on his face. "Water it is, then."

He snags two glasses and fills them while I approach the island, placing the letter on top. He turns to face me, and his stare drops to the envelope. He pauses, then places both glasses on the island, one on each side of my letter, and raises his eyes to meet mine.

I clear my throat and my hands anxiously worm into my front pockets as I meekly offer, "For you."

Grady reaches forward, dragging the paper across the granite countertop with the tips of his fingers. Once it's in his possession, he lifts it, his eyes inquisitive.

He definitely doesn't seem angry anymore.

Maybe I still have a chance?

I nervously shift my stance. "You can read it."

He seems to pick up on my nervous energy, because his expression falls serious as he takes a seat and hooks his finger under the flap to open it. The cream-colored paper is extracted.

I watch nervously as he begins to read. His face gives nothing away with the exception of a clenched jaw as he reads, which later relaxes toward the middle of my letter. I remain silent, watching his reaction to my words.

Once he's done, his eyes remain trained on the paper held in his hands, absorbing everything I've shared. Once through, he remains silent as he creases the letter between his thumb and forefinger and places it gingerly back into the confines of the envelope.

Only then does he raise his eyes, and as he does, glistening, caring eyes meet mine. I grind down on my teeth, but my tears are stubborn. They surge, coating my lashes.

I clear my throat and finally remove my hands from my pockets, gesturing toward him as I say, "Well, that's it. Now you know everything."

Grady shakes his head, disengaging his gaze from mine to look back at the letter in his hands. "I suspected, but I didn't know. Not for sure."

"You suspected?" I inquire, already realizing his answer before he speaks it out loud.

His eyes remain locked in the direction of the island. "The first time I ever touched you, in Krav Maga, remember?"

I know exactly to what he's referring. "You put your hands on my waist, and my entire body froze."

"It did." He finally looks back to me, his stare furious, yet equally heartbroken. "I'm trained to recognize these things, Cass. I just . . . *fuck*. I hoped it hadn't happened to *you*."

My mouth dips into a sad smile and I shrug. "Well, it did. But like you said, I think you knew that. And honestly, I think *I* knew that you knew, but I wasn't ready to admit it to myself yet." I pin him with my gaze. "That's why you gave me Aubrey's card, isn't it?"

Grady's mouth lifts into a rueful smile and he dips his head slightly in affirmation. He exhales deeply before adding, "I followed you, you know. I was worried when I couldn't get hold of you. So I got your parents' names from Spencer and tagged their address. I just needed to know you were okay."

He clears his throat. "I was outside your house that morning, when you went to the cemetery. You were upset, angry, so I followed you. I stayed in my car, watching from the periphery while you cried, but when you rose to your knees and pleaded, *goddamn*, Cass . . . it took every bit of restraint I possessed not to get out, haul you into my arms, and bring you home with me."

He becomes blurry in my vision as I watch his pained expression.

"It was him, wasn't it?"

I nod, the movement ripping the tears from my eyes. They begin to flow freely, coating my cheeks in damp warmth.

He mirrors my gesture, his head dipping downward before he continues. "I waited for you to finally get back to your apartment. I wanted to ask you about it, but as soon as you opened that door, I knew you were already gone. Too far for me to grab hold. And I blamed myself. I was so pissed, so angry because I was losing you right in front of my eyes. I spoke out of anger, and I'm sorry for that."

I laugh and wipe a tear drifting down my face. "If *anyone* spoke out of anger, Grady, it was me. I said things I can never take back. Horrible, awful things. Then you left and I rationalized it. I convinced myself it was for the best, that it was better for you not to have to deal with my baggage, with my pain, with my past. Things I couldn't even deal with at the time." A shy smile crosses my face as I shrug. "But when I woke up, and I saw my belongings in front of me, then Roger staring at me with his beady eyes, all I could think was I really *hope* Grady Bennett waits for me to finish falling. I wasn't able to admit that to myself for a really long time, but it's true. I think at that moment, somewhere in my consciousness, I knew I would make it, that I would conquer my fears, but I wasn't ready. Not then. It had to be my decision to make."

I grin, then pull up the bottom of my shirt, exposing my reason for coming tonight. I could've easily left the letter for Grady to read on his own, but I really wanted to show him this.

My smile broadens until my cheeks ache, and I feel giddy as a teenager as I hook my thumb in my jeans and tug them down gently, displaying the fresh ink on my skin.

Right above my hipbone is the image of a parachute, just as I remember when I looked up from beneath Grady, watching as it caught air and flared open. The top is a very light orange and morphs gradually into a deep red toward the bottom, symbolizing not only my very own spark, but the way Grady makes me feel. The color of warmth.

And in paying homage to the shade of his sapphire eyes, the very eyes I found my initial focus in, are two words written in navy blue right in the center.

Landed strong

"I landed strong, Grady. I was in one hell of a free fall, but I found my strength and righted myself. It was *you* who helped me to be able to do that. You made good on your promise and with the help of Dr. Miller, of *Aubrey*, you put me in the position to be guided slowly, safely, until my feet finally hit the ground. And when they struck, I felt pure power with the knowledge that I had faced my fears and conquered my own personal hell. I landed strong because of you."

I lower my shirt and release my jeans, shrugging my shoulders. "So, thank you. That's all I wanted to say. That's why I came. I just . . . I needed to see you for no other reason than to let you know I landed the fall and to thank you for getting me there."

And I really hope you still love me.

Because I do still love you.

I will always love you.

Grady remains seated, his expression stoic, giving nothing away as he watches me nervously tug at the bottom of my shirt. I hold his stare, and when he says nothing, disappointment drowns any hope I had for his forgiveness. For his love and acceptance. For a future.

Our future.

I will always love you.

My thumb flies over my shoulder, indicating the door. "I'm just gonna go ahead and go . . ."

The edge of his mouth quirks slightly. "So there's *no* other reason you came then?"

I grip my bottom lip with my front teeth and lift my shoulders. A nervous rush of energy erupts through my system. "I mean, well, I had hoped—"

"Come here." Grady rises, the chair screeching with his movement. Persistent eyes lock onto mine, brimming with intensity.

Another wave rushes through me and giddy excitement pricks my veins. I don't move an inch, though. I remain where I stand, but my bottom lip is pulled from my teeth as I give him an ornery grin.

Grady's brow lifts, he raises his hand and crooks his finger. "Come here. *Please.*"

My feet make the decision for me. They're insistent in their strides as they pick up pace, and once I'm within launching distance, I fly into his arms. My arms wrap around his shoulders as he catches me, squeezing me tightly in an embrace. One arm hooks around my waist, while the other positions his hand at the base of my neck. He weaves his fingers into my hair and his warmth floods my body as he holds me securely against his chest. Soothing heat from his mouth sifts through my hair when he presses his lips to my temple, the sensation increasing as he releases a long, contented breath.

We grip each other tightly, our bodies pressed firm with our lengthy embrace.

I. Have. Missed. This. So. Much.

God, how I have missed him.

"I'm so fucking proud of you, Cass."

His mouth hits the shell of my ear with his whisper and my throat clogs, not with sadness, but with pride in myself.

Suddenly, his body tenses within my hold and he presses away, his arms still clenched tightly around me as he squints down at my face. His eyebrows are pressed together, clearly confused as he inquires, "Wait . . . who's Roger?"

I laugh—*really* laugh—and its release is freeing as the rush of air leaves my chest. "I have so much to tell you. A lot's happened over the past three months. And it all started with Roger, the green, plastic paratrooper. The stubborn bastard who wouldn't crash no matter how hard I threw him."

A full grin remains on my lips as I toss Grady a very *Grady*-like wink.

His face relaxes and his mouth curves beautifully before he states, "You're so goddamn beautiful when you smile, but when you *laugh*, it steals my fucking breath every time."

He leans his forehead against mine, centering his lips just centimeters from my mouth as he whispers, "I love you so much. These months apart haven't been easy for me, knowing you were fighting battles on your own, but I knew you could do it. And you were never really alone, Cass. I was watching, making sure you were landing safely, because I knew as soon as you hit that ground, sweetheart, you were mine. You *are* mine. And regardless of what you said in your apartment, you *are* my purpose. There isn't anything I wouldn't do to keep you safe."

Just like that, I turn into a girly puddle and melt to the floor.

And I love it.

I love *him*.

He closes the distance and captures my mouth, his full lips grazing mine ever so tenderly as his soft tongue gently probes the seam. I open for him, angling my head to the side as he does the same. Our mouths fuse as we wordlessly communicate the depths of our love for each other with each moan, with each growl, with each press of our bodies, as though we can't get close enough.

Hours later, when we've shed our clothes, along with every last one of our vulnerabilities, we communicate much the same way. With each gentle trace of his fingers along my skin, with each tug of the hair wrapped around my fingers, with each clench of my body and each low rumble I receive in return, we continue to express our love through action.

No words are necessary.

But a very distinct one comes to mind.

Home.

I feel as though I have not only found myself—found I can love myself—but as though I have finally found my home.

And as he holds my stare from above as he pumps his length slowly into my body, he takes his time to show me how much he loves me. He gently runs his fingers up and down my body as if he simply can't *not* touch me. He reacquaints himself with the softness of my skin, with the texture he'd missed so much. He tells me how he had waited patiently for me from afar, how hard it was to wait, having already tasted me. And after he takes his time touching my skin, he shows me exactly how much he's missed my taste. He kisses me senseless, tonguing and sucking me into oblivion. *Ecstasy.* Every action is a demonstration of how precious I am to him. He fills me completely, in heart, soul, and body. He consumes me with his passion, his need, his desire. And I let him *take* me.

I offer myself completely, everything I am, because much like the song we danced to for the first time in this very apartment, he is *mine* and I am *his.*

Forever and always.

Thank you, Grady Bennett, for waiting for me to land strong.

Thank you for believing in me and guiding me to safety.

And thank you, most of all, for showing me what love is.

For teaching me the meaning, the unadulterated beauty of the emotion, as it exists between the two of us . . .

The way it was meant to be experienced.

Home.

Chapter 34 ✵
The Last Letter

Uncle Alan,

This last letter, my letter to you, will serve as my voice. I remained silent for too long, hiding your secrets because I thought I shared in the blame.

This is my absolution as I choose to provide it for myself. My chance to take back my innocence, my choice in what happened to me, what you saw fit to take as your own, without consequence.

I am finally writing to you to say aloud the ramblings of my mind as they're poured onto paper, so I may find some sort of peace once I lay this letter to rest in the same soil that covers your lifeless body and houses your malevolent soul.

I will never understand why you did the things you did, or said the things you said. I don't think any person in their right mind can ever really wrap their head around the actions of a pedophile. Of a person who preys on the innocence of children, who feeds off of it with absolutely no remorse, for the sole purpose of their own sick gratification.

I hope to never understand. I pray I am never witness to the darkness that twisted your mind, because I've had a hell of a time dealing with my own.

Yours would undoubtedly seal me in that grave right alongside you.

But that's the funny thing about choosing to live. About making the decision to change your life, to take a different road, a more difficult path in order to reach where you deserve to be.

You're dead now, and because of your own choices, you're lying right where you should be.

And because of mine, my new choices, I'm living.

Really living.

It's not always easy. Some days are harder than others. Some mornings I wake up, still feeling heavy and burdened, because in all honesty, I will never be able to completely erase your presence or your actions from my mind.

But there are so many other days when I don't. When I open my eyes, warmed by the sun and the excitement of staring into the eyes of a man who loves me unconditionally, every piece of me, regardless of the damage you caused.

Those days, when I wake up in his arms, safe and secure, loved . . .

I refuse to take them for granted.

I choose to live.

I choose to laugh.

I choose to love.

I choose to smile.

You took so much from me, but my choices? My happiness? Those you can't have.

They're mine.

You also tried to take me too, but guess what?

You can't have me either.

I'm too strong.

I found my voice, my own vindication for your senseless actions.

I will right your wrongs.

And one day, I pray I will find the strength to completely rid your existence from my mind. But until that day comes, I will keep traveling my path. The one I chose, not you. I will walk with my head held high, with a smile on my face, and with love—real love—in my heart.

Because that is *my* choice.

Good-bye, Uncle Alan

Cassandra

One month later, I'm bent at the knees with my hand splayed on the dirt now covering my letter. Sitting back on my heels in front of his headstone, a surge of strength flows through me. Minutes go by as I silently read the letter in my mind, announcing each word proudly to the man beneath my feet.

I don't cry. I simply shake my head at the senselessness before rising on my feet.

A warm hand curls around mine, helping me as I stand, and I turn to meet those caring eyes watching my every move.

The corners of my mouth tip upward, forming a thankful smile, and I lean into Grady's arms, allowing him to provide the warmth I need right at this moment.

"So proud of you, Cass."

His lips brush my forehead, then he drops his hand, linking my pinky with his as he turns to lead me out of the cemetery. I grin to myself, tightening my finger as we walk together, away from my past and into our future.

Epilogue ✦

One year later . . .

Eighties rock pounds relentlessly from the speaker beside me, and I grin widely at Grady as he skates toward me, coming from the direction of the DJ booth. His eyes crinkle at the sides with his smile as he approaches. Masterfully, he circles once before coming to a stop a foot in front of where I stand.

"I can't believe you wanted to come here," he shouts above the music.

I laugh, then respond. "It's full circle. Where we started."

He smiles, then takes my hand into his, leaning into me as he speaks. "So fucking proud of you."

I never knew I needed those words until my Grady said them to me. Now, I feel delight in them.

My cheek presses against his with my smile and I nod my acceptance of his compliment. His beard tickles my skin as I press my lips just above where it frames his gorgeous face. I smile as I inhale his scent.

"Thank you for giving me a fucking phenomenal epilogue, Grady Bennett. For being the perfect hero. And for giving me my very own happily-ever-after."

He mirrors my gesture, smiling contently against my skin. "It's your story, sweetheart, I'm just lucky to be living in it."

He releases me then wheels backward and gestures toward the floor.

"Dance with me?"

Grady's eyes light with amusement when a familiar Foreigner song begins to play. I couldn't *not* smile if I tried.

I nod eagerly, then press off my skates to follow his lead.

My eyes quickly find Spencer skating circles around Dalton, already on the floor. Her mouth forms the words as she shouts them at the top of her lungs and I shake my head, laughing as I listen to the lyrics.

Looks like love finally found them both.

Mrs. Locke—well, Mrs. Lawson—catches my attention next. Her smile is peaceful as she watches her daughter skating on the floor. After a beat, her stare slides from Spencer to capture mine. Her grin widens and she winks, signaling her approval of my accomplishment.

I smile back at her, watching as Detective Lawson snakes his arm around her waist from behind to whisper something in her ear that makes her laugh. My happiness for her stretches clear across my face before I break away from watching them to carefully focus on my footing.

After a couple successful steps, I lift my gaze, which lands on Aubrey and her husband, Kaeleb, as they guide their three-year-old daughter, Adley, carefully around the slick floor. Her blonde curls bounce as she flees from her parents, clearly having none of their assistance. I grin as Kaeleb looks to Aubrey in a way that tells me Adley resembles her mother very much.

That grin continues to widen as I watch the couples and their unequivocal happiness. My own joy takes flight, knowing everything is as it should be. That *I'm* right where I should be, doing exactly what I should be doing with my life.

And it has nothing to do with hair.

Although I do miss my clients terribly, I made the choice earlier this year to embark on a new journey. A new vocation, so to speak. In fact, it's the reason we're all gathered here tonight.

I train my gaze on one pair in particular, angelic giggles somehow rising above the blaring music as they hit my ears.

I eventually gave Spencer her birthday present. It was belated, but only because it was a work in progress.

With the support of Aubrey, Spencer, and of course Grady, I decided to try my hand at writing. And when I did, there was no turning back. I was completely captivated as I wove the words together, laughing and crying with the characters as they told me their story.

I published my first book six months ago.

It was a beautiful tale of two children who unknowingly fell in love one day as they watched a simple sunset together on a front porch. A story of their resilient friendship as they grew into young adults, the undeniable growth of their feelings with each passing year, and sadly, soon after finally caving to those feelings, their separation as one's haunting past threatened the other's future. It was a story of redemption, as after five long years, they still remained *Under the Influence* of their love, finally making their way back to each other.

A true love story as witnessed by my eyes, yet told by them.

Their story, my gift to Spencer.

But tonight, as we all celebrate together, I just hit publish on my *second* book.

My book.

My story.

My secrets, unleashed, when my own life was *Out of Focus.*

So many thoughts and feelings have swirled through my mind for years. Talking with Aubrey and sharing with Grady have not only been cathartic and provided necessary healing, but allowed all the jumbled words to find their position on the pages.

You see, once I found my voice, I knew exactly what I intended to do with it. So, with the publication of my second book, I did just that.

Why have a voice if you're scared to use it?

I've lived in fear for the majority of my life, but I refuse to remain silent anymore.

I wrote my story for all to read, in my own voice, in hopes that if I can just reach one person, if I can relay the message that they're not alone, then I've somehow made sense of a senseless act . . . of any kind. Tragedies happen all too often but remain hidden underneath a terrifying blanket of secrets. A devious blanket of lies. An agonizing blanket of pain.

As I look at those gathered here to support me, my family born not of blood, I know I've finally landed on the road I was meant to be traveling all along.

I was plucked from that path, thrown into a free fall for years, but eventually I found my way. All it took was a pair of blue eyes, loving arms, my own strength, and the unwavering support of those around me to help me land strong.

What will it be for you?

Everyone has a story.

I can only pray mine has helped someone come to terms with their own.

Are you that person?

And if so, what do you plan to do with *your* story?

If you hear me, if I've spoken to you, then I leave with you the same four words that changed my life.

The choice is yours.

THE END

Other Books by
L.B. SIMMONS

Chosen Paths Series

Into the Light
Under the Influence
Out of Focus

Mending Hearts Series

Running on Empty
Recovery
Running in Place

Acknowledgments

First and foremost, a huge thank you goes out to my readers. I know I tell you this all the time, but your energy and excitement are contagious. You keep me going, keep me motivated, keep me writing. Each one of your messages of support and love for my characters is invaluable. The fact that out of all the amazing books out there, you choose to spend your valuable time reading mine, well . . . it's such a surreal feeling. Thank you.

My darling husband and our girls—As always, thank you for your patience. I know it's not easy when I take time away from all of you to dive into my stories and create my worlds. The fact that all of you are so supportive, as well as incredibly forgiving, means so much to me. I love all of you with every piece of my heart.

Luna Sol—Woman. We did it! You are such an amazing friend to me. I am truly blessed to have you in my life. Your support and iron fist keep me going when so often, I want to give up. Your love for my characters is something I will never forget or take for granted. Thank you for standing by me always.

Jena Eilers—Ah! SIX BOOKS! I love you so much! Thank you for believing in me when I first began this journey, and for continuing to believe in me with each new book I write. You are the definition of a true friend, and I don't know what I did to deserve you in my life, but I'm gonna keep you forever! Thank you for ALL that you do!

Hang Le with Designs by Hang Le—You did it. Again. You created a cover for this story that is beyond perfection in its beauty, as well as its symbolism. Thank you for your never-ending patience, and for listening to my ideas without screaming for me to shut up and to just let you work. LOL! You are so brilliant, and I am blessed to work with someone of your creative ability.

Marion Archer (Making Manuscripts) and Karen Lawson (The Proof is in the Reading)—Mere words are not enough. I was so nervous, so worried I wouldn't be able to do this story justice. You not only believed in me and encouraged me but pushed me to get

Cassie's journey to a level I am so proud of. Thank you for taking the time to "get me there." LOL! Thank you for truly loving my characters. It makes all the difference in the world.

Marisa A. Corvisiero of Corvisiero Literary Agency—Thank you so much for believing in my writing. Your excitement and faith in my storytelling ability make me smile on a continuous basis. I am blessed to have you in my corner, and I have the utmost faith that this year will be our year!

I hope I didn't forget anyone, but chances are I did. Please know that I appreciate every single reader, every blogger, every friend, and every family member who come together to support me as I release new books into the reading world. Without you by my side, my journey on this writing path would have ended years ago. Thank you, each one of you, from the bottom of my heart.

About the Author

Two Sons Photography

After graduating from Texas A&M University, L.B. Simmons did what any biomedical science major would do: she entered the workforce as a full-time chemist. Never in her wildest dreams would she have imagined herself becoming a *USA Today* bestselling contemporary romance author years later.

What began as a memoir for her children ended up being her first self-published book, *Running on Empty*. Soon after, her girls were given reoccurring roles in the remainder of what became the Mending Hearts series.

L.B. Simmons doesn't just write books. With each new work, she attempts to compose journeys of love and self-discovery so she may impart life lessons to readers. She's tackled suicide, depression, bullying, eating disorders, as well as physical and sexual abuse, all while weaving elements of humor into the storylines in an effort to balance the difficult topics. Often described as roller coaster rides, her novels are known for eliciting a wide range of emotions.

Connect with the Author

L.B.'s Website:
   http://www.lbsimmons.com/

L.B.'s Facebook Page:
   https://www.facebook.com/lbsimmonsauthor

L.B.'s Twitter Page:
   https://twitter.com/lbsimmons33

L.B.'s Instagram:
   https://www.instagram.com/Lbsimmons33/

Contact L.B.:
   http://www.lbsimmons.com/contact-me